The GOOD DEED

THE CHANDLER HORDE - BOOK ONE

MARY A. NASON

THE GOOD DEED

Mary A. Nason

may trigger a PTSD response in some readers. There are many resources for victims of domestic violence. See the *Links and Resources* page at the end of this book.

This book is dedicated to all the seasoned ladies who appreciate mature spicy characters

And to the brave men and women who have lost a loved one to violence or alcoholism and carried on —

You deserve a happily ever after!

QUOTES

If we remembered everyday that we could lose someone at any moment, we would love them more fiercely and freely, and without fear — not because there is something to lose, but because everything can always be lost.

— MICHAEL FIORE - DIGITAL ROMANCE

Someone who deserves you sees your imperfections. They know you're moody, strong, and hard to handle. And not only do they appreciate it, they also wouldn't change it. . . Even if they don't like it all the time.

— CHARLES J. ORLANDO

When you find someone who breaks you open and makes you feel things, you fight for them.

— TARRYN FISHER

She's got the eyes of innocence, the face of an angel, the personality of a dreamer, and a smile that hides more pain than you can imagine.

— UNKNOWN

Grief, I've learned, is really just love. It's all the love you want to give but cannot. All of that unspent love gathers up in the corners of your eyes, the lump in your throat, and in that hollow part of your chest. Grief is just love with no place to go.

— SECOND FIRSTS – FACEBOOK

Crawl inside this body, find me where I am most ruined and love me there.

— Rumi Lazuli

I still believe in love. I still believe that in spite of your painful past, you can still meet someone tomorrow who would love to build a beautiful future with you. I still believe there is someone out there tailor made to love you how you deserve to be loved. I still believe that you can go from being in a relationship that feels like a nightmare, to being in love with someone who feels like a dream come true. I still believe that someone can still see the best in you, even when you only see the worst. I still believe that you can wake up with joy in your heart and peace in your spirit. I still believe that you can meet someone who will never leave your side during a difficult time. I still believe that you can meet someone who wants to add value to your live. I still believe that you can meet someone who wants to bring your smile back and make you laugh again. I still believe that you can still fall in love . . .

— IG@woodtheinspiration

ACKNOWLEDGMENTS

Thank you, Mr. Ray for the storyline based on your adventure while out looking for a Starbucks in Casper Wyoming during KallypsoCon 2016. I hope you like what I did with it.

Thank you, Patti Lee Swigart, for being my friend during your loss and all the political insanity. This book is for our angels, Abigail Angelique and Annie Rene. They're playing with Baby on the other side of the Rainbow Bridge.

I planned to take a break after publishing my first three books in the Second Chances series, but I got ambushed by a brokenhearted lawyer while I waited for my coffee to brew. He wouldn't shut up, and I had no choice but to sit down and take dictation. Then *she* started in on me so I had to write her story, too. Just when I thought I was finished, another couple showed up. Of course, they all got their happily ever afters — and so much more.

As the saying goes: no good deed goes unpunished. This is a story about a man's search for redemption and a second chance at love, a woman's courageous triumph over brutality, and their search for justice.

For immediate release

KEYWHOLE GROUP ANNOUNCES $2 MILLION TRADEMARK SETTLEMENT

Carson, California, February 17, 2003: Keywhole Group, a wholly owned subsidiary of ALL NET USA, Inc. was awarded $2 million in damages today in a trademark and copyright lawsuit against iKeywhole, an SEO software company owned by sole proprietor, Stewart Sheldon.

"Corporations invest huge sums of money developing and growing their brands. Registered trademarks are valuable assets that must be protected. Intellectual property is copyrighted for that same reason. Let this be a warning to other businesses that ignorance of trademark and copyright law does not absolve any company, no matter how small, from the repercussions of violating these laws." said Michael Chandler, Esquire, senior counsel for ALL NET

According to a company spokesperson, Mr. Chandler received a high six-figure bonus from ALL NET for his tireless work.

1

A plan formed in Stewart Sheldon's mind. Here was a way to end all his problems and take that bastard down at the same time.

That cold-hearted, sleazy, bastard in a thousand-dollar three-piece suit, that slimy snake who destroyed his life would suffer just like he was. People, especially lawyers, didn't get to treat hardworking, honest, law-abiding, taxpaying business owners like him like ants to be stomped on. No, Mr. Chandler would get what he deserved.

He loaded his computer in his junk car and drove to the closest pawn shop where he exchanged it for a gun and a small box of bullets—he only needed two. Then he went home, packed up whatever he had left, and said goodbye to the house his children had grown up in.

He moved into a cheap motel that charged by the week. He wouldn't be there long, just until Christmas Eve morning. Then he would give Mr. Michael Chandler, Attorney at Law, a gift that would keep on giving for the rest of his miserable life.

He spent the next month wrapping up his affairs and changing beneficiaries on his various insurance policies to his two children. It wasn't much, but no way in hell was his ex-wife, the woman who had promised for richer or poorer, and left him as soon as the poorer part kicked in, no way was she going to get everything and his life insurance, too.

While the drunken motel manager was passed out, he let himself into the office and used the computer to write the goodbye letter and attached the press release. Now it was just a matter of watching and waiting.

Every morning of the week before Christmas, he parked on the street that slimy bastard lived on, and he watched. He knew when Mr. Michael Chandler, Esquire, went out for his morning jog. He knew how long it took, and he knew how much time he would have.

That morning, that final morning, dawned clear and beautiful as only a Southern California December day could. It was the perfect day for what he had planned. He hid in the bushes and watched the poor unsuspecting scumbag leave for his morning jog. And when the bastard turned the corner, he let himself in through the unlocked door.

He heard a woman's voice from upstairs. "Michael? Are you back already?"

Perfect.

2

There was a new home under construction two blocks down, and Michael had been thinking about doing some remodeling. Maybe he could get some ideas. But as he neared the construction site, a woman, probably around his age, ran out to the front yard, screaming. She was battered and bloody and collapsed on the grass, crying.

He froze. He couldn't just jog past. He had to stop and help her. He didn't think about his own safety or what might happen if the person who'd done that to her came outside with a weapon. He had to help, so he knelt down next to where she sat bleeding and sobbing. "Are you okay? Do you want to call the police? Is anything broken? Do you need the paramedics?"

Her tears mixed with the blood that dripped down her chin. "Am I okay? Do I look okay? I think this time he broke my nose. He's never hit me this hard before. And I'm afraid if I call the police again, it'll just make him angrier. And I ran out without my phone."

"Let me call the police for you. And I'll stay here until they arrive. I'm a lawyer, although I practice corporate law, but I should be able to persuade them to arrest your . . .?"

"Husband. My loving *husband.*" Sarcasm dripped from that word the way blood still dripped from her nose.

"Are you willing to press charges? Because without that, they'll only hold him until Monday, at most."

She wiped her nose on her sleeve which spread the blood and her tears all over her face and her shirt sleeve. *"Ow!* Shit! That hurt, and now I'm a bloody mess." She needed a tissue, and he didn't have one. "I've done that before, pressed charges, and he always gets out. He already has misdemeanors. If it's a felony this time, they'll still only hold him until he makes bail. Well, one way or another, I'm not doing this again."

He called 911, explained the situation, and five minutes later a police cruiser arrived. By then the blood from her nose had stopped dripping, and she'd stopped crying. "What's your name?"

"Elaine Jeffers, and my soon-to-be ex is Dan Jeffers. I can't thank you enough for stopping to help. Most people don't want to get involved, and I really appreciate this, but I don't want to keep you from whatever you were doing. And I didn't get your name."

"Michael Chandler. My wife, Sandy, and I live nearby. I was just out for a jog to the coffee stand to get a latte for her. She's still sleeping so she won't expect me back right away."

The paramedics arrived a few minutes later, cleaned up her face, and gave her an ice pack for her nose while an officer questioned her. They arrested Dan Jeffers who didn't put up a fight.

He gave his statement while the husband sat, handcuffed, in the back seat of the cruiser looking like nothing had happened. Probably figured he'd be out on bail before dinner. But since it was Christmas weekend, arraignment wouldn't be until Monday or Tuesday which bought her at least a few days of peace, anyway. He felt sorry for her. He and his brothers adored their mother and learned to respect women by watching how their father treated her.

After the cruiser left, she thanked him. "It's nice to know there are still people like you in the world. Your wife is a lucky woman. I'm going to change and go down to the police station to press charges. I'll be okay. You go get your wife that latte, and maybe we'll run into each other again."

"If you're sure you're okay . . . I don't have any business cards with me, but you can find us in the phonebook if you need to. Michael and Sandy Chandler on Hemingway. Take care of yourself!"

He continued his jog to Roasted, got two eggnog lattes, and walked home. When he turned the corner onto his street, there were five police cruisers with lights flashing, and a white van parked in front of his house. The marking on the van read *Coroner,* and the front door was open. A man in a white coat was pushing a gurney with a body bag onto the porch.

What the fuck?

He dropped the cups in the street and ran to the door only to be blocked by a uniformed officer. "Hey! This is my house. What happened? Where's my wife?"

A man, probably a detective since he wore street clothes, turned to him. "Your name, sir?"

"Michael Chandler. My wife's in there. What the fuck is going on?"

"Sir, step away from the door."

"Look, Detective, if that's what you are, this is my house, and I'm going in there!"

"You can't do that, sir."

"Why the fuck not? I want to talk to my wife, NOW!"

"I'm sorry, sir, but that won't be possible. Do you know a Stewart Sheldon?"

"Who?"

"Stewart Sheldon. We found a letter addressed to Michael Chandler next to his body."

"I don't know anyone by that name. This has to be some kind of mistake. And what do you mean *next to his body?* WHERE THE FUCK IS MY WIFE?"

"Let's go over to my car and I'll explain everything."

Dread and terror battled in his gut, and a wave of nausea threatened, but he followed the detective. When they got to the car, he turned and faced the front door ready to run to her as soon as she came out.

Where is she?

"What happened?"

"Neighbors heard gunshots. When officers arrived, the front door was open. They found a white male lying on the living room carpet dead from a single gunshot wound to the head. The letter was laying near the body. Officers found a female victim on the bed in the upstairs bedroom dead from a single gunshot wound to the chest. I'm very sorry, sir."

No!

"I don't believe you. I want to see her. This is all a mistake. It has to be! Whoever you found, it's not her. It *can't* be!"

"Please follow me."

They approached the gurney as it was about to be loaded into the coroner's van. "Is that the female victim?"

"Yes, sir."

After a nod from the detective, the coroner unzipped the body bag enough to reveal her face. "Is this your wife, sir?"

All the air in his lungs vanished. He couldn't catch his breath. He couldn't talk. He couldn't think. There was the face of the love of his life. He fell to his knees and cried out to the God he'd so devoutly worshiped all his life, "Why, God? Why her?"

"Sir, is there anyone you can call?"

He couldn't stand, couldn't answer, just pulled the phone out of his pocket and handed it to the detective.

"Anyone with the last name Chandler."

"Okay. Hey, Greg? Can you help Mr. Chandler back to my car? We can't go in until the crime scene guys finish, and he can't sit here."

"Sure thing. Come with me, sir."

Like a robot on autopilot, he followed the officer back to the detective's car. He waited, hoping he'd wake from this nightmare and be back in bed watching her sleep. He couldn't wrap his head around the idea that she . . . His brain shut down. He had no idea how long he'd been sitting there when the detective came to get him. Everything seemed to move in slow motion.

"We can go in the house now. And your brother is on his way."

"Which one? I have five."

"The one who answered the phone. I don't remember which one finally did."

When they got to the doorway, he couldn't cross the threshold. He didn't want to see where the man's body had lain. He didn't want to walk into his house knowing she wasn't there, that she would never be there, again. He was going to lose his mind, and he needed to hit something.

The detective waited for him to calm down. Finally, after taking several deep breaths, he walked through the doorway. Other than the large bloodstain on the carpet, there were no other signs of violence. "Can I look in the bedroom?"

"Yes, but prepare yourself. There was a lot of blood."

He followed the detective up the stairs and down the hallway to the big master bedroom with the French doors and the king-sized bed with the brass headboard. He'd put those doors in, himself. And he could remember the day they christened that bed like it was yesterday. After sucking in a deep breath, he walked in and looked around.

Thank God he hadn't eaten anything.

Even if he replaced the blood-soaked mattress, he'd never sleep in that bed again. He wasn't even sure he'd ever sleep in that bedroom again. Actually, he didn't think he'd ever *sleep* again.

"Your brother is here so I'll be downstairs, but Officer Ross will remain."

"Hey, Mike. Wow. This sucks. I thought the cops had the wrong number when they called. It's so hard to believe. Mom and Dad are on their way. Should be here in about fifteen minutes. Mark's on a fishing trip so he won't find out until tonight. Everyone else is making plans to get here as fast as they can. Jesus, Mary, and Joseph. Look at all the blood. I'd hate to have to clean that up."

How like the *runt* to be so unsympathetic. His spoiled brat of a brother never cared about anyone but himself.

Another officer appeared at the bedroom door. "Mr. Chandler? Detective Kelly needs to talk to you about the letter."

He took one more look at the last place he'd seen her alive then followed the officer and the *runt* back down to the living room. Who could have done this? "Is that the letter?"

The detective held it out to him. He took the poly bag by one corner as if the evil it contained could somehow escape.

On the other side of the letter was a newspaper clipping of a press release from a case he'd won last year. He remembered the case because he'd gotten a huge bonus, the biggest one he'd ever received. It was big enough to buy a little beach cottage down near Oceanside when he retired. They had just browsed the real estate ads the other day, not that he planned to retire soon, but just to get some ideas.

Then he read the letter.

Mr. Chandler,

I'm sure you don't remember me, and I know you never bothered to find out what losing that lawsuit did to me, and I can bet you wouldn't care, anyway. You wouldn't care that I lost the house I raised my children in. You wouldn't care that my wife left me and sued for divorce — the day before Thanksgiving. You wouldn't care that I lost my business and the software program I'd poured my life's blood and all my money into. All you cared about was winning that case for your corporate masters — a company that makes in one week everything I'd worked for all my life, everything I lost that day in court.

I have nothing left to lose, and now I won't have to deal with the pain anymore. But you, sir, will spend the rest of your life knowing that because you took everything I had, you drove me to take everything you had and leave you with a lifetime of guilt.

See you in hell.

Stewart Sheldon

A tear rolled down his cheek as he read the signature.

"Hey, Detective! What happens now? Our parents and brothers are on the way over."

"Well, the crime scene team have what they need, but we need to secure the house until the case has been closed. I'll have an officer go with you to pack some of Mr. Chandler's things while I ask him some questions. It'll probably take a few days, maybe a week, for us to clear the house."

☒

"Mike! Sit down before you fall down! I'm getting you a drink."

He collapsed on his parents' couch and shivered with emotional pain as the enormity of what happened crashed into him again. When John handed him the shot of Irish whiskey, he knocked it back and held out the glass for more. What he *really* needed was the whole fucking bottle.

"Do you know what I did? I ruined that man's life, and while he was murdering my wife, I was helping another woman whose husband had just beaten her. I should have been home. If I'd been there, this wouldn't have happened! This is all my fault! *Oh,* my God! How am I supposed to live with this? Without her?"

His mother sat down and held him while he cried in anguish, and when his crying slowed, he sat up and wiped his eyes with his sleeve. His father who was always stern and strict with a house full of active, usually unruly boys, held his arms open. He stood only to collapse against the hulk of a man everyone said he looked the most like. His sobbing started again. He expected to cry forever. He only pulled away when his mother tapped his shoulder and offered him another shot of whiskey. Why didn't she just leave the bottle?

"I'm calling Father Timothy. I know there's no way to understand God's will or why He took Sandy, but maybe he can help."

Through all the . . . chaos? Tragedy? Shock? Prayer sounded like a ridiculous waste of time. No savior, no saint, no rosary, none of it would bring Sandy back.

"I don't think this is a good time for anyone to talk to me about

God's will. If this was God's will then I don't want anything to do with Him." He knew that upset her, but damn it all to hell, he didn't give a fuck. He should have been there. Then Stewart Sheldon could have killed him, too.

3

"I'm so sorry about Sandra, and I want to help you deal with your grief."

"Thank you Father, but you know what would really help me right now? Answers. Tell me why this happened. Why did He let that man kill my wife, an angel who never hurt a soul? What was His decision-making process? What facts did he gather? How did he determine it was time for her to die? What was the payoff? That's what I want to know!"

The man he'd known since before his first communion was quiet for a few seconds before he answered. "There is no way to know God's will. We can only have faith that God had a reason for choosing her. But asking ourselves why — why this person and not that person — well, we're not meant to know that. But that's part of the grieving process. When you no longer ask why but just accept that there *was* a reason, then you'll be on the road to recovery."

"So God gets to make these arbitrary decisions, and we just have to accept that there's a good reason, and we don't deserve to know?"

"Well, yes. That's what faith is. Knowing that everything does happen for a reason. Tell me, when was your last confession? I know I should know this, but I suspect it's been a long time. Am I right?"

How long had it been? Weeks? Months? That wasn't something he wanted to say in front of his mother. But confession was supposed to be good for the soul, right? Maybe it would help with the ton of guilt that was strangling him.

"Yes, it's been a while. And yes, I'll come." He blinked back tears. "Sandy and I were planning to go to confession this afternoon so we could take communion tonight at Midnight Mass. So, you want to hear my confession? Tell me, when do you have a free hour or two in your schedule?"

"Anytime, you know that. Do you think you can do that?"

He was ready to try anything, but he didn't hold much hope that confessing his sins to a celibate priest would help much. How could a priest possibly understand this kind of loss? And reciting the same prayers over and over again wasn't going to help, either. But what the hell. If confession didn't work, he could always drink himself to death.

⚡

"Father bless me for I have sinned. I have no idea how long it's been since I last confessed." He paused looking for the right words, but there weren't any so he just blurted it out. "I killed my wife."

"Michael, you didn't kill Sandra."

"Well, it might as well have been me. I ruined a man's life, and he took vengeance by murdering my wife and destroying *my* life. If I'd had any compassion for him that day in court, if I had asked for a reasonable amount, maybe he wouldn't have lost everything and been so despondent. And to make matters worse, while Sandy was dying, I was waiting with another woman for the police to arrive and arrest *her* husband for domestic battery. I should have been home. It should have been me. Look, I don't know why I'm even here. There's nothing that can take this guilt from me. Not a hundred *Hail Marys* or a thousand *Our Fathers*. God may forgive me, but *I* never will. I'm sorry I wasted your time, Father." He stood up.

"Michael! Sit. Down. That's not how it works. If you'd known that man was coming and left the house, anyway, that would be a very different matter. But you didn't know — you couldn't know what would happen. You said you helped someone, and that's why you weren't home?"

"I was jogging and heard her screaming. Then I saw her run out of a house. She was covered in blood so I stopped to help and offered to wait with her until the police came. I guess it's true. No good deed goes unpunished. I helped a stranger while my wife paid with her life because I was good at my job. Don't you see? This is something prayers just aren't going to fix."

"You're right. Empty prayers won't fix this. What will, though, is forgiving yourself. And I don't think you're going to do that here. Can you take time off from work?"

He laughed. "Are you kidding? I'm their *boy wonder*. Their golden boy. I set my own hours unless I'm due in court."

"Take a leave of absence. Go on retreats. Work in missions. Help the homeless. Don't sit around waiting for an answer that will never come. Find some meaning in your life, some purpose. God doesn't blame you. Your sin is blaming yourself and not having faith that God knows what He's doing. I want you to pray to Saint Mary Magdalene in your own words and invite her into your heart that you may find peace."

He recited the Act of Contrition, and Father Timothy recited the Prayer of Absolution and Benediction. Then he left the confessional, found a statue of Saint Mary Magdalene, and knelt. He didn't know what to say or how to say it. If God knew what was in his heart, he shouldn't have had to say anything. So he sat there hoping Her healing love would enter his heart and take away his pain.

Of course, it couldn't be *that* easy. He felt nothing. No peace. No understanding. Nothing. After waiting for half an hour, he gave up and went back to his parents' house.

His mother was busy cooking for tomorrow's big Christmas dinner. When he walked in, she looked at him with concern. "Well, how did it go?"

"I don't know what you were expecting, Mom, but I'm pretty

sure it didn't happen. Father Timothy absolved me for blaming myself for something I didn't do. But I don't think it helped. He suggested I take time off from work and make myself useful to mankind. I'm not so sure about that second part, but I definitely need to take time off. In fact, I'm thinking about resigning."

"Resigning? Why?"

"Because of who I am when I'm at work. I'm ruthless. I'm cold. And I have no compassion or empathy for anyone. My focus is on winning money for the corporation I work for and getting paid for it. *That's* the man who got his wife killed. That man cost me the love of my life. I don't want to be that man anymore. I *can't* be him, and my position as senior counsel requires that I *be* that man. And if I go back to being him, then nothing about losing Sandy will have made any difference. Do you understand?"

"Yes, sweetheart, I do understand. But take some time to think about this before you do anything permanent."

There was no point thinking about it. That's the way it had to be. That's the answer Father Timothy wanted him to find. As long as he blamed himself, there would be no peace for him. So he placed the blame where it belonged — with God.

Σ

A week after Sandy's funeral, he walked down the hallway to the corporate vice-president's office to submit his resignation. Word had spread throughout the office grapevine. If he hadn't been so numb, he would have screamed at the barrage of sympathy. Everyone was *so sorry*. He was in their *thoughts and prayers*. Everyone offered to *help* in any way he needed. And none of it made a fucking bit of difference. His wife was still dead.

He knocked on his boss's open door.

"Come in, Michael." The man jumped to his feet and reached over the desk to shake his hand. "I know you've heard this hundreds of times already but I want you to know how sorry I am, how sorry I was to hear what happened. And I want you to take all the time you need. And if you need grief counseling, my assistant can arrange that."

Grief counseling? Yeah, that'll help.

"Thank you, Ray, but that won't be necessary. I came in because I wanted to give this to you in person." He handed the manila envelope to the man who had hired him as a junior attorney all those years ago.

"I know what this is, and before I open it, I want you to think about this first. You're the best litigator we've ever had. You've won cases for us when I thought for sure we'd have to settle for pennies on the dollar. You've saved this company millions, and we don't want to lose you. *I* don't want to lose you. So take some time off. Travel. Grieve. Whatever you need to do, and when you're ready to come back, your position will be waiting."

"I've already given this a lot of thought. I've had nothing else to do since that day *except* think. I can't do this anymore. When I'm in court, I become another person. Someone cold and calculating. That's not who I want to be, and if I'm going to make any sense out of this, I have to find the real me. I have to come to terms with who I was. And I have to find some way to live with knowing that who I was caused this. So thank you for the offer of time but I won't be needing it. That's my letter of resignation, effective immediately. Anyone on my team will be able to take over my pending cases. It has to be this way for my sake and for Sandy's memory. I appreciate all you've done for me, and I thank you for all the opportunities you and ALL NET have given me, but I have to go."

Ray opened the envelope and read the letter. He took a deep breath and said, "I'm sorry. I truly am. This was such a tragedy. And I understand. If someday you want to come back, we'll always have a position for you. I wish you peace, my friend. Please stay in touch." He stood, came around the desk, and put his hand out.

He shook his manager's hand knowing it would be the last time. "Thank you for understanding. I'll leave my badge, my phone, and the company credit cards with your assistant." He left his expensive

Italian leather briefcase with everything in it and walked away from his life as a corporate attorney.

It was a warm January day. The sky was clear, and the sun shone. The smell of the ocean, the sound of the waves, and the warm breeze called to him. He hoped for a few minutes of quiet. Just a few minutes without the accusing voices that now lived in his head constantly reminding him what a piece of shit he was.

He stopped by his too quiet house to change and grab his surfboard. Then, after spending the day letting the waves beat him up, he detoured to a liquor store and bought a six-pack and a bottle of Writers' Tears Irish Whiskey. When he got home, he showered and then sat on his couch and cried like a baby. An hour later, he called the local Chinese restaurant and ordered Kung Pao Chicken for delivery.

☐

4

H e lost track of time during his self-imposed purgatory. The only thing that changed was the restaurant he called each day. He couldn't go out. He couldn't sit still. Reading was out of the question. And the only way he got the voices to shut up was by watching NCIS or getting drunk until he passed out. Yeah, he drank too much, but damn it, he needed it or he'd blow his brains out.

One night, after a few beers — he couldn't remember how many — he ventured out to the local bar. He knocked back several shots of whiskey and got into an argument with a man who was verbally abusing a woman. Other than the flashing red lights, he had no memory of what happened or how he got home. And the next morning he woke up with a black eye and no idea where his car was. Now the voices had something else to chide him about.

He drank to shut them up. He drank more to forget what he did when he was drunk. Then he drank to get over the hangover. And every day he started all over again. His only sober moments were Tuesday nights at eight o'clock or the days when NCIS reruns were on. It was an endless, vicious cycle.

⌛

The doorbell woke him from his nap. He looked like hell and didn't give a fuck. He tried to ignore the noise, but it kept ringing and then knocking started. When the knocking turned to pounding, he gave up. Whoever it was, he had no intention of letting them in. He just needed the noise to stop. He opened the door to find Father Timothy looking concerned. "What can I do for you, Father?"

"May I come in?"

"Look, now's not a good time."

"I think this is the perfect time." The priest pushed past him and walked into the living room strewn with takeout containers and empty beer cans and whiskey bottles.

"Sorry. I gave the maid the year off. What do you want?"

"Your mother called me. She's very worried. She hasn't been able to reach you."

"I turned in my phone when I quit. I haven't bothered to get another one because I don't want to talk to anyone. Thank you for your concern, Father, but tell her I'm fine."

"You're not fine. From the looks of things, you're in a very dark place, and I want to help you."

"Why doesn't anyone listen to me? Of *course*, I'm in a dark place! *I* put me here. I'm dealing with this the best way I can. I just can't make the voices shut up!"

"So you're drinking in order to — what? Forget?"

"Yeah."

"And how's that working for you?"

Cussing out the old priest sounded like a good idea. Maybe then he'd leave. "It's working just great. Fucking great. Can't you tell? Look, I'm sorry I'm not following your stages of grief very well but I'll be okay. Tell my mother I'm fine."

"I'm not going to lie to her. You can if you want. You don't come to confession anymore so why not? If I'd known you were going to do this, I wouldn't have suggested you take time off from work. It looks like all you've done is wallow in self-pity."

Hitting the priest would probably buy him eternal hellfire and damnation although that might be a step up from where he was.

"I think you should get away. Go on a spiritual retreat. Find some peace, maybe even some answers." Father Timothy pulled a card out of his pocket and handed it to him. "This is a good place to start. They host many different groups, some are men only, some are women only, and there are a few mixed events. I would like to see you sign up for a men's recovery weekend."

"A recovery retreat? Recovery from what? Retreat from what? My life as it is now?"

"Recovery from your grief. And recovery from alcohol. I think you have a drinking problem."

"No, Father. I have a *living* problem. Look, I appreciate your concern, really I do. But I'm fine by myself."

"Okay, Michael — for now. But when you hit bottom, you know where to find me. Just please, think about what I said. Get away from here and all the memories. Go someplace where breathing won't hurt so much. Will you consider it, please?"

"Yes, Father. I'll consider it."

"God be with you, my son." The priest made the sign of the cross and left.

God be with me? Why the hell would He start now?

He locked the door, pulled the drapes closed, and made his way through the bottles and trash to the wet bar where he poured himself a tumbler of straight whiskey. Then he sat on the couch, and as he sipped the drink, he listened to the voices tell him what a piece of shit he was. Over and over they told him he was a murderer, and he didn't deserve to live. But through the noise, there was another voice, a quiet soothing voice. It almost sounded like Sandy. "You can't kill yourself because of me. Go find peace. Forgive yourself and find a purpose."

He looked at the now half empty glass.

I feel better already.

The glass slipped from his hand as he fell into a drunken, dreamless sleep.

5

Three months and one dismissed misdemeanor drunk driving charge later, he drove up Scenic Highway 1, California's beautiful winding road along the Pacific Coast. The road was just made for his little sports car, and with the top down and the wind in his hair, he almost felt normal.

The retreat center was in San Juan Bautista. Some of the photos on their website were of the mission and the historic little town. The retreat center was in the hills overlooking the Salinas Valley with its farms and vineyards. There were hiking trails in the hills and the town was full of shops and historical landmarks. And it was over four hundred miles away from everything that reminded him of Sandy's death.

He turned off the highway onto the one lane, winding, teeth jarring road that looked and felt like a minefield. Somehow, his BMW Z3's suspension held together. A canopy of tree branches covered one stretch of potholes. It was like driving through a tunnel of green. Then the view opened to pastures with horses and cattle and several run-down barns. He parked in a dirt lot and walked into the small office to register. "Hi, I'm Michael Chandler. I have a reservation for the retreat this weekend."

"Yes, Mr. Chandler. You're in room 47. We don't use locks here so there's no key. If you have anything of value, be sure to lock it in your car. You'll be sharing a room with Mr. Kevin McNally. There are bed linens and pillows already on the bed and towels and soap are in the bathroom. The rooms are very small so I suggest you leave anything you don't need in your car. The dinner bell rings at six and Father Devon will give a welcome presentation and hand out the agendas. Our cell reception is spotty but we do have a wireless network, albeit, a slow one. The password is *faith*. I hope you enjoy your stay. Feel free to wander around the grounds. There are trail maps in the gift shop next to the cafeteria."

He was sharing a room? He hadn't shared a room since college. He found the room which was unoccupied. Very small was an understatement. *Postage stamp* would be more accurate. He claimed the bed by the window and was grateful the FAQs on the retreat's website listed what *not* to bring. The dresser had one drawer, and the closet was large enough to fit two coats. The bathroom, however, was huge, or maybe it just seemed that way since the shower was smaller than the closet.

After he unpacked, he put on his trail running shoes and headed outside. The grounds were quiet, peaceful, and very green, something he wasn't used to. Rain was a regular occurrence in Northern California unlike where he lived. He began the path of the Stations of the Cross that circled a small pond. It was peaceful but not very inspiring. The prayers had lost their meanings. Still it was a nice walk.

When the dinner bell rang, he jogged to the cafeteria. It was Friday, and the meal was baked halibut with rice pilaf and steamed asparagus. He filled his plate and found an empty seat at a table. The food was much better than he'd expected.

Father Devon stood and introduced himself, said grace, and as the men ate, he explained a little about the weekend's events: meetings, presentations, and Mass.

He could have done without the Mass.

The men at his table chatted and made small talk, something he just wasn't up to. After dessert, he excused himself and wandered through the gift shop. It was full of inspirational books, souvenir trinkets, carved rosaries, and children's bible toys. He thought about buying some for his nieces and nephews, and maybe something for his mother, but that could wait until Sunday.

He made his way back to the main building and took a seat in the chapel in front of a large crucifix hanging on the wall above a simple altar. There was a time when that would have brought him comfort and inspiration. Now it just looked like a statue of a bleeding man in agony. It certainly didn't communicate love and compassion. It evoked fear and guilt which was exactly what he'd hoped to get away from.

This was a mistake.

He was just about to leave when a man in his sixties who looked a lot like Santa Claus in street clothes, approached him.

"Hi. I'm Kevin McNally. Father Devon said you're my roommate."

"Michael Chandler." They shook hands.

"So, Mike, we all have a story, a reason for being here. I'll tell you mine if you'll tell me yours."

The man seemed sincere and genuinely interested. That wouldn't last long. "I ruined a man's life. He killed my wife and committed suicide in my living room, and now I drink to forget. So, what's your story?"

Kevin was silent for a few seconds. He should have left in disgust, but he didn't. "Well, you're in the right place. And I hope by Sunday you'll have a different perspective. My story? I drove in a drunken blackout one night, rolled my car, and my wife died instantly. Spent two years in San Q for vehicular manslaughter. Then I spent six months on probation and had to attend AA meetings once a week. That was thirty-three years ago. Haven't had a drink since that night. If you want to talk about anything, I'm a good listener. We're all gathering in the fireside room in a few minutes. There's a big fire, coffee, and I understand Father Devon is going to tell his story."

Kevin left him to think about how similar their stories were.

How long had it taken that man to get over his guilt? It was comforting to know there was someone else there who had known the same hell of guilt and shame.

He found his way to the fireside room where chairs had been moved to form semi-circular rows facing a massive stone fireplace. Men of all ages milled about getting coffee and sodas before finding seats. He didn't need anything to keep him awake. The voices took care of that, and now he didn't have any alcohol to shut them up. But a cup of hot chocolate sounded good. It reminded him of happy times at night on the beach with Sandy. He blinked back tears and found a seat in the back where he wouldn't be in anyone's line of sight. He was an imposter. He didn't belong, and when everyone found out what he'd done, they'd tell him to leave.

Father Devon spoke of his days in Belfast, Northern Ireland, and his involvement with the Irish Republican Army. He'd been a Protestant then, an explosives expert, his job was blowing up buildings and killing Catholics. He talked about his crisis of conscience and the priest who took in an angry, bleeding young man and gave him sanctuary while the police searched for him. He talked about how that priest helped him escape to America. And he talked about how God entered his heart and showed him light and love and how all mankind belonged to God. He talked about finding forgiveness in his own heart and how he vowed to devote his life to bringing comfort to any suffering soul who needed it. And that's how he became a priest and wound up at the St. Francis Retreat Center.

The things that man had done! Yet, as he spoke, he glowed as if filled with the Holy Spirit. But Father Devon had fought for a cause he'd believed was right and justified. And that was very different from being a cold-hearted, blood sucking, life destroying murderer. Yes, it was an inspiring story but he couldn't relate.

After the evening prayer, everyone mingled or wandered around the building in solitude. He took that opportunity to slip outside. The night was clear and the Milky Way was beautiful. He made himself comfortable on a wooden swing around the corner from the doors where no one could see him. He listened for the sounds of wildlife. According to the center's website, animals and birds roamed the area including the occasional bobcat, although they tended to stay away from the humans. He heard rustling and snuffling in the stillness but it was too dark to see anything. Whatever it was, it wasn't interested in him so he closed his eyes.

Maybe it was exhaustion, maybe it was the spirituality of the place, or maybe he just dreamed he heard Sandy's voice. But when he opened his eyes, there was no one there.

"There you are. It's supposed to get down close to freezing tonight. Don't you think you should come in?"

"I heard her. I don't know what she said, but I heard her voice."

"Who?"

"My wife. But it was just a dream. Yeah, I should go to bed. It was a long drive and I'm hallucinating. I need some sleep. I hope you don't mind I took the bed by the window."

"Nope. Come on."

They walked through the almost empty fireside room and down the hallway to their tiny room. It was too warm, so he opened the window a bit.

"Is that okay?"

"Yeah, I prefer it a little cool. I'm going to take a quick shower. I'll try to be quiet, but there are earplugs next to the bed if you need them. In case you're asleep when I get out, I'll see you in the morning and we'll talk. Breakfast is at eight."

"Okay, thanks. I doubt I'll sleep much."

He changed into sweats and stretched out on the narrow twin bed with its mattress that should have been replaced fifty years ago. It was so soft, and the springs were so worn out, the middle sagged almost to the floor. He closed his eyes and listened to the shower run. It was strange hearing someone else after living alone.

§

"Mike, wake up!"

"Huh, what? What time is it?"

"Eight. You need to get up if you want breakfast."

How could it be eight? Had he really slept through the night? How long had it been since he'd been able to do that? "I have to shower and change."

"Don't bother. No one else has showered yet. You're dressed. That's good enough."

He dragged himself out of bed and followed Kevin to the cafeteria where he found hot coffee and a room full of cheerful men. Breakfast was scrambled eggs, bacon, toast, oatmeal, fresh fruit, pastries, orange juice, grapefruit juice, and, of course, more coffee. It must have been the fresh air and the peacefulness of the place because he couldn't remember the last time he'd been that hungry. He was just finishing up a second helping of eggs and toast when Father Devon addressed the room.

"This morning we have two workshops to choose from starting at ten. One is about dealing with grief. There are different kinds of grief. There's losing a loved one to death, losing a family due to separation and divorce, losing a job and livelihood, and losing one's faith. That workshop will be in the meeting room on the other side of the gift shop. The other workshop is on religion versus spirituality. Are they the same or different? Are they mutually inclusive or exclusive? Can you be one without the other? That workshop will be in the chapel.

"Following those, there will be meetings for two different recovery programs, Alcoholics Anonymous for those of you who have or think you have a problem with alcohol, and Alanon for those of you who are trying to deal with someone else's alcoholism. Both include some background on how the twelve steps can be used to solve most problems. Check the blackboard in the fireside room for the locations. After that, we'll meet back here for lunch, followed by two hours of free time. By now you've noticed our food here is exceptional. Still there are some who use the lunch hour and free time to go into town and do some exploring. We'd like to give the kitchen an idea of how many lunches to prepare. So how many of you plan to stick around?"

About half the room raised their hands and Kevin leaned over. "Let's go into town. There's a great cantina with authentic Mexican food and the mission and museum are very interesting."

"Okay, sure." He didn't care one way or the other. He was just along for the ride.

"So, which workshop are you going to attend? I think I'll go to the one on grief."

"Yeah, I was thinking about that one, too. But the other one sounds like something I might need more."

"Okay, if I don't see you, meet me in the fireside room after the AA meeting. We can drive or walk."

"I think I'd like to walk."

"Great! See ya later."

He finished his coffee and considered which workshop to attend. Too bad they were at the same time. And why had Kevin assumed he would attend the AA meeting?

"Excuse me. Michael, right?" Father Devon stood next to Kevin's empty chair.

"Yes, Father."

"May I join you? We have a few minutes before the workshops start."

"Yes, please."

He sat down. "You're Catholic, right?"

"Yes."

"Are you practicing?"

"Not for the last few months. I've had some problems. Actually, I'm struggling."

"Would you like to talk about it?"

Did he want to talk about it? Not really. But he would have to, eventually. "Well, in a nutshell, I ruined a man's life, and while I was doing a good deed, he took revenge by murdering my wife. Then he committed suicide in my living room."

"I see. And why do you think you ruined this man's life?"

"I don't think. I know. He left a note next to his body telling me what I did to him. I was a corporate lawyer, and because of me, he lost everything, and his note said he wanted me to suffer the same way he had."

"You said this happened while you were doing a good deed?"

He related all the events that took place that day and expected the priest to express some kind of judgment.

"Do you blame God?"

How did he know? "Yes. Yes, I do. My wife was the kindest, most considerate, and the most loving person I've ever known. She had a pure heart. She was beautiful inside and out, and I was the bastard who made a living out of ruining other people and their companies. It should have been me. My priest said there's no way we can understand why God chooses one and not another. We just have to have faith. I'm finding that impossible right now. It's too arbitrary. Someone like Sandy who did everything right, not because she had to, but because she was that kind of person, how can there be any reason for God to take her? If there's no reason, then there's no point in having faith. I'm starting to feel like there is no God, or if there is, He doesn't care as much as all the religions say He does. I know this sounds pretty sacrilegious, and I'm sure I've shocked you."

"Not at all. There wouldn't be much for priests to do if we only ministered to perfect Catholics. I understand how you feel though. When I was in Ireland fighting with the IRA, I killed many people — not by my own hand, but I set the explosives. I robbed women of their husbands and children of their mothers and fathers. I did it because we believed we were fighting for a cause. I believed Catholics were the enemy. I was, like you, someone who ruined people's lives."

"Then how could you convert to the enemy?"

"I was pretty badly injured by one of our own bombs. It detonated early, and I didn't get away fast enough. This was near a Catholic church, and the priest dragged me inside, bandaged my wounds, and told me he forgave me. It was the most ridiculous thing I'd ever heard. But as he talked, I began to understand. The police were looking for me and he hid me until things cooled down.

During that time, I learned that God is God of all things and all people. God doesn't care if we kneel or stand when we pray. He doesn't care what words we pray with or what language we use. What He cares about is that we live in His light. He's not even that big on us obeying his commandments. That's why He sent His only Son to take away our sins. Forgiveness is ours. All we have to do is ask for it."

"You sound like Father Timothy. And all that may be true but it's going to be awhile before I forgive Him for taking her. And right now I'm still not sure He exists."

"He does, but you will learn that for yourself. You were brought here to start on your spiritual path. I believe God has a purpose for you but you must find it. No one can tell you how or why. All I ask is that you keep an open mind. *Oh*, my goodness. It seems we've been talking for quite a while. You've missed the beginning of the workshops. But I think you needed this chat more."

"Thank you. You've given me a lot to think about."

"Are you going to attend one of the meetings later?"

"I haven't decided yet. Father Timothy thinks I have a drinking problem, but it's more of a living problem."

"I think the AA meeting would be good for you. It'll help you decide if you really do have a problem with alcohol. I think that meeting is in the library. And Michael? Feel free to talk to me or any of the friars. We all have pasts. As they say in AA, *No guts, no story.*"

He stood, said the Benediction, and hurried off to the fireside room.

That was a lot to take in, but he'd take the priest's advice and go to the AA meeting. All he knew about AA was what he saw on TV.

He finished his coffee and went back to the room to shower. Father Devon had given him a lot to think about.

6

"Welcome, everyone. My name is George and I'm an alcoholic."

The twenty men in the room answered, in unison, "Hi George!"

George read the preamble and something called the responsibility statement. "*I am responsible. When anyone, anywhere, reaches out for help, I want the hand of AA always to be there, and for that, I am responsible.* In that spirit, is there anyone here, in their first thirty days of sobriety, who would care to introduce themselves by their first name only? This isn't to embarrass you, but so we can get to know you better."

Well, why not?

He raised his hand, and when George nodded to him, he stood. "My name is Mike, and I think I'm an alcoholic — at least that's what my priest said."

"Welcome, Mike. Maybe you'll hear something that will help you decide for yourself. Feel free to talk to any of us after the meeting. Anyone else?"

No one else? He was the only one? Or was he the only one brave enough to speak up? Hell, he wasn't even convinced he was an alcoholic. After all, he hadn't had a drink in a week. Didn't that prove something?

He sat through the meeting, listened to story after story, and identified with some of them. Some, like Kevin's, hit too close to home. But Kevin's drinking caused the accident that killed his wife. *He* hardly drank at all when Sandy was alive. It wasn't until she died that he crawled into a bottle of oblivion.

After the meeting, several of the men approached him. It was overwhelming, and he looked around for an escape. He found Kevin near the door to the garden. "Can we get out of here? I feel like a steak in a cage full of hungry lions."

Kevin chuckled. "Let's go. You're a newcomer and, yeah, you're fresh meat, and some of them will try to talk to you later. They just want you to know you're in the right place. We believe that if a person has to ask if they have a problem with alcohol, they probably do."

It was a brisk two-mile walk into town, and they found a Mexican restaurant with a courtyard and outside seating. While they waited for the server to take their orders, a table of young people — maybe in their twenties — did a round of tequila shots. He was acutely aware that he could never drink again for the rest of his life if he joined AA. Definitely not a good selling point.

After they ordered lunch, the group of young people got up to leave. There were several half empty beer mugs still on the table, and the sight triggered something inside him, something he couldn't name, but it felt a lot like anger. How could they leave without finishing their beers?

"Does that bother you?"

"What?"

"All those mugs with beer still in them? It's okay. It still bugs me. We call that *alcohol abuse*. For us, it's inconceivable that anyone would willingly leave a half-finished drink. It's like when someone says they've had too much and are starting to feel it. Well, isn't that the whole point?"

It seemed funny in a sick sort of way which made him uncomfortable. So rather than think about it, he watched a rooster strut around pecking the ground for crumbs.

After lunch, they wandered in and out of the shops, and he bought a few souvenirs for his mother and his nieces and nephews. They took a quick tour of the mission museum, lit candles in the chapel, and then walked back to the retreat center. "What's on the schedule for this afternoon?"

"There's a lecture on spirituality and meditation and then Mass before dinner."

"Will there be confession and communion?"

"*Hmm.* I doubt it. Probably not enough time."

That was fine with him. He was already well acquainted with his sins, and his penance and absolution never worked. It should have been him in that body bag. How was he supposed to live under the weight of all that shame and guilt? And as for meditation? Might as well just give the voices in his head a bullhorn.

This whole weekend was a waste of time. "I think I'm going to skip all that and go for a hike."

"Are you sure?"

"Yeah. It's either that, or I'm going to leave. All this God stuff is too uncomfortable right now. I'm still angry, and that's something I have to work through myself." What he *really* wanted was a drink. No. If he was being honest with himself, he *needed* one.

"Okay, Mike. Be sure to get a trail map before you go. And you'll want to be back before dark. There are bobcats up in the hills."

They said their goodbyes when they neared the center. Kevin carried the shopping bags to the room while he detoured to the gift shop.

It was still clear and crisp out, and even though they'd just walked almost five miles, he still had more antsy energy to burn. He had at least three hours until sunset so he chose the long trail. Ten feet up the trail, he could still hear the voices of the men gathered in the patio area. One man claimed he was born an alcoholic, another said he didn't have his first drink until college, but that one drink had started his obsession. Well, *he* was grieving for his dead wife, and for the time being, he needed the comfort of an occasional oblivion. It was temporary.

A whistle pulled his wandering mind back to the moment. It sounded like it came from the hills above. A hawk glided directly toward him. The bird of prey didn't mean him any harm, although how he could know that, was a mystery. When the huge bird circled overhead, he laughed. Wouldn't it just figure that this hawk had picked him out to shit on? Talk about a message from God!

He shielded his eyes from the sun's glare and looked up in time to watch a wing feather float down in front of him. He picked it up. It beat being shit on but was it really some kind of message?

He had barely enough signal to look up the meaning. According to a list of totem animals and their meanings, a hawk was a messenger. It brought intuition, victory, healing, nobility, recollection, cleansing, visionary power, and guardianship. Well, that sure covered a lot of things, but *messenger* and *healing* seemed the most relevant. He did a little more searching on hawk feathers.

Hmm. According to federal law, it was illegal for anyone to possess a feather from a bird of prey.

So what the hell does that mean?

So did the hawk give him a gift? A message? Or was he being setup for an arrest? And if it was a message, what was it trying to tell him? He closed his eyes and saw Sandy's smiling face. He didn't believe in the supernatural, and getting caught breaking a federal law would get him disbarred, so he put the feather back where it had landed. Then he took a photo with his phone so he could ask someone about it later.

When he reached the top of the trail, he had a panoramic view of the valley and the town below. He recognized the spot from the website. With at least two hours until sunset, he sat down to rest and enjoy the view. The silence was palatable. The voices had stopped! When did that happen? He closed his eyes and attempted to meditate.

When he opened his eyes, it was dark. His watch read six-thirty. What the fuck? He tried to call the center to let them know where he was but his cell phone battery was dead.

Great. They'll send out a search party.

He hiked down as best he could with only the moon to light his way. Every once in a while, he heard rustling and snuffling but it was too dark, and he became disoriented. Was he walking in circles? Then he almost stepped on the feather. He was on the right trail and only a half mile or so away from the Center. This time he picked it up and tucked it inside his shirt. If it was that big of a deal, he could put it back tomorrow.

The lights from the center weren't very far, so he jogged the rest of the way.

"Mike? *Oh,* thank God! We were just about to go out looking for you! Are you okay? What happened?" All five men in the search party spoke at once, and he kind of wished he was back on that quiet hillside with the bobcats.

"I'm fine. I just lost track of time is all. But I could use some food. Is the cafeteria still serving?" Kevin pulled him into a bear hug which was a complete invasion of his personal space, but the man had worried about him so he let it go.

"Yeah, there's still food. Come on."

7

"So how was your hike? Did you learn anything?"

Did Father Devon somehow know about the feather still tucked in his shirt? "I'm not sure what you mean by *learn anything.* It was just a hike."

"*Hmm.* I thought the old hawk might have a message for you."

"Old hawk?"

"There's a hawk living in the hills, and there are some who say it's the spirit of an Indian who jumped off the cliff hoping to communicate with his dead wife before he hit the ground. It's just a myth, really. But some people report finding feathers and having vivid dreams of loved ones who have passed."

Well, hell.

He kept the fact that he had the feather to himself.

"You missed Mass. There will be another one tomorrow morning at seven. After breakfast, we'll have a panel discussion on the Prayer of St. Francis. You know the prayer?"

"Yes. And there's a wallet card in the welcome packet."

"Of course." The priest hesitated. "So, there's nothing you want to talk about?"

"No, Father. I just want to finish eating and go to bed. I'm not used to all the fresh air and exercise I got today."

"Will I see you in the morning?"

"I'll definitely be here for breakfast, and I'll probably stick around for the discussion, but I need to get home sometime tomorrow. It's a long drive."

He finished eating and walked back to their room. Kevin wasn't there, so he pulled the feather out of his shirt and carefully packed it. Part of him wanted to believe it meant something but the other part of him was skeptical. He'd hoped to find some peace and maybe some answers this weekend, but so far, he'd only found a feather and more questions.

After a shower, he climbed into the sagging bed.

"Sweetheart?"

"Sandy?"

"You need to find your purpose."

"Why did you have to die? Why wasn't it me? God, I miss you so much."

"You can't move forward until you find a way to help."

"Help? Who? How?"

"You need to help them."

"Who? I don't understand!"

"You will."

"Don't go, Sandy! I love you! Please don't go!"

"I'm always here. And I'll stay until you find your way to the one who will love you the way I did. Have compassion for yourself. Forgive yourself. It wasn't your fault."

He bolted up. His heart pounded and sweat poured off him while he shivered and gasped for air. Kevin was snoring, and the room was dark. He checked the time: A few minutes after five. Going back to sleep now would be impossible.

Find a way to help them. Who? And how? *Someone who will love you the way I did.* Not possible. He got dressed, pulled on his jacket, and tiptoed out. Just past the pond was a gazebo that overlooked the valley. He sat on the bench and closed his eyes. He needed answers.

Maybe he should just chuck it all and drink himself to death. Or maybe he could run away. The payout from the life insurance policy

Sandy had insisted on getting would arrive any day. If he sold the house, he could travel the world for at least two years. Maybe he could find some answers somewhere else. As soon as that thought crossed his mind, he heard her say, "What you need is closer to home."

Hearing her voice loosened the vise around his heart, and the burden of guilt he was so used to carrying seemed a little lighter. He hadn't felt spiritual in a long time. He hadn't felt a lot of things in a long time. He wasn't even sure he could call himself a Catholic anymore. But he went to Mass, anyway. That would make Father Timothy happy.

☒

"Here's my card. Call me anytime you want to talk. And here's the phone number for the AA office near you. It's close enough you could probably walk there."

"Thanks, Kevin. Thanks for everything. I'll keep in touch."

"I hope so. And I hope you find what you're looking for. God speed, Mike."

God speed? No, he wasn't looking forward to the drive home. It wasn't a home anymore, anyway. *Oh,* what the hell. He was so close, he might as well drive up to San Francisco and see the sights.

He lowered the convertible top, cranked the heater, and hit the freeway. It was a beautiful drive, but as soon as the Golden Gate bridge came into view, he had to stop and raise the top. Who was it that said something about the coldest winter they'd ever spent was a summer in San Francisco? To be fair, it was just the first weekend in June so not summer yet. Still, he was used to Southern California where it was summer all year long.

He took the long way around the city and found an expensive hotel overlooking Fisherman's Wharf. He got the last room, unpacked, and walked down to the wharf. The aroma of steamed crab and clam chowder that permeated the chilly air made his stomach growl.

He walked into a restaurant on Pier 39 and ordered clam chowder in a sourdough bread bowl and a glass of cold, crisp white wine. The wine was excellent, but he finished it before he finished the chowder, so he ordered another glass. He had one more glass before he left. The soup had been delicious and satisfied his hunger, and he wasn't the least bit drunk so he went looking for a liquor store for a nightcap.

It was almost dark when he found a store. He bought an expensive bottle of wine, a bottle of Writers' Tears Irish Whiskey, some snacks, a corkscrew, some plastic cups, and a souvenir shot glass. Then he made his way back to the hotel.

The bathroom had a nice big tub with a big screen TV which seemed a little over the top. So with a full cup of wine and the remote control, he made himself comfortable in the tub. When the cup was empty, he got out and went to get the bottle and tried not to slosh the water when he climbed back in. It was lukewarm, so he turned on the hot water. When he ran out of wine, he cracked open the Writers' Tears.

The bed was heaven compared to the tiny twin with the sagging mattress, and his body melted into it.

He heard pounding but was too tired to find out where the noise was coming from. Probably just construction somewhere. Then the bed shook.

Earthquake?

He opened one eye and found a man in a gray uniform standing at the foot of his bed. A Hispanic woman who looked like a housekeeper stood next to him.

"Mr. Chandler!"

"*Huh? Wha?* Who're you? What's going on?"

"Mr. Chandler, you've been locked in this room for three days. A locksmith had to remove the deadbolt just so we could get in. The hotel manager wants you to leave. Now."

Three days? Leave? He sat up but had to hold on to his head to keep it from exploding and spraying brain matter everywhere. What the fuck happened? He'd just gotten comfortable in bed with a cup of whiskey.

Nausea hit his gut like a baseball bat. *"Uh,* excuse me." He barely made it to the bathroom. When the dry heaves passed, he realized he was stark naked which was good since he was sitting in a large puddle of water. He rinsed his mouth, splashed some cold water on his face, and with a towel around his waist, he walked out to face the hotel security guard. "I'm sorry. I haven't been feeling well."

Yeah, that's it. Don't pay any attention to the empty bottles and the open bags of chips and cookies.

"Mr. Chandler, you need to pack up, settle your bill, and go."

"Yes, of course. Just let me clean up and get dressed." What the hell time was it?

"We'll wait in the hall."

They wanted to escort him out like a fucking bum? Fine. Whatever. After the security guard and the housekeeper left, he stood in the puddle of water and brushed his teeth. Why was there a puddle of water?

He'd meant to have the hotel laundry clean his clothes, but apparently that had been two days ago. At least his jeans and sweat-shirt were relatively clean and not too wrinkled. He found his watch. It was seven.

Shit.

He finished packing, including the not quite empty whiskey bottle, and walked out with his eyes downcast. He was beyond humiliated, but it was his own fault. And he wasn't even sure how it happened. He hadn't meant to get drunk. All he'd wanted was to relax, but something happened during dinner. Why did he buy the wine and whiskey? Why had it seemed like a good idea at the time?

The people at the front desk sneered at him like he was a drunken street bum. According to the day manager, he'd called the concierge Monday night and demanded a pack of cigarettes and a call girl, which was a damned lie. He'd never smoked a day in his life, and he'd never hired a hooker before, and there was no way he'd demand anything like that. As far as he knew, he'd slept for two days.

He still didn't understand what the big problem was. He guaranteed the room with a credit card when he checked in. What difference did it make how long he stayed? He was perfectly willing to pay for the extra days plus a large tip for the housekeeping staff. But the manager said he wasn't welcome at their hotel again. And after a phone call, probably from the housekeeper, the manager said the damage estimate was two thousand dollars.

Two thousand dollars? Damages?

As the manager read off the list, his stomach threatened another round of dry heaves. He'd let the tub overflow, pulled the desk phone out of the wall, and urinated in bed.

And the hits just kept on coming.

Yeah, he wouldn't be going back there again. Fuck. He wouldn't be going back to San Francisco again. All he'd wanted was to check out the wharf area, grab a bite to eat, maybe buy a few souvenirs, and get a good night's sleep.

After settling the bill, he grabbed his bag and quickly left the lobby. Valet already had his car waiting out front. The hotel couldn't get rid of him fast enough.

The voices started as soon as he put his car in gear so he cranked up the music to drown them out on the long drive home. He stopped twice to fill up and grab something to drink. He needed a beer to settle his stomach and stop the shakes, but after everything else that had happened, the last thing he needed was to get pulled over with an open container. He settled for ginger ale.

By the time he got home six hours later, the shakes were much worse and parking in his garage was a challenge. Before he did anything else, he grabbed a Corona from the fridge and gulped it down. Then he opened another one, sat on his couch, and tried to process everything that had happened. The retreat had helped. He'd learned a lot, and he wouldn't forget the experience with the hawk. He'd made some friends, and although he didn't come away with any answers, at least he was somewhat clearer on the questions.

He winced and shuddered as the memory of the disaster in San Francisco overwhelmed him. He'd heard the term *pitiful and incomprehensible demoralization* in the AA meeting. That described him perfectly. And he didn't even know how it happened. He'd blacked out one other time back in college — and there was that night he got into the bar fight. Shit, he never had a problem with alcohol until Sandy died.

He turned on his phone, something he forgot to do when he left the retreat, and found six voicemails, five from his mother and one from Father Timothy.

Fuck. He was supposed to be home Sunday night, his mother had started calling Monday morning, and now it was Wednesday. In her last message, she was frantic and wondered if she should call the highway patrol and start checking hospitals. He dreaded calling her, but if he didn't, she'd probably come over. And then she'd get on his case about the trash and dust. Father Timothy just wanted to know how the weekend went.

Might as well get it over with.

"Hi, Mom."

"Michael! *Oh,* thank God! Are you okay? Where have you been? And why didn't you call me back?"

"I'm fine Mom. I decided to check out San Francisco while I was up north. I'm sorry I didn't call. I guess I forgot to turn my phone back on after the retreat."

And I was out cold, drunk in a trashed hotel room.

"So, how was it?"

"The retreat? It was okay. I learned a lot, got a lot of exercise, *oh,* and I picked up some souvenirs for you when we walked into town."

"Did you go into the mission?"

"Yeah, it was pretty interesting. It's still a church and there's a pretty extensive museum next door."

"Listen, I want you to come for dinner tonight."

"Tonight? Why tonight?"

"I'm having Father Timothy over, and he asked about you. He's a little concerned."

Fuck.

"Concerned about what?"

"He's worried you're not grieving right."

"I didn't know there was a right way and a wrong way to grieve when your wife's been murdered."

"I'm sorry. I didn't mean you were doing it wrong. I guess there are several stages and it's a process. He thinks you might be stuck between guilt and anger. Anyway, I'd love to see you."

"Who else will be there? Any of my brothers?"

"No. Everyone's too busy to visit dear old Mom and Dad these days. So, you'll come?"

Fuck.

"Yeah, sure. What time?"

"Well, you can come over whenever you want, of course, but dinner will be at six-thirty. Okay?"

"Yeah, okay. That'll give me time to do some laundry. I'll see you then."

"Love you."

"Love you, too."

Fuck.

Well, at least he didn't have to call Father Timothy.

He finished his beer, tossed the empty bottle into the overflowing recycle bin which knocked another bottle to the floor, and unpacked. He put the feather in a safe place and got a load of laundry started. Then he removed all the price tags from the gifts and put everything in a bag. Next was a much-needed shower.

He had about two hours before he had to leave, so he grabbed his laptop and a beer and sat down on the couch.

He wasn't sure what he was looking for other than he needed to move. Everything about this house reminded him of Sandy. He could probably get a million for it. The house was in good condition, and he hadn't broken anything major, yet. He didn't owe that much on it — maybe four hundred thousand. That would leave him with a nice down payment, and he would have plenty of cash in the bank from Sandy's life insurance. If he got a decent interest rate, he could handle the mortgage on a small place, maybe down by the water. But that meant getting a job.

The retreat and the feather and the peace he'd briefly felt came back, but he needed more. Maybe he should put off the house thing and go find himself somewhere. He had nothing else going on, anyway. All he needed was to not do anything stupid beforehand.

8

"Hi, Mom."
 She rushed to him and threw her arms around his neck. Then she pulled back and examined his face. He cringed when one eyebrow went up. She always could see right through him. "What's wrong?"

"What do you mean?"

"You know what I mean. I'm your mother, and I know something's wrong."

"Well, of course, something's wrong."

"Not that. Something else happened. Tell me."

Fuck.

She always knew. His brothers had gotten away with everything, but she always knew when he'd done something wrong or something bothered him. And there was no way in hell he could tell her about San Francisco. He had to change the subject. "Nothing happened. I'm just tired. The bed was about a hundred years old and sagged so badly, I thought my butt would hit the floor. Anyway, look what I brought you. And there are some toys for Luke's and Matt's kids, too."

She took the bag as she continued to eye him. Then she stirred the spaghetti sauce, turned down the flame, and went through the bag as his father walked in.

"Michael."

"Dad."

"Want a beer?"

"Sure." The word was out of his mouth before he knew it. One wouldn't hurt. In fact, it would probably steady his nerves and help him deal with all the questions that were coming.

"So, how was it?"

"Relaxing."

"Was it at a church? Your mother said something about St. Francis."

"It's a monastery and a retreat center. Jesuit brothers run it, and Father Devon led the retreat."

"So, a Catholic thing?"

"Sort of. There were men there from other religions, too."

Hmm. So why did you wait until today to call your mother?"

Fuck.

"It's a new phone, and I guess I forgot to turn it back on when I left the retreat. I took a ride up to San Francisco since I was so close."

"Oh? So, what did you do for two days?"

What the fuck is this? High school?

"I wandered around, saw the sights. You know."

"Hmm."

Just as he started to sweat, the doorbell rang. "That must be Father Timothy. I'll get it." Anything to get out of that kitchen.

"Father. Please come in."

"Well, Michael. Good to see you. Here, this is for your mother."

He took the wine bottle from the priest and shook the man's hand. "Can I get you something?"

"How about a wee shot o' Irish?"

"Coming right up." He hurried to the kitchen and gave the wine to his mother "Here. This is from Father Timothy." Then he grabbed the whiskey from the cupboard along with two shot glasses. Before anyone could say anything, he ducked out of the kitchen and hurried back to the living room where he set the glasses on the coffee table and poured two shots. The priest raised an eyebrow but didn't comment.

"Good health and long life to you."

"And to you. Cheers!" It burned on the way down, but when the warmth flowed through his limbs, his skin fit again. He took a deep breath and let it out slowly. That was his first deep breath since Sunday night at the restaurant. At least that's the last one he remembered. "Another?"

"No, I think I'll wait. I need some food in my belly. Wouldn't do for a priest to get drunk, would it?"

"I suppose not. Well, I'm not a priest." He poured another shot for himself, knocked it back, and felt even better.

I still have some of that bottle left over. Maybe I can duck out of here early.

"Father Timothy! Welcome! I see Michael's already gotten you a drink. Can I get you anything else?"

"Dinner would be good. I'm famished, and wonderful smells are dancing out of your kitchen."

"*Oh*, Father, you have such a way with words. Michael, can you help me set the table?"

"Sure, Mom. Be with you in a sec." He poured one more shot for himself, knocked it back, put the cap back on the bottle, and bounced into the kitchen to get the silverware. When his hands were full, he tried to close the drawer and dropped a knife. As soon as he picked it up, he dropped another. After the fourth one fell, he let go of everything in frustration and looked down at the pile of cutlery on the floor unable to figure out what to do.

"Michael! What on Earth!" His mother stooped to pick everything up, dumped it all in the sink, and began to wash each piece.

"I'm sorry Mom. Some knives slipped, and when I tried to catch them, I dropped the rest. I'm really sorry. God, I'm so sorry. I don't know what's wrong with me." Jesus, he was crying!

His father sneered. "Well, I know what's wrong with you. You're drunk."

"Samuel! Michael is not drunk. He's just tired. He's been under a lot of stress lately."

"Stress? He just got back from a spiritual retreat! How can he be stressed already?"

"Excuse me. I don't mean to intrude, but can I talk to Michael in the living room?"

Fuck.

Now the priest wanted to get on his case. He wiped his eyes as he followed the man into the living room. Jesus, he needed another shot. His parents were fighting, and it was about him. Something else to add to the list of fuckups for the voices to use against him.

"Sit down, please."

Shit.

"I watched you with the whiskey, Michael. You took three shots to my one, and you still have a beer."

That's right!

As soon as he finished it, he wanted another but Father Timothy kept talking.

"What happened in San Francisco?"

"Nothin'! Why does everyone think somethin' happened? Jesus H. Christ! Why can't you all jus' leave me alone? Don't you all have anythin' better to do?"

"Michael! You do NOT use the Lord's name in vain!"

"For cryin' out loud. This ain't fuckin' Sunday school, and I'm not a kid. If I wanna swear, I'll swear. Look, I'm not doin' this right now. I'm goin' home." He stood and staggered to the door.

"Please don't go!" His mother was holding on to his arm, crying, and he was at the breaking point.

"Leave me alone, God damn it! Jus' leave me alone! Why can't you all jus' leave me alone?" He fell to his knees and cried out, "God help me! I don't know what's wrong!"

"You're a drunk, that's what's wrong!"

"Samuel, please. Mary, you two go back in the kitchen, and let me talk to Michael alone."

"You're babying him, Father. He needs to man up. Yeah, his wife died. Yeah, it was tragic. But that was what? Almost six months ago? He needs to get a grip. He's not the only man who ever lost his wife."

"Samuel! In the kitchen, NOW!"

Great. Now his mother was pissed. She never yelled like that, and it was his fault. Just another fucking thing to add to the list of things he fucked up.

"All right, all right. I'm coming. Talk some sense into him, Father. He's going to kill himself if he keeps this up."

Father Timothy reached down to help him up. He swayed and fell on the couch.

"Okay, I want the truth. What happened?"

"I doan know, Father. I doan know. Everythin' was okay, really. When I left the retreat, I felt better'n I have since . . . since before that day, so I drove up to Frisco. I doan know how it happened. I doan even 'member most of it. I jus' had wine with my soup, an' I stopped on the way back to my room an' picked up more wine and a bottle of whiskey. That was Sunday. This morning, they kicked me out. I doan 'member nothin' else. They said I demanded cigarettes an' a hooker. A hooker! Me! An' I trashed the room. An' *oh*, my God, I pissed in the bed! I'm so 'shamed, and I doan know why it happened!"

"Don't you?"

"No, I doan!"

"It's called the *phenomenon of craving*. You can't have just one drink. It changes something in your brain, and you have to have more. It's an addiction."

"I'm not some addict."

"But you've been drinking a lot since Sandy died. It was probably always in you, and her death triggered it. You need help."

"I need for everyone to leave me alone. I jus' wanna die, maybe drink myself to death."

"Yes, you could do that, but that's a mortal sin. Besides, think about what it would do to your family. They love you, and I know it's hurting them to see you like this."

"Mom, maybe, but not dear ol' dad. You heard him. I jus' need to man up, get a grip, forget I lost the only woman I ever loved — the only woman I'll ever love. Well, I can't. I'm not a man like him. I'm just a fuckup."

I wonder how many rosaries for saying fuck to a priest. Add another one to that fucking list.

"I'm sorry, Father. I shouldn't have said that."

"Do you think, as old as I am, I've never heard that word before? You're upset, you've had too much to drink, and you're still grieving. I think God will forgive you, but I don't think your mother would, so you might want to watch what you say around her. Now, what are we going to do?"

"Do? 'Bout what?"

"About your drinking. I think you need Alcoholics Anonymous."

"I went to a meeting at the retreat."

"*Oh?* And what did you think?"

"I think those people have real problems. But I'm not like them. I drink 'cause it was my fault that man murdered my wife."

The old priest sighed. "It doesn't matter *why* you drink. What matters is what happens to you *when* you drink. Where's your phone?"

"Why?"

"I want to look something up."

He handed his phone to the priest who punched in several words, read the screen and said, "There's a meeting right down the street in a half hour. I've been to this one before but on a different night. I'll take you."

"But what 'bout dinner?"

"I'll explain it to your parents. They'll understand. This is more important. Go wash your face with cold water while I tell them. *Oh,* and I'm driving, and we're getting you a coffee on the way. No more whiskey!"

He was almost sober when they walked into the back room of the Lutheran church. What was it with AA and churches? Wasn't it supposed to be spiritual and not religious?

There were several people gathered around a coffee pot. Some of them looked like they'd just come from jobs at a bank, and some looked like homeless street people. Many of them knew Father Timothy who insisted on introducing him to everyone when all he wanted was to find a chair in the back of the room and hide.

It started like the meeting at the retreat, but they read from something called a *big book* which didn't look any bigger than most books. Some of it didn't make any sense, but some of it almost sounded hopeful. When they asked for any newcomers, he stood up. "My name's Michael, and I'm an alcoholic." He sat and wiped his eyes as everyone said in unison, "Hi Michael. Welcome! We're glad you're here."

The president, or whatever he was, asked, "Would you like a phone list?"

"*Uh,* I guess so." A trifold meeting schedule made its way around the room, and each man wrote his name and phone number on the back. He leaned over and whispered, "No women?"

"No. Men work with men. Women work with women. Avoids all kinds of problems that way."

It was just as well since he was really uncomfortable at the thought of talking to women. The meeting guide was for the South Bay area, and on the back were fifteen names and phone numbers. They didn't know him, but they were all willing to help him. "So, what's in it for them?"

"What do you mean?"

"Why would they want to help me? What do they want in return?"

"They don't want anything from you."

"Bullshit. Everyone wants something."

The leader was speaking. "We will now practice the seventh tradition which states *we have no dues or fees, we are self-supporting through our own contributions.* This money goes toward rent, coffee, and literature."

He leaned over to the priest and mumbled, "Here it comes. This is the entry fee, right? How much?"

"There is no entry fee. Put a dollar in the basket for the coffee you're going to drink, if you want."

When the basket got to him, he pulled a twenty out of his wallet, but before he could put it in the basket, the priest stopped him. "How about just five dollars? You're welcome here. You don't need to buy your way in."

After a short coffee break, the meeting resumed. A bald man covered in tattoos and piercings, who looked like a cross between a street thug, a pimp and a tatted Mr. Clean, introduced himself as Bruce, which sure didn't fit his homey gangsta persona. He talked about some of the things he'd done, the bottom that got him to sober up, and what his life was like now. Why would anyone talk about such awful things like that in front of a room full of strangers? At least the retreat had been a controlled environment of men.

After the man finished speaking, everyone clapped like he was some sort of a celebrity. Then he called on others to share, and they talked about similar situations. And people laughed! They laughed at the sickest, most disgusting things.

Suddenly, the room got quiet, and people turned to look at him. The man had called on him! Well, he'd show them. When they heard what he did, they'd tell him to leave. The whole thing was phony, anyway. These people didn't know what kind of man he was, but they were about to find out. "Yeah, so, like I said, my name is Michael, and I'm an alcoholic. But I'm not like you. I drink to forget that I ruined a man's life, and he killed my wife for revenge." Then he sat down.

That should do it.

The room buzzed, and the gangsta said, "Michael, you're

welcome here no matter what you did. Please stick around after the meeting. I'd like to talk to you."

What?

What could a street thug possibly tell a successful corporate attorney like *him?* Except he wasn't a successful corporate attorney, anymore. He was a smug, egotistical drunk looking down on these sober people from his own gutter.

When the meeting was over, the group formed a circle and said the Serenity Prayer: "God, grant me the serenity to accept the things I cannot change, courage to change the things I can, and the wisdom to know the difference." Then they chanted "Keep coming back, it works."

It sounded like a school cheer. Rah, rah. Go sobriety. Yay! He dismissed it as cultish just as several people surrounded him, including Bruce, the Mr. Clean gangsta.

"Let's go get some coffee and talk."

"Thanks, but I can't. I'm with Father Timothy."

"I don't think he'll mind. I'll give you a ride home."

The priest smiled, waved, and left.

Great.

He followed Bruce out to his broken-down Gremlin or Pinto or ancient VW bus, but stopped, and his mouth dropped open. The tatted pierced gangsta unlocked a new Lexus LX 470 SUV!

"Yeah, you're probably wondering how someone who looks like me wound up with a Lexus. I get that reaction a lot. No, I didn't steal it. Get in, and I'll tell you the rest of my story."

Well, this ought to be interesting.

"So, the uncensored story of what it was like. I was a gangbanger because that's what the men in my neighborhood were. I got popped many times for petty theft, minor assaults, all the things you'd expect from a teenage wannabe gangsta. I had my pick of the neighborhood girls. And I was always drunk. It was kinda fun until I turned eighteen. Instead of weekend vacations in juvie away from my shitty home life, I was spending months in county jail where I got hooked on drugs. In jail, you can't be picky. You do whatever's available. You might say I was an equal opportunity addict. When the Third Strike Law kicked in back in '94, I was already well on my way to a long prison sentence. That happened when I got arrested for bank robbery. I was the lookout, but the other guys copped a plea, so I did, too. I spent seven years out of a ten-year sentence in San Quentin in maximum security."

"How long have you been out?"

"Eleven years."

"Seven years is a long time to be incarcerated, but you seem to be doing okay, so I guess you're not a hardened criminal."

"Quite the opposite. I took advantage of every minute, every opportunity, and every state rehabilitation program. Got my GED inside and bachelor's degrees in computer science and criminal justice, and a master's degree in law enforcement. I wrote my thesis on Cyber crime. But the best part? I'm a partner in a private investigation agency. We specialize in computer forensics. Between the police and the big financial companies, we pull in over two million a year."

Well, that explained the Lexus.

After they were seated at the coffee shop, Bruce went into more details about alcohol and drug addiction. After about an hour, the tattoos, piercings and bald head faded away, and all that was left were bright, intelligent, black eyes and a warm smile.

"So, tell me your story."

He told him everything starting with what he'd done to Stewart Sheldon and what that man had done in return.

"Wow. That's tough. I've never been in a relationship, let alone married. I can't imagine what it must have been like, especially under those circumstances. And I can definitely understand why you wanted to numb out. But, I'm guessing since you came to a meeting and announced yourself as a newcomer you're ready to join the living again?"

"It's funny you should put it that way. I've been drunk off and on, mostly on, for just about six months now and figured that's the way it would be until I drank myself to death. But after what I heard tonight, and now listening to you, I feel almost hopeful."

"Well, you should. You've been through something most people will never understand, but there are some who will. And there are others who need to hear what you have to share. I'd be willing to bet you'll find a way to use your experience to help others. In the meantime, consider me your sponsor. We'll meet weekly while you work the steps, and I want you to call me daily, just to check in. Can you do that?"

Could he? It sounded like a commitment and follow through hadn't been high on his priority list lately. But since his way wasn't working, he agreed to give Bruce's a try.

⚜

They went out for coffee after Bruce gave him his sixty-day chip. He'd finished the first three steps but drew a blank at Step Four, *Made a searching and fearless moral inventory of ourselves.* Whenever he tried to write his inventory, the image of Sandy on that stretcher, and how she died for his sins, paralyzed him. He told Bruce about the hawk feather that he shouldn't have taken. "Sometimes I think I hear the bird telling me to take it home. Sometimes I dream Sandy's holding it out to me. And I think I need to do something with it soon."

Bruce had some native blood in him and told him about the vision quest he went on when he got out of prison. "I think it would be a good idea for you to go on a spiritual journey to return the feather and let the rest happen."

Let the rest happen?

"I have a friend from prison I've kept in touch with. He's now legal counsel for a tribe up in Oregon. I'm going to call him and see if he can arrange a vision quest for you."

"How is that going to help me with my fourth step? Every time I pick up a pen I see her lying on that gurney, and I remember that if it weren't for me, my wife would be alive and by my side instead of . . ." He couldn't finish the sentence and fought back tears for a few seconds. "It's so obvious it was my fault. What else is there to write?"

"Don't worry about your fourth step right now. I think, when you get back from your vision quest, you'll see things differently."

He doubted that. But he still had nothing else going on, so why not?

9

"Okay, you got everything? Tent, sleeping bag, flashlight, rain gear, tarp, shovel, hatchet, food, utensils, tobacco, fabric and string for prayer ties, the feather, and lots of warm clothes." Bruce rattled off everything on his list.

"Yeah, *Mom*, and underwear and a notepad and plenty of pens, too."

"Good. There's wood at the site. Use what you need and pay Sal on the last day. Now just follow the map and call him when you get close. He'll meet you at the market and lead you to the site because you'll never find it on your own. You have the vision quest book with the suggestions of things to do and your Big Book, but I want you to leave your cellphone in the car. There's no reception there."

"Yes, *Mom*."

He was grateful for Bruce's help in putting together a sort of wannabe vision quest. Any self-respecting Native American would laugh at his *car camping* preparations, but this was as close as a white man like him would get to the real thing. He drove away just before dawn and thought about his intentions, what he hoped to get out of this wilderness experience — alone in the woods with no contact with the outside world for seven nights.

Shit.

Fear and excitement ganged up on him. The last time he went camping, he'd been a boy scout, but that was with twenty other boys and three adult men. This time, he was on his own with nothing but what he'd crammed into Bruce's Lexus.

Fourteen hours later, he met up with Sal at the small market. He stocked up on energy bars and two cases of bottled water. He had a filtration pump, and would be near a stream, but felt better knowing he had easy access to plenty of water. Bruce wanted him to take a rifle and hunt his food, but he drew the line there. He'd never had to live off the land, and he'd starve if he had to look into Bambi's big brown eyes and pull the trigger.

His mother had given him a big pot of homemade Irish stew, and he had a fishing pole if he needed more food. Besides, the fast was three days and nights out of the seven. Food wasn't what worried him. He was a city boy about to spend a week in the wilderness, alone.

He followed Sal's Jeep into the woods and stopped when they arrived at a clearing. He would never have found it on his own, and if anything happened to Sal, he'd never find his way out.

The firepit had plenty of cooking stones and a grate, and the site was level and smoothed of small rocks and pebbles. It was obviously well used.

"So, this is where I leave you. I'll be back on the eighth day. Don't bother with your cell phone. There's no service out here. This is sacred ground for personal vision quests only. The tribe knows you're here, so no one will bother you. And there's a natural force field around the area that only admits animals, but they're usually friendly. The stream is just past those trees. It's clean, but if you need water, use the pump, anyway, just to be safe. And it's snow melt, so don't spend too much time in there. Hypothermia can sneak up on you. You can pay for the wood you use when I come back. And keep the tarp over it. It rains a lot here. Good luck, and I hope you find what you're looking for."

"Thanks. I hope so, too."

He spent the last hours of daylight setting up camp and getting a fire going. After he put the pot of stew on the grate to heat, he walked down to the stream. It looked so refreshing, a dip to wash off the dust from the campsite seemed like a good idea. There were no signs of other people, and Sal had assured him no one would disturb him, so he stripped off his clothes and dove into the water. The icy cold shocked the air out of his lungs, and he surfaced sputtering and screaming, "FUCK!" which echoed down the stream and back.

No shit it was snow melt! Dust or no dust, if he stayed in that water, he'd freeze to death in minutes. He scrambled out, grabbed his clothes and ran back to the fire. "Not a great way to start my adventure. Shit, that was cold. I need to dry off and get dressed. And I'm already talking to myself. Terrific."

When he crawled out of the tent in clean clothes, his stomach growled from the aroma of the stew. When it was hot enough, he scooped some into a camp bowl and grabbed a bottle of water and a spoon ready for a feast. It was a big pot and would sit on the side of the firepit to stay warm. His mother's stew always tasted better with each reheating, and he had other food to supplement it with.

By the time he finished clearing the eating area, the moon lit up the campsite. He sat on the folding camp chair, leaned back, and studied the sky. The only sounds were the crackles of the wood as it burned.

⌛

"This is beautiful, Michael. Thank you for bringing me here."

She appeared ethereal in the firelight, like an angel. "I miss you so much, Sandy. And I'm so sorry I wasn't there for you."

"It wasn't your fault. Please stop blaming yourself. You couldn't have known."

"But I should have. And I don't know how to live with this."

The wind in the trees whispered, "Help us," and he bolted up. Sandy was gone, but in her place was a little raccoon. Well, Sal did say the animals were friendly.

"Looking for a free meal? Sorry, buddy. Dinner's over."

"I'm not here for dinner. You have something that belongs to a friend."

How can I be losing my mind already?

"What do you mean?"

"You have a feather. It led you here for a reason. But it's served its purpose, and now it's time to return it to its rightful owner."

"And how do you propose I do that? I found it a thousand miles from here."

"Leave it by the fire. Hawk'll come for it."

Yeah, he was losing it, and he still had seven full days to go. He closed his eyes and tried to visualize Sandy again, but when he opened them, it was dawn and the beginning of his first full day. "I slept outside all night? I wonder what time it is. Probably five-thirty or six."

Shit. He'd answered himself, again.

He looked at his wrist where his watch should have been, then remembered Bruce told him to leave it at home, something about interfering with the energy of the area. And it's not like he had any appointments to keep or places he had to be.

Bruce's old percolator took a while to brew, so he fried some eggs in an old pan and toasted two slices of bread on the hot stones. When the coffee was ready, he poured some in a well used but not so well washed cup. Then he ate his breakfast feast and thought about what the raccoon had said.

What the raccoon said . . .

Right.

He got the feather from the back of the SUV and placed it next to one of the larger stones that circled the firepit. Then he finished his fried egg sandwich and coffee.

After cleaning up the campsite, he eased into the folding chair with his notepad and a pen and tried to formulate his question. What did he want? He wanted to know why. Why what? Why did Sandy have to pay for what he did?

He waited, but there was no answer. Then he could swear the trees whispered, "Help us."

"It's either the wind in the trees or I'm losing my mind. First, my dead wife talks to me. Then I carry on a conversation with a raccoon as if I do that all the time. And now I'm waiting for a hawk to come get his feather. And I'm expecting some kind of answer to a question I don't even know how to ask. I suppose I could start with who keeps asking for my help? And what am I supposed to do about it?"

He waited. But there was still no answer.

He spent the rest of the morning making prayer ties out of tobacco and little squares of colored cloth tied together with one long length of string. The vision quest book said to ask his question with each pouch, so as he tied the knots, he asked *why*.

When his stomach told him it was lunchtime, he had a hundred little pouches. He was supposed to burn them that night, sending his prayers skyward with the smoke. Each day he had to make prayer ties, and each night he had to burn them. On the last day, he was supposed to receive his answer. That would be after three days of no food so no doubt he'd have some kind of hallucination, if he even lived that long.

After he ate some stew and drank a bottle of water, he cleaned up the eating area, dragged his sleeping bag outside, and laid down for an afternoon nap in the warm sunlight.

☒

"Thank you for keeping my feather safe. I hope it helped."

"Yes, it did. Thank you for letting me borrow it."

"You will find your answer . . . and so much more. But you have a lot of work to do first. It won't be easy, but it *will* be worth it."

"I'm so lonely, though. I miss her so much."

"We know. But you need to be alone right now. Don't worry. It won't be forever. There is someone for you, but she's going through her own trials. When you're both ready, you'll find each other, and you'll do great things together. You'll help many people. Now I must go. Enjoy your stay in our woods."

"Wait! I don't understand! Who is she? What are we supposed to do?"

He woke up shivering. It had been warm when he laid down in the sun, but that was hours ago. Now it was dusk, and a cold breeze had come up. He carried his sleeping bag into the tent and put on a jacket. Then he scooped out a bowl of warm stew, grabbed some rolls and a bottle of water, and ate dinner.

It wasn't until he straightened up the campsite that he noticed the hawk feather was gone.

When the sky was dark enough, he got the prayer ties, held them, and asked, "Why?" Then he dropped the string of little pouches in the fire and watched and listened as they burned and crackled and released their smoke and his prayers to the heavens. It was his second night alone. Tomorrow he would make more prayer ties. By then he hoped to have a real question. And according to the book, he should gather small rocks and pebbles to make a medicine wheel in the dirt.

His body had released some of the stress that had weighed him down, and he struggled to keep his eyes open. When he couldn't fight it anymore, he crawled into the tent and into his sleeping bag. He woke to the sound of rustling outside the tent. When he peeked out, there was Mr. Raccoon trying to get into the pot of stew.

"Hey! I told you that's not for you. That's *my* food. Go find your own."

"That's exactly what I'm doing. You're in my territory, and you left this out. We're opportunistic scavengers, you know. But fine. Keep your old stew. I see you met Hawk today. Tomorrow you'll meet other friends."

"Wait, *what*? What other friends?"

"Friends with messages for you. Don't worry. It's all good."

Easy for him to say. He's not the one carrying on a conversation with a raccoon.

His second full day dawned with a loud *clank*.

"What the h —?"

Two squirrels were trying to tip over the percolator he'd prepared the night before.

"Beat it! Scram! Vamoose! Shoo!"

They'd gotten into some of his food, but there was still plenty left. "Guess I should put everything in the car at night, so they're not tempted by the smell." He stopped moving and let out a deep sigh. "I'm talking to myself, again. This just keeps getting better and better."

He spent the morning making prayer ties. Then he rinsed off in the freezing stream and brushed his teeth. On his way back to camp he gathered pebbles for the medicine wheel. One of the small rocks looked like an opal. It would make a good reminder of this adventure, so he put it in his pocket.

He used a stick from the woodpile and drew a circle on the ground. Then he drew geometric shapes in each quadrant of the medicine wheel. The shapes were supposed to symbolize aspects of his question, but he still didn't know what the real question was. And he couldn't draw to save his life so his shapes looked more like doodles.

Someone or something was watching him as he worked. Then he heard chittering. Two squirrels sat on a branch in a nearby tree. "What's up, you little shits?" Thank God they didn't answer him in English. They just chittered away as if they expected him to understand what they were saying. Or maybe they were just laughing at him.

He picked up his blank notepad and pen and sat in the camp chair, but still, nothing came to him. Maybe if he took a walk along the stream, something would come to him.

It was cool in the shade of the trees, and the air smelled like rain. About a quarter of a mile downstream the smell turned into reality, and by the time he got back to camp, his clothes were soaked through, and the fire was out.

He changed into sweats in the tent and waited out the storm by sketching a new medicine wheel on his notepad since the rain was obliterating his first one. No big loss. It hadn't been very good, anyway.

Nature and hunger drove him out into the downpour just long enough to make a run for the latrine pit, and on his way back he grabbed the pot of stew, a spoon, and a bottle of water before he ducked back inside the dry tent. He had plenty of other food which would stay nice and dry in the back of the SUV. And in the morning when it stopped raining, assuming it stopped raining, he planned to take an inventory and maybe make a sundial.

When he finished the last of the stew, he put the empty pot outside the tent and changed into dry clothes. He crawled back into his sleeping bag where he listened to the rain beat on the waterproof rain fly. The whole situation seemed like a dismal failure. At least before, he could drink and numb himself from reality. Stuck in the tent in the dim light, he tried to sketch a new medicine wheel. When it was too dark to see, he reached for the battery-operated lantern. And . . . surprise! It didn't work.

Terrific.

"You *do* understand you're on a journey, and you haven't reached your destination yet, right?"

"Say what?" All he could make out in the darkness was a white stripe. This had to be another one of those dreams. Maybe the stew had gone bad. If it wasn't a dream, no amount of icy water would wash the skunk scent off.

"You came here for answers to questions you can't express. And you *will* find the questions, as well as the answers. It hurts now, but growth usually does. Think of it like a caterpillar splitting its skin. That's gotta hurt something fierce, but from that comes its rebirth as a butterfly."

"Great. I'm splitting my skin, and I get to be a butterfly. Not sure that's what I signed up for."

"You want to know why your wife died. No one can answer that, so stop asking. You have to find a way to turn your tragedy into something meaningful."

"So instead of asking why, I should ask how?"

"That would be a good place to start."

It was almost dawn on his third full day when he woke up with an intense need to relieve himself. The rain had finally stopped, so on his way back to the tent, he grabbed a few dry logs and the waterproof matches and got another fire started. As soon as the coffee was ready, he filled up his mug and crawled back into the tent.

His analytical mind kicked in, and he made a list of his talents and abilities, hoping to see a pattern that would point him in the right direction. It was close. He knew it. But there was something missing, some small detail that eluded him.

After finishing his coffee, he found a stick in the pile of wood, faced what he was pretty sure was north, and drew a circle in the mud with tick marks for the hours. He estimated it was about 5:30 and drew a line indicating where to stand. If he got it right, when the sun came up enough to cast a shadow, it would point to seven, give or take a few minutes.

He cleaned up the kitchen area, laid his wet clothes from yesterday and last night on the large stones next to the fire, munched on a muffin, and thought about what he needed to get done for the day. He needed to formulate his question as a prayer for the prayer ties, and he needed to re-make the medicine wheel. And he needed to write. And if the ground dried out enough, he wanted to explore the area beyond the point where he'd had to turn back yesterday, before the deluge.

By the time he finished his chores and was ready for the hike, the shadow from the sundial pointed to three. Dinner that night would be his final meal until the last day of his quest. He planned to make the rest of the fried egg sandwiches and finish the perishables that wouldn't keep for four more days. And if he could find a nice green stick for the marshmallows, dessert would be s'mores.

The air was chilly, but the sun was warm. Steam rose from the still damp soil which gave the forest an eerie feeling that seemed appropriate for a vision quest. When the shadows grew long, he turned back to camp. He found a damp wooden stick and a lump of what looked like turquoise. He'd read about medicine bags, buckskin pouches for keeping objects like rocks that were symbolic of important occasions or revelations. Now he had two stones for the pouch he'd make when he got home.

When he got back to camp, he was starved. Not as starved as he would be though. This dinner was the last food he would taste until the final day so he tried to savor every bite. The s'mores brought back memories of that night he and Sandy spent on the beach snuggled in front of a bonfire toasting marshmallows.

"Babe, I wish you were here. I miss you so damn much. I know I have to move on and find some meaning to all of this, but it's so hard."

Shit.

Crying. Eating s'mores and crying. Alone in the woods. How the mighty corporate attorney had fallen.

When it was time to burn the prayer ties, he lit yesterday's and today's strings, asked for directions on how to turn his pain into something positive and useful, and watched the smoke carry his prayers upward in the moonlight. He didn't expect answers, but at least he'd put the questions into words. Then he slouched down in the camp chair and watched the sky.

"It's good to see you're finally getting it. You've been beating yourself up for too long. We've been hoping you'd realize it wasn't your fault."

This just keeps getting better and better.

He was about to have a conversation with a deer. Maybe he should invite the whole gang for a party. Maybe a potluck? He smiled, wondering what dishes his animal companions might bring. "So, Mr. Deer. How many more of you are there, anyway? So far, I've had conversations with a raccoon, a hawk, and a skunk, and I've been laughed at by a couple of asshole squirrels. Either I'm losing my mind, or there's something weird going on."

"You're not losing your mind, and there's nothing weird about it. You came to us, remember? We're giving you what you asked for."

"And what's that?"

"A direction. Or did we get that wrong? Because if we did, now would be a good time to let us know. We *do* have other vision quests scheduled."

"No. You didn't get it wrong. It's just . . ." How did one explain feelings to an animal that wasn't supposed to talk?

"Let go of your need to figure everything out. Of course, none of this is rational. Animals don't talk, at least not to people. So just go with it and put your mind at ease. You're not going crazy. You're so close to figuring it out, but here's a hint. You blamed yourself for what Stewart Sheldon did. If you had had more compassion for him, maybe he wouldn't have taken revenge. Compassion is key."

"Key to what?"

"Your path."

"That's it? That's all you're going to give me?"

A cramp in his leg woke him. As usual, they'd left him with more questions than answers.

This was the beginning of his three-day fast. Nothing but water until the last day. The headache hit that afternoon, just as he finished that day's prayer ties.

Caffeine withdrawals and no food.

Goody.

The vision quest book said to drink plenty of water and he still had a case and a half of liter bottles. He pushed through until it was just a dull ache behind his eyeballs. Maybe a dip in the ice-cold stream would help.

Shivering violently certainly took his mind off the headache, and he hunkered down next to the fire to dry off and warm up. Then he got dressed and started writing.

It began as a letter to Sandy, and by page twenty-three, he'd finished his fourth step. He was thorough like the Big Book said. He listed everyone he had a resentment against, what he thought they did to him, and what his part in it was. And he even listed God. It was an eye opener. Getting it all down on paper released more pressure inside his chest. The ache around his heart eased. It wasn't gone, but breathing didn't hurt so much.

He waited for the sun to set and then burned the day's prayer ties. This time, he focused on asking for the directions to get to his path. His thoughts were a little clearer which was interesting since, without food, he should have been dazed. Instead, a strange kind of buzzing energy flowed through him.

When it was too dark to see, he crawled in the tent and into his sleeping bag. He wanted to sleep under the stars, but it was too damned cold, and he didn't want to waste wood keeping the fire hot enough. He was asleep as soon as his head hit the pillow.

"So, how's it going?"

How is it going? Shouldn't they already know?

"How did you get in here?"

"Does it matter?"

"Kinda, yeah. But I suppose this is all in my head, too. I mean, you're a bear. You should be pillaging my campsite and eating my toothpaste, but you're in my tent talking to me."

The bear laughed.

Wait, a minute. Bears laugh?

"You had a breakthrough today. You got it all out, and you feel better, don't you?"

"Yeah, I guess I do. So, what's next?"

"After turning yourself inside out, you should feel some healing and strength. You see where this is going, right?"

"Starvation or a sanitarium?"

"You're not going to starve. The fasting is only three days, and you've already made it through one. Look at me. I hibernate all winter. No food, no water, just sleep. Then I wake up every spring ready to mate."

"I am *not* talking to an imaginary bear about my non-existent sex life."

"Don't worry about it. You're not ready yet, anyway. And *she* sure isn't."

"She?"

"If you were meant to be celibate, you'd already be a priest."

"You got that right. I mean, I think I'm still Catholic, but a priest?

Uh, no. Can't see myself listening to other people's problems all day."

"That's funny."

"What is?"

"You'll see. So, yes, to answer your question. There's a *she* for you. But you both still have a lot of work to do. Your paths are very different, but your destination is the same, and when you're both ready, you'll find each other. In the meantime, you still have to figure out what your purpose is."

"How about a hint?"

This time the bear's laugh was so loud, it woke him up. But the noise didn't stop. In fact, it sounded like a car horn.

What the hell?

He scrambled out of the tent and ran to the SUV where he found wrappers and bits of energy bars scattered on the ground. He heard chittering over the blaring horn.

Asshole squirrels!

They'd eaten through the floorboard and chewed through something that shorted out the horn. Then the little shits got into his food.

The blaring brought his headache back, front and center. Now he had to figure out how to shut the horn off without coffee to wake up his brain cells. Didn't newer cars have fuses dedicated to specific functions? He popped the hood, found the fuse box with labels, and sighed with relief when he pulled the fuse for the horn — and the noise stopped.

Thank-you-Jesus!

What a rude way to start his fifth day.

He closed the hood and got a bottle of water from the back of the SUV he would be paying a shitload to clean and fix. The little shits ate his energy bars but couldn't get into the water bottles, thank God. So much for breaking his fast on the last day.

The little bastards chittered their laughter, so he grabbed a rock and threw it at the tree branch. "Yeah, you better run, you future moccasins!"

He carried the case of water into the small tent. It took up a lot of space, but he didn't want to take the chance of those four-legged ear muffs chewing through the plastic.

Since he couldn't have coffee, he woke himself up with a swim. He was almost used to the freezing cold water now. It was refreshing and did the trick. As he warmed himself by the fire, he thought about what the bear had said.

What the bear said . . .

"You really are losing it, Michael. And you're talking to yourself again."

Sigh.

He wrote down all the animal visitors and what he could remember of their conversations. "No one's going to believe me."

The raccoon told him about the hawk. The hawk took back the feather that had started him on this quest and gave him encouragement. The second raccoon — or was it the same one? — he said there would be other animals with messages. Not exactly what he'd wanted to hear at the time. The skunk said he had to split his skin and become a butterfly in order to be reborn. The deer talked about letting go of his preconceived ideas and learning compassion. And the bear told him there was a *she* and he'd have sex again. It all led to only one answer.

Forty-two?

He giggled. The answer to life, the universe, and everything, according to Douglas Adams. It was so simple. Why hadn't he thought of it sooner?

Delirium. Terrific.

It stuck in his head, and when he made his prayer ties, he asked, "What is the answer to life, the universe, and everything?" Without coffee, cognitive thought was just too difficult, and there was no way he was going to make it to sundown.

Might as well get it over with.

He burned the prayer ties and crawled in the tent for a nap.

It was dark when he woke to feel something slither into his sleeping bag. "SON OF A BITCH!" He scrambled, barefoot, out into the icy cold night.

"Hey! Where'd you go? Don't you know it's freezing out there? Come back in here where it's warm."

"You're a fucking snake, and you're going to bite me, and I'll die because I'm stuck out here alone."

"I promise not to bite you. Besides, I'm not real, remember? Look, we need to talk."

He had to face down his fear and climb back into the warmth of the tent, or stay outside and freeze to death. The warm tent with the snake won. However, he refused to snuggle with it and sat as far away from the reptile as the little tent allowed. "Okay. Lay it on me. What's your message?"

"You know, by now you should be welcoming us, but instead you're getting cynical. What's wrong?"

"You're kidding, right? What's *wrong*? Well, for starters, I'm sharing my tent with a talking snake. Besides you, I've had meaningful conversations with five other animals. Two asshole squirrels ate most of the food I was saving for the last day, and they damaged my friend's SUV, which seeing as how it's a Lexus, will probably cost me at least a grand and possibly his friendship. Yeah, I guess when you put it all together, it's not all that bad."

"There's no need for sarcasm, Michael. Remember, this was all your idea. Well, except for those asshole squirrels. And I'm thinking they'll probably make a tasty late-night snack for me when we're done here. Anyway, you're so close to your goal. Now is not the time to give up. You're going through an initiation of sorts. A transformation. This is what you wanted. To be someone your wife would be proud of. To make amends for how you treated others. To somehow make things right. And you will. When you leave here, you'll know what to do. And you'll see. It'll all be worth it. You'll look back on this week with gratitude and joy. You'll even smile. And you'll honor your wife which I think is very important to you. Am I right?"

More than anything, he wanted to be the man she'd always thought he was. "Yes, you're right. This whole experience reminds me of the serenity prayer. I'm coming to accept the things I did since

I can't change them. I'm working up the courage to fix what I can, although I still don't know exactly how. And I suppose the wisdom to know the difference will become clearer."

"By George, I think he's got it!"

A loud growling woke him.

Now what?

He peaked outside and saw . . . snow? The growling got louder and seemed to come from his stomach.

And so began the sixth day of his quest.

With three inches of snow on the ground.

In August.

Fuck.

There was no way he could have anticipated snow, but at least the drinking water was in the tent. Damn. He hated to admit it, but if it hadn't been for those asshole squirrels, the water would have frozen. At least the hot coals kept the firepit from being buried, but the ashes were a soupy mess.

He sat up slowly while stars and grayness filled his vision. He had to hold it together long enough to get the fire going again or stay in the tent for the next twenty-four hours, which sounded like a damn good idea. Other than make and burn prayer ties and maybe write a bit, there was nothing he needed to do, even if he could.

However, *Nature* doesn't care how cold it is when she calls, and he had no choice but to get dressed and brave the freezing temperature just to take a leak. The icy fresh air revived him, so he got the fire restarted. Thank God for waterproof matches and dry wood. He was going to owe Sal a fortune.

Despite the cold, it was nice out. Crystal clear, brilliant blue sky, and when he held still, the sun warmed his face. Being California born and bred, snow was a novelty. If he had to shovel sidewalks and driveways and commute in the slush, he'd probably feel differently. But at that moment, it was damn pretty.

He poured a bottle of water in the coffee pot and put it on the fire to warm up. When the water was hot enough, he took the pot and a cup and all the materials to make the prayer ties into the tent.

Tonight was his last night. Wait. Hadn't he just gotten there? When he finished the prayer ties, he crawled out, stood up to stretch, saw stars, and face planted in the snow.

He didn't recognize the office filled with bleeding and bruised women. They were crying. Then he saw Sandy. "You have to help them. No one else will."

"Help them, how?"

"You'll know."

The scene changed to what looked like a conference room. There were two women seated at the large table. One woman had horrible burn scars on her face, and part of her nose was missing. The other woman seemed familiar, somehow.

It was dark when he came to, shivering, and his teeth chattered so hard, his jaw ached. He could have frozen to death, and no one would have known. He got the fire going again, burned the prayer ties, and one last time he asked for the answer to what his purpose was and how to go about it. Then, with the last of his energy, he crawled back in the tent.

"Congratulations. You made it."

"Made it? In case you didn't notice, I damn near froze to death today. I can barely raise my head without hearing my blood pounding in my ears. And I'm afraid to go out to take a leak in case I pass out again. So, okay, I made it. Where's my prize?"

The falcon was silent for a minute, and he wondered if the bird changed its mind.

"Your prize is a new beginning. Your prize is passion and leadership. Your prize is knowing you can rise above and conquer anything that stands in your way. Your prize is your purpose."

"And what's that?"

"You mean you still haven't figured it out? Not too bright, are you . . ."

"Look, today I could have died from exposure. You can't expect me to be sharp as a tack."

"Haven't you heard their cries?"

"You mean the voices that say *Help me?*"

"The women who are begging you to help them. Yes, them."

"How am I supposed to do that?"

There was no answer. Typical.

He opened his eyes to bright sunlight, and the snow had melted. How late was it? He needed to pack everything and clean up the campsite. And he needed to figure out what he would tell Bruce about the trashed SUV. He sat up slowly, waiting for the dizziness to hit. It didn't, but in its place was a new mental clarity. And if he'd wanted to, he could probably shoot sparks from his fingertips.

He got dressed and went out to start the coffee and load the SUV. When he opened the hatch, there were two undamaged boxes of energy bars laying on top of everything. They hadn't been there before, but nothing about any of this surprised him.

First things first.

He built up the fire, made coffee, and feasted on the bars. Then he got to work. There wasn't that much to do since he'd tried to keep the site clean. And there was no sign of those future moccasin-liners, either. He popped the hood and put the fuse back hoping the horn wouldn't start blaring. It didn't. But the really weird part, if it was even possible for something to *ever* be really weird again, was there was no damage to the SUV.

No. Nothing would ever surprise him again. This was what the deer meant by *going with it.*

He gulped the last of the coffee and grabbed the pot to go wash it out in the stream. As he walked toward the water, a breeze picked up, and a torn piece of newspaper wrapped around his ankle. It was a news story about a woman whose husband had thrown a pot of boiling water at her which scarred her face and chest. The bastard got a six-month suspended sentence and left the state. The woman had massive medical bills, received no restitution, couldn't work, and committed suicide after being hounded by collection agencies.

And there it was. The answer.

He picked up the sparkling stone that lay in the dirt in front of his tennis shoe and added it to the other two in his pocket.

10

Bruce poured so much creamer in his coffee, he might as well have ordered a glass of milk. "I take it the vision quest was a success?"

"That's an understatement. Looking back, I can say it was a once in a lifetime learning experience, and I need to make a medicine bag." He was still walking on air after being back a week. In AA, they call that a pink cloud. Well, his was magenta.

"Want to tell me about it?"

"Yeah. So, I know this'll sound crazy, but each night I had a conversation with a different animal. The rational part of my brain says these were just dreams and that would mean it was my subconscious doing the talking. But the way I felt when I woke up each morning, and the final answer sure didn't seem like it all came from my imagination. And they told me things I could never have come up with on my own, some things I still refuse to accept."

"So, what's the answer to life, the universe, and everything?"

"Ha-ha. I asked, and it's still forty-two. No, it took me a few days to figure out what the question was, and one of the animals, the snake, I think, said it had to do with how to help others and be a man my wife would be proud of."

"And?"

"Well, this is the *really* unbelievable part. I was waiting for Sal to show up, and the wind kicked up, and a piece of newspaper wrapped around my ankle. It was a news story about a woman who committed suicide because she couldn't work and couldn't pay all the medical bills from when her husband threw a pot of boiling water at her."

"And?"

"And I'm going to become a civil litigation attorney and help victims of domestic violence sue for restitution. And I need to make a pouch for the stones I found."

⌛

It didn't happen overnight. He went back to Loyola Law School and took accelerated courses in family law, tort law, and criminal law, which was almost as difficult and complex as the contract law he originally specialized in. He had no life outside of school, AA meetings and Tuesday nights with NCIS, but that was fine with him. Social lives were overrated, anyway.

He attended church regularly, and prayers were meaningful, again. His mother insisted he come to Sunday dinner after church. He went but dreaded it since his father liked to argue. Civil law paid virtually nothing compared to what he'd made as a corporate attorney, a fact his father loved to remind him about. And he planned to charge on a sliding scale based on the client's ability to pay. It was never about the money.

He'd invested most of Sandy's life insurance and had a diversified portfolio and money in the bank. He should have already sold the house, but now he was too busy to look for another place to live. Instead, he focused his efforts on opening his law clinic.

⌛

It had been a year since he listened to Bruce at that first AA meeting, and he was eating Sunday dinner with his parents and Father Timothy.

"So, Michael, how's the studying going?"

"Well, Father, I'm learning a lot. It's a very different type of law."

"Yeah, cheap law for losers. Good to know your expensive education is paying off."

"Samuel!"

"No, that's okay Mom. He's right. The people — men and women — I hope to help have been seriously injured, physically and emotionally, and in many cases, they have nothing but scars and enormous medical bills. Their abusers may get jail sentences, but that doesn't pay the bills."

"So, you're going to sue a man for every penny he's worth and who cares about *his* situation or if she provoked him, is that it? Doesn't that make you no better than an over-educated ambulance chaser?"

"Samuel, that's e-NOUGH! Michael is trying to honor Sandy's memory by helping those who can't help themselves. I would think you'd be a little more supportive!"

"Mom, it's okay."

"No, it is NOT okay! I think what you're planning to do is wonderful."

"Well, he'll have to give up that beach house and that fancy car, since he won't be making any money."

"I have every intention of downsizing my life. Sure, it would be nice to stay near the ocean, but it's not a life or death thing. And I expect to get a lot of referrals from Legal Aid. Besides, not everyone is poor."

"Whatever. Anyone need a beer? Wine? Michael?"

"No thanks, I'm good with water."

"Yeah, that's another thing. Why did you stop drinking everything?"

"Because I had to."

"Can't hold your liquor anymore, *eh?* You just need willpower, self-control."

That was the one thing he absolutely refused to talk to his father about. He didn't need any lectures on self-control or willpower, and as much as he hated to hurt his mother, he had to set some boundaries.

He stood up and placed his napkin on his plate. "Mom, thanks for dinner, but I have to go."

"What? No! You haven't finished your dinner! And I got an ice cream cake for dessert, your favorite."

"Thanks, but I can't stay."

"Hear that, Mary? He hasn't changed since he was a boy. Only thinks about himself."

No, Dad. That's John.

"Yeah, so Mom, I'll call you sometime this week. Father Timothy, it was nice to see you. Will I see you Friday night?"

"Absolutely. Wouldn't miss it."

"What's Friday night?"

He ignored his father's question. "I'll call you, Mom." He had no intention of telling his father about his one-year anniversary in AA on Wednesday. The people in his home group were arranging a celebration dinner after Friday night's meeting, and he was grateful for their support. His father would *not* be there to ruin it for him.

There was another reason for celebrating. Friday, he would receive certificates of completion for the law courses. That was something else he had no intention of sharing with his father who still resented the private school education they'd paid for. All of his brothers had gone to trade schools except the *runt* who'd gone to a state university and gotten a degree in Exercise Science, a fancy name for PE

He still had his license to practice law in California, so he didn't need to take the bar exam again. And technically, he hadn't needed to go back to school at all. But he learned about torts and the criminal justice system and victim's rights so he could better represent his future clients. Besides, he enjoyed school even though his classmates treated him like an old man.

He got two blocks away from his parents' house when his phone rang. The display read *Mom,* so he pushed the speaker button.

"Mom?"

"Michael, I'm so sorry. I don't know what's gotten into your father. He hasn't been himself lately, and he's sleeping on the couch tonight. I want you to know how proud I am of you, and I know he's proud too, in his own way. Now, what's this about Friday?"

Great. His parents had a fight because of him. "I'm getting my one-year AA chip Friday night. I'd love it if *you* could be there, but not Dad. This is very special to me, and I don't want him there making his snide remarks in front of my AA friends. I hope you understand."

"I do. It's a shame, but I understand. And I will be there if you'll tell me where."

"I don't want to cause any more tension and arguments between you two."

"Don't worry about that. I can handle him. I've had lots of practice. Does Father Timothy know where?"

What did she mean by *lots of practice?* "Yes."

"Then I'll go with him."

"Thanks, Mom. This means a lot to me. *Oh,* and I didn't get a chance to tell you, I finished all my coursework. Next week I'll go scouting for an office and start advertising."

"That's wonderful! Sandy would be so proud of you!"

Sandy.

He'd been so busy, he'd forgotten about his dead wife. "Listen, I have to go. I'm driving, and the last thing I need is to get pulled over."

"Okay, honey. I love you, and I'm sorry about your father."

"Love you, too, Mom."

When he got home, he sat on the couch in the dark and closed his eyes. Guilt washed over him. How could he have been so busy he forgot about her? He couldn't visualize her anymore without looking at a photograph. Loneliness joined the guilt. "God, Sandy,

I'm sorry. Baby, I miss you so damn much, I've just been busy trying to be a man you could be proud of."

"I was always proud of you. You know that."

"That was before I realized what I was. Someday, I'll find a way to make it up to you."

"I know, honey, I know. But you're well on your way. You know everything happens for a reason. Always remember how much I loved you, and I'll be here — until you're ready for her."

"Her? What do you mean?"

There was no answer, and when he opened his eyes, it was dawn.

⌛

"And now it's time for everyone's favorite part of the meeting. We give out chips to celebrate milestones along the road of sobriety. Is anyone here celebrating thirty days? Sixty days? Ninety days? How about six months? Nine months? Wow, tough crowd! Okay, what about . . . *hmm* . . . one year?"

"My name is Michael, and I'm an alcoholic, and Wednesday I had one year clean and sober." He walked to the podium as everyone clapped and cheered. He waited until the room got quiet. "You can't possibly know what this means to me. Okay, maybe some of you can. I came to you a year ago drowning in grief and Irish whiskey, and thanks to this program, working the steps, a great sponsor, and you, my AA family, I stand before you a new man with a purpose. It hasn't been easy, but it's sure been worth it. Thank you all for being here, and I'll take another twenty-four."

Bruce handed him a shiny AA medallion with a big number one on one side and the serenity prayer on the other. Then the gangsta thug gave him a big hug while everyone clapped. When he got back to his seat, his mother was wiping her eyes. "Don't cry, Mom. This is a good thing."

"Yes, of course, it is. These are happy tears. I'm so proud of you."

"I'm kinda proud of me, too. By the way, the man who gave me my chip is my sponsor, Bruce."

"Bruce? He looks more like a bruiser."

He laughed. "Yeah, I thought he was some gangbanger gangsta pimp when I met him the first time. But he's an awesome guy. You'll get to talk to him at dinner."

"Dinner?"

"Yeah, didn't Father Timothy tell you? We're going out to celebrate after the meeting."

"*Oh*, dear."

"What's wrong? Is it Dad?"

"Well . . . yes. I sort of didn't tell him where I was going. He just assumed I went to church."

"Mom, you can't lie to him for me. And you'll shock Father Timothy if you actually have something worth confessing."

"I didn't have any choice. I wasn't going to miss this, and I couldn't take the chance of your father trying to stop me or wanting to come along and then making a scene. And this is definitely worth a rosary."

He doubted her penance would be anything more than a *tsk, tsk* and a *Hail Mary* to make her feel better. "Well, I'm glad you're here. Looks like the break is over. We'll talk to Father Timothy after the meeting and see what he says."

Later, when they were seated at a table in the restaurant, Father Timothy whispered, "We won't call it a lie. It's just a little fib for a good cause. Don't worry about Samuel. I'll talk to him."

"*Oh*, I'm afraid that'll make things worse. He's not very happy with me lately, and he hates when outsiders interfere." She rubbed her left arm.

What was *that* about?

"Don't worry, Mary. I'll definitely talk to him. It'll be okay."

"I hope you're right. He's been worse since February. It's always bad in February but this year . . . No, I'm sure everything will be fine."

Had his father always been so closed minded? The man was

strict but loving when he was growing up. He couldn't remember ever hearing his parents raise their voices to each other, and he hated the idea that somehow, he'd caused problems between them. He watched Bruce entertain his mother with some of the more colorful parts of his story and waited for her reaction. What if she didn't approve of him hanging out with ex-thugs and felons?

"My goodness, Bruce is such a character. And what he's accomplished! Very inspiring. We must have him over for Sunday din—*hmm*. Or maybe not."

"It's okay, Mom. I'm just glad you don't disapprove."

"Would that stop you from being friends with him?"

"He's my sponsor. He saved my life. The vision quest was his idea. So no, it wouldn't stop me, but it would be something I couldn't share with you."

"Well, don't worry. I like all your friends. You're an adult and quite capable of making your own choices. Still, we might not want to spring him on your father all at once."

The next day he contacted a commercial real estate agent to start the search for office space and a residential agent about selling his house.

The day he and Sandy had signed the papers they'd celebrated with champagne in bed. No more Sandy. No more champagne. And soon, no more house.

11

He set up shop in a small office in a strip mall in Torrance and bought a small beach house right on the Strand. The seller was going through a nasty divorce, something that was all too common in the Los Angeles area. The owner didn't want his wife to get her hands on half the profit, and the price was so low, whatever profit there was went to the agents. As a result, he got a steal. It was exactly what he needed. Lying in bed at night listening to the waves soothed his soul. Too bad he didn't have more time to surf. Someday.

The local Legal Aid office had a huge backlog, and the manager was more than happy to refer cases to him. He gained a reputation for being successful and word spread. He never sued for more than what was fair for his clients, enough to cover their past and future medical bills and loss of wages while recuperating. If it involved children, he made sure there was better than adequate support. Juries never had issues with reasonable claims, and he usually won the full amount. Once in a while, a jury would even award more.

By Thanksgiving, there were too many cases and not enough hours in the day. Most evenings all he wanted to do was collapse. He hated turning away anyone who had already been turned away from Legal Aid, so he started the search for a partner much sooner than he'd expected to. Thanksgiving dinner was crazy. His father was on his case all evening. He stuck around for the meal, and with his mother's blessing, he left early.

As busy as he was, he fought the same anxiety he'd faced the first Christmas without Sandy. His mother insisted he spend the holiday with the family, but just the thought of it made him *thirsty*. It was what Bruce called a *slippery situation*. He tried to get out of it, but good old Mom was like a dog holding on to a bone. He planned to get a convenient case of the flu until she suggested he bring Bruce. It would probably end in disaster, but it would be kind of fun to watch his father go head to head with Bruce who still looked like a combination of Mr. Clean, gangsta, thug, and pimp.

Christmas Eve morning was tough, but he went to a few meetings and made it through. He spent Christmas Eve in church, even went to confession so he could take communion at Midnight Mass, something that made his mother very happy. His father had spent most of the evening playing with the younger grandchildren and left him alone.

Christmas Day was the disaster he knew it would be, but it sure kept his mind off the two-year anniversary of Sandy's murder. His father and Bruce traded snide remarks and insults the whole time. Father Timothy tried to keep the peace amidst the chaos of children amped up on Christmas cookies. His brothers got into their usual competitions. And through it all, Bruce kept his cool. It seemed like his father was baiting Bruce trying to get him to throw a punch, probably so he could have Bruce arrested for assault. But the man didn't take the bait. It was a good learning experience in patience.

The last thing he saw as he and Bruce escaped out the door was his mother aiming an old BB gun at his father. Definitely, a Christmas to remember.

☒

By January 2007, he and his new partner already had a backlog and had started the search for a third partner. Domestic battery was becoming almost as common as vicious divorces. The violence seemed to escalate, maybe because of the economic downturn. There was no shortage of cases, and although they charged a sliding fee scale and often worked pro bono, the money poured in.

His life was simple. Work took up most of his time, but he always had time for AA meetings, church, and his one guilty pleasure, NCIS.

He made a difference in the lives of people, mostly women, who had survived incredibly cruel and brutal attacks. By the following year, he had four partners, and they were just about ready to add a fifth.

He tried not to think about what the bear said about the *she* the bear had told him about.

His life was good. Not wonderful, but satisfying.

☒

Christmas Eve morning, 2014, ten years after Sandy's murder, he sat in the confession booth. He didn't have much to confess since his life revolved around making a *living amends* to society. Then Father Timothy asked him a question he didn't want to think about.

"Michael, I know I don't have to remind you it's been ten years since you lost Sandy, but have you given any thought to dating?"

Dating? No, and the idea made him slightly queasy. "Why would you ask me something like that?"

"Because you've been single and focused on your work all this time. Man was not meant to be alone, and ten years is a long time to grieve."

"I don't really grieve anymore. But it was always Sandy. I don't remember what dating was like before her, and I'm not sure how it works now. Times have changed. Look, Father, I know you mean well, but I'm very happy with my life, and I don't feel any need to change it."

"Are you afraid?"

"Afraid? Of what?"

"Afraid of falling in love with a woman and losing her the way you lost Sandy."

Was that it? Sometimes he missed the feel of soft, warm skin against his so much he could almost taste it. But then the memory of the body bag on that gurney quashed any desire to find someone. "No, I'm not afraid. I've just been too busy."

"You understand the penance involved for lying to a priest during confession, right?"

Geez. He shouldn't be surprised. The old priest had known him since he was a child. Might as well be honest. "Okay, so, yes. But every time I think about it, I remember that day, and I get scared."

"I can understand that. But you need to overcome that fear. There's someone out there for you. Let down that wall."

"Bruce tells me that all the time, and then he reminds me no dating in AA."

"Why?"

"I think his words were, *We're here because we're not all there.* And my favorite, *Two sickies don't make a wellie.*"

The priest laughed. "Well, it doesn't have to be someone in AA. Find some interests outside of work and meet other people. Put yourself out there. The more you do, the more comfortable you'll feel."

"See, that's the thing. It's not work to me. It's a vocation. Yes, it's time-consuming and sometimes it's frustrating, but it fills my needs."

"Try to keep an open mind. Maybe she'll walk into your office one day. Who knows?"

If she walked into his office, it would be because she needed his legal services, and that would be an ethical violation. But he humored the priest. "Okay, Father. I'll keep an open mind."

After the priest blessed him, he left the confessional, recited his penance, and went home to catch a nap before Mass. He wasn't the least bit surprised when Sandy appeared.

"Father's right, you know."

"I'm not ready."

The Good Deed

"Yes, you are. You've been ready for a long time. You have to move forward, my love."

"I have been."

"Yes, you changed your entire life. You have a purpose, and you and your partners have helped hundreds, maybe thousands of people find justice. But it's time to let me go so you can find her."

"How can you say that? You're my wife!"

"No, Michael. I *was* your wife. I've been gone a long time, and you've been alone for too long. It's time to move on."

"I don't know if I can. I don't know how."

"It's easy. You just do it."

He woke with a start to the obnoxious ringtone he'd assigned to his mother so he wouldn't sleep through her calls. "Hi, Mom."

"Michael?"

"Yeah, Mom. What's up?"

"Can you come over? I need you."

The trembling in her voice put him on high alert. "Be right there."

"Thank you."

When he arrived, the most important woman in his life was pacing the kitchen floor holding a bag of frozen peas to her eye.

Rage and nausea flowed through him.

What the fuck?

"Mom! What happened?"

"It wasn't his fault. He was drunk, and I shouldn't have said what I said. It's been building for a long time."

"*Oh,* my God! Dad *hit* you?" She pulled the bag of frozen vegetables away from her face, and he saw her swollen eye. Then he saw red and his hands clenched in fists.

"I provoked him, and I shouldn't have. He's been having a hard time. He hasn't been feeling well, and the doctor has him on all kinds of pills. And he was drinking."

"Where is he? I'm going to kill him."

"Don't say that! I don't know where he is. He ran out of here, and I heard the car screech out of the driveway."

His fists clenched and unclenched and he vibrated with rage. "I'm going to find him, and then I'll show him what it feels like."

"No! That's not why I called you."

"Then why *did* you call?"

"I'm having thirty people, including children for Christmas dinner tomorrow, and I can't let them see me like this."

"Why not?"

"Because it'll embarrass your father, and your brothers will react just like you are right now."

"Good! He should be a lot more than just embarrassed. He should be in jail. As for my brothers? You bet they'll be pissed off. You didn't do anything to deserve this. No woman or man ever deserves this. I think you should call the police and press charges!"

"*Oh,* my Lord! I couldn't! He's my *husband,* for better or for worse! I just need help tomorrow. I should be able to cover up the swelling, or maybe I can get an eye patch and just say I have an infection or something."

"Geez, Mom. You're going to cover for him? What happens if he does it again?"

"I won't give him a reason."

That's when he lost control. "Won't give him a REASON? YOU DIDN'T GIVE HIM A REASON THIS TIME!"

"Michael, please don't yell at me!" She collapsed into a dinette chair and broke down in tears.

He made his mother cry. Wonderful. He needed to get a grip. "I'm sorry, Mom. Tell me, what can I do? What do you need?"

"I need you to tell your brothers what to expect so they'll behave, and I need you to be here early tomorrow morning. I don't know what will happen with your father, but I do know I won't stand for any violence from you or your brothers."

"But you'll stand for violence from your husband? Damn it, Mom. I'm sorry. I just can't stand the thought of him laying a hand on you."

"This wasn't the first time, and it probably won't be the last. Your father has a temper. He has for a long time. He's a good man unless he's had too much to drink, and that's not very often, usually just around John's birthday. Something I do sets him off, and I've never been able to figure out what."

This wasn't the first time? This wasn't the first time his father had hit his mother? Where were he and his brothers when it happened before? How did they not know? He needed to talk to someone before he did something he would regret and lose his license to practice law. "Okay. I'll talk to them, and I'll be here bright and early. But you have to promise me you'll call me if he comes home drunk. Okay? Do you promise?"

"Yes, I promise. And thank you."

"What are you thanking me for?"

"For coming when I called."

"You're my *mother*. I'll *always* be here for you!"

"Are you going to Mass tonight?"

"Yes, I'll be there. What about you? If he doesn't come home, what will you do?"

"I'll be there no matter what. Ice packs should keep the swelling down, and it'll be dim inside the church. I'll get one of your brothers to drive me."

"Call me if you need anything."

"I will."

He sat in his car and tried to compose himself before he made the calls. He didn't want to explain and listen to the same swearing five different times, so he invited them over — just them. No kids, no spouses. When he told them it was about Mom, and it was serious, they all agreed to come. He set the Chandler Horde powwow for five o'clock. That way they could all get home to their families in time for Christmas Eve festivities before going to Mass.

Father Timothy had to be his next stop.

After reciting the preliminaries, the old priest chuckled and said, "Well, Michael, what could you possibly have done between this morning and now that you would need to confess again?"

"I swore at my mother about my father."

Silence.

"Go on."

"He hit her, Father! He was drunk, and he hit her. She called me, and I went over there, and I saw my *mother* holding a bag of frozen peas to her eye! And all I wanted to do was hurt him. And she said this wasn't the first time. And I don't know what to do with this!"

The priest was silent, again.

"Father?"

"Yes, Michael. I'm here. I want you to pray to Saint Monica. It needs to be something from your heart, not a *Hail Mary* or an *Our Father*. Saint Monica is the patron saint of alcoholics. I'm not saying your father is one, but he has a serious problem. Pray that he receives healing and mercy from our Lord. And pray for yourself, too, that you may find compassion for his suffering as you once suffered."

He recited the Act of Contrition, and after the priest blessed him, he walked into the church, found a pew, and kneeled. But the words wouldn't come, so he focused on opening his heart. He used to be where his father was. But to the best of his recollection, he had never been violent except for that bar fight, and that was because he was drunk and watched a man verbally abuse his date. But there *were* other times he'd blacked out, so it was possible.

He had about a half hour before his brothers would arrive, so he stopped at a store and picked up some sodas. He didn't keep alcohol in his house, and although some of them would want a beer, or maybe something stronger after they heard what he had to say, they'd have to settle for a cola.

The *old man* and the *runt* were the first to arrive and bombarded him with questions, but he refused to tell them anything until the others got there. They didn't have to wait long before there was a commotion at his front door. Matt, Luke, and Jimmy all tried to get through the door at the same time, just like when they were boys.

After they found places to sit, he told them what happened, and their reactions were the same as his. After everyone calmed down, they discussed what to do about it. "Mom doesn't want us to do anything. She just wanted you to know so you wouldn't make a big deal about her eye in front of the grandkids. And she wants your promise that you won't retaliate in any way."

"Not retaliate? You're kidding, right?" Mark barely held his anger in check. And the others all yelled at once, echoing the *old man*.

It looked like it would be up to him and Father Timothy to keep the peace. "Look, if you can't control yourselves tomorrow, she doesn't want you there. This is *Mom*, and she needs our support. Can you guys be civil?"

One by one, they agreed not to make a scene, and one by one they left. That went better than he expected. Of course, he *had* held back that little tidbit about it not being the first time which would have really set them off. They could be rowdy when they got together and had one too many beers, but none of them was the violent type, and all of them adored their mother. There was no way any of them would hit a woman. However, never in a million years would he have believed his father was capable of it — if he hadn't seen her eye.

Most of his clients were women whose husbands only hit where the marks and bruises wouldn't show so the police wouldn't believe them. Was that what his father used to do? Was that why he and his brothers never saw the signs? Was that why his father showed up with bouquets of flowers for no reason? Had there actually been a reason? And she said it usually happened around John's birthday. Why? The *runt* was his favorite. He was spoiled and got away with just about everything.

He resolved to be more sympathetic and sensitive. And he resolved to be more compassionate. His father was a sick man, just like he had been.

He showered and dressed for Midnight Mass, and when he walked into the church, he found his family taking up three pews. Someone must have gotten there early to save all those seats. But his father was missing. "Shove over. I need to sit next to Mom."

"No way. I got here first."

"Luke! Stop acting like a child and go sit with your family."

His brother sulked and moved. Once Luke was out of earshot, he leaned in closer. "Dad?"

She stared straight ahead and shook her head.

"No call?"

Again, she didn't look at him. Just shook her head.

It was almost midnight. His father had been gone for twelve hours. "Did you talk to Father Timothy?"

She nodded.

Well, at least she'd done that. He didn't ask her what the priest said. It wasn't any of his business, but he could imagine. "How did you get here?"

"John picked me up."

"I'll take you home."

She sighed when he took her hand. She'd always stuck up for him when his brothers or his father picked on him. He didn't think of himself as her favorite, but they had a bond she didn't seem to have with the others. His heart ached for her. Fifty-two years of marriage, and it looked like this would be their first Christmas Eve apart.

She was silent as he drove her home; he took her hand and squeezed it. "It'll be okay, Mom."

"He's never stayed away this long."

"He's probably sleeping it off in his car somewhere."

"I hate that idea."

So did he.

They were two blocks from his parents' house when his cell phone rang, so he pushed the speaker button to answer. "This is Michael."

"Is Mom with you?"

"Yeah."

"Take me off the speaker."

There was something in Mark's voice . . . "Hold on." He pulled over and pushed the button to switch to the handset. "Okay, what's up."

"You need to get to Harbor General. Dad was in an accident, and it doesn't look good."

Shit.

"Okay, we'll be right there." He disconnected and turned to the woman next to him. "That was Mark. We need to go to the hospital. Dad's been in an accident."

She stared straight ahead. "I know."

"What do you mean, *you know?*"

"I felt it while we were in church. And he's not going to make it either, and I never got a chance to forgive him and tell him I still love him." A tear slid down her cheek.

"Mom, you have to stay positive! The hospital isn't too far. We'll be there in a few minutes. Hang on."

The emergency admitting clerk said the doctor would be out to give them an update. He could tell from the way the woman lowered her eyes when she spoke. It wasn't going to be good.

Christmas Eve strikes again.

While they waited, he called Father Timothy. He didn't want to use the term *last rites,* but the priest would hear it in his voice.

Three hours later, he dropped his mother off and sped home to pack a bag. He would spend Christmas Day with his mom but there would be no celebration.

As he drove back to his parents' house, he heard the bear's voice in his head reminding him there was a *she* out there for him.

Not a chance in hell.

"Fuck you."

☒

He still couldn't get over the idea that the man who looked like a skinhead gangsta pimp was getting married tomorrow. It had only been a few months since he and his friends had been out celebrating his ten-year sobriety birthday. Bruce had walked in with a beautiful, classy lady on his arm. He'd nearly dropped his club soda when the man introduced her as his fiancé. He knew Bruce had been dating someone, but he had no idea it was that serious.

Cathy was the perfect woman for Bruce, and it was obvious to everyone how in love they were. For a second, a twinge of jealousy and envy grabbed at his heart. But only for a second.

It had been two years since his father's car accident. His mother managed by keeping busy with church events. She even worked part time for Father Timothy who was getting on in age and was a bit forgetful. It was great seeing her interact with the world again, and he spotted several silver-haired gentlemen trying to catch her eye every Sunday morning. After the way his father had treated her, any man who even thought about courting her would have to submit to a psych eval first.

Sometimes, late at night, he wondered why he couldn't find someone.

What a stupid question.

He couldn't bring himself to go out and look. Besides, his thriving law firm and their caseload took all his time and energy. There were eight-partners now, and since they'd added wrongful death suits, they were swamped.

That part of his vision quest, all those years ago, had come true. The other part hadn't, and as far as he was concerned, it wouldn't.

The next day he would be a groomsman at his best friend and sponsor's wedding.

What a mind blower.

12

Despite the physical and emotional pain, Elaine had sat in that witness stand and told her story, and now the jury would decide her future. Fear or freedom. If she still believed, she would have prayed, but he'd beaten that out of her.

During their so-called happy marriage, Dan Jeffers had slapped her around, sometimes in her sleep and usually because she was snoring. But when it was more than a slap, Elaine called the police. Each time he was convicted of misdemeanor battery and spent a day or two in jail until his lawyer got him out. Each time he agreed to attend anger management classes. Each time she could have had him sent away for six months in the Los Angeles County Jail. But each time she believed his promise never to hurt her again, so her lawyer always agreed to the terms.

Dan was ten years older and a successful businessman when they met. He romanced her and flattered her and showered her with flowers and gifts. Her parents approved of him and thought he was a great catch. She married him right out of high school with his promise that she could attend college part time as long as she fulfilled her *wifely duties*. At the time, she didn't know what that meant. She learned the hard way after dinner one night, shortly after their marriage.

She told him she planned to register for some classes at the local community college.

"No."

"No?"

"That's what I said. No."

"Why not?"

"Because you can't even keep up with taking care of me and this house. It's filthy. I'm embarrassed to invite anyone over. And dinner is usually late and tastes like shit. So, no. You don't have time for school. Besides, what would you study? You're not that smart."

Not smart? She'd graduated high school with a 4.0 GPA and scored in the top two percentile on her SATs! She could have gotten a full scholarship to UCLA and tested out of her first year! But he'd charmed her into marrying him, instead. "I do *too* keep the house clean. I vacuum and dust every day. You always have clean, pressed clothes, and you can practically eat off the kitchen and bathroom floors. What part is filthy?"

Instead of answering her, he stood up from the dining room table, grabbed her by her hair, and dragged her into the living room. Then he pushed her face down until her nose hit the corner of the hardwood floor. "There. See that?"

"*Ow!* You're hurting me! I don't see anything! Let me go!" She struggled to get away, but he just pushed her face in harder.

"It's a God damned cobweb!"

It was in the corner near the floor and about two inches long. She'd missed it because it was so small. He let go of her hair and slammed her head into the wall.

She never asked about school, again.

After that, she was meticulous about keeping the house clean, laundry folded, his shirts and pants ironed, the bathrooms — including the walls and floors — spotless, cupboards and the fridge full of his favorite foods and drinks, and with a new cookbook, she had a gourmet dinner on the table every night when he got home. Considering everything she had to do each day to keep him happy, he'd been right. She had no time for school.

He still found reasons to slap her around. But he never left any marks as long as she kept up with her chores and never asked for anything. The two times he lost his temper and hit her hard enough she needed stitches, she'd called the police. Both times the jury found him guilty of misdemeanor spousal abuse. After he paid the fine, they released him. Then he would he treat her like a queen, but it never lasted long. He brought her flowers for their anniversary, but he hadn't signed the card, and the flowers were wilted.

After the last beating, she got a restraining order. It prohibited him from all contact, and he had to maintain at least a three hundred-foot distance from her and anything having to do with her. But after anger management classes and a sincere apology, including diamond earrings, she let him back in, and he immediately raped her.

After that, as long as she *behaved*, her home life was tolerable.

Until Christmas Eve morning.

She hadn't felt well, and the toast was a little darker than he liked which sent him into a rage. He cornered her in the kitchen and punched her in the face. As she'd tried to back away, he punched her again, hard enough to give her a nosebleed and knock her to the floor. Then the kicking had started.

Her ribs still hurt as she sat in that courtroom listening to the lawyers, and there was an emptiness where her womb had been. Memories of that day were a blur. Somehow, she'd gotten away, or more likely, he'd gotten tired of kicking and left her in a fetal position on the floor. As soon as he left the room, she'd run out the front door screaming for help. A nice-looking man about her age had come to her rescue. He called the police on his cell phone and stayed with her until they arrived, took her statement, and arrested Dan.

Now it was over. The jury found him guilty of Felony Willful Infliction of Corporal Injury and sentenced him to four years in Corcoran Prison. As the bailiff led him out of the courtroom, he screamed, "I'll get you, Elaine! You'll pay for this, you bitch!"

Pay? She'd already paid with her uterus. She hadn't known she was pregnant until she miscarried in the ER. The damage from the

beating had been so severe the doctors had to perform an emergency hysterectomy to keep her from hemorrhaging to death. She'd
paid, all right.

Dan was on his way to prison for four years, and she looked
forward to freedom. Yes, there was a possibility of early parole, but
the prosecutor assured her she would be notified well in advance
and a restraining order would be in place. The court awarded her a
decent settlement for her pain and suffering, and thanks to a good
divorce lawyer, the judge ordered Dan to sign a quitclaim which
gave her the house and all the contents. The judge also ordered him
to arrange automatic spousal support payments while he was in
prison.

What was that nice man's name? He said he was a lawyer, and
he and his wife lived a few blocks away. Michael. Michael Chandler.
She wanted to find him and thank him again for his help and
support. When she got home from court, she searched for him on
the internet. According to LinkedIn, he was an attorney at a large
corporation, but when she called, they told her he no longer worked
there. There weren't any listings in the white pages, either.

She Googled him and found a link to a news story about a
murder.

Son of a bitch!

According to the story, Mr. Chandler's wife had been murdered
the same day Dan had beaten her for the last time. By the time she
finished the article, devastation enveloped her, and she couldn't stop
crying.

Someone killed that poor man's wife while he was helping me!

Short of hiring a private detective, she couldn't track him down.
Guilt took up residence in her stomach and heart, and she hated her
ex-husband even more.

☒

As soon as she got her maiden name back, it was time to register
for school. She aced the entrance exams and qualified for a scholar-

ship specifically for women who had suffered physical violence in domestic relationships. It wasn't much, but it was something.

She'd always had an aptitude for numbers so it made sense to get an accounting degree and become a CPA. It paid well and knowing when Dan got out, he'd stop the monthly payments, she needed to support herself. The coursework was relatively easy, and she enjoyed her time in the classrooms. At home, when she didn't have her nose in a textbook, she held yard sales and put the house up for sale. To avoid a hefty capital gains tax, she calculated a paper loss and rolled everything into a Roth IRA. At night and on weekends she indulged in her one guilty pleasure — NCIS reruns.

She found a cute little cottage that was in foreclosure and up for auction. It was too small for most people, but she got it for back property taxes which meant she could cover the monthly payments out of her support payments with a little left over. She was set financially and congratulated herself with new bedroom furniture. Living alone was heaven compared to the hell she'd endured with Dan.

School kept her busy, and when she wasn't studying, she gardened and decorated and swooned over Very Special Agent Leroy Jethro Gibbs. Her home was her haven, and no matter what happened during the day, when she got home at night, kicked off her shoes, and put her feet on the coffee table, she smiled.

She made friends with some women in her classes. As they were eating lunch one day, one of them asked if she ever thought she'd marry again.

"Sure. When hell freezes over."

"So there's still a chance?"

"Funny. Well, if *he* ever shows up, and that's a really big IF, he'll have to go through a battery of psychological tests. Charm, good looks, and a bank account don't matter if he's a wife beating bastard."

"You know, there are dating services that pre-screen the men."

"The prescreening I'm talking about is the same as for a government *eyes only* security clearance. Besides, right now I need to stay focused on getting my degree, my CPA license, and starting my accounting business. I don't have time for dating." She didn't want to think about it, either. She pitied the first man she agreed to go out with if he so much as held her hand too tightly.

"There are several support groups for battered women, you know. Maybe you should think about joining one."

Now that sounded like a good idea. How did other women cope in mixed social situations?

13

She breezed through her exams and took accelerated courses during the summer. By the time winter break came along, it was time for a change of scenery. Her battered women's support group had planned a wellness retreat, and as much as she loved her little cottage, she needed a change.

She and the other eleven women were going on a six-day retreat in Sedona, Arizona. The website had information on all the services and classes, and it sounded like just what she needed. She hoped to come back even more empowered, but mostly she wanted to get back in touch with the feelings she'd blocked. She still had no intention of ever dating, let alone getting married again.

She was so hyped about the retreat she had a hard time sleeping the night before, and when she finally slept, her dreams were jumbled with impressions of hospitals and Dan and forest animals. At some point, she'd been beaten so badly she knew she was dying and woke in a cold sweat.

It had to be all the stress from finals. At least, she hoped that was the cause. She didn't believe in premonitions or foresight or any of that hocus-pocus stuff, anymore. Real life had turned her into a staunch atheist.

Yeah, this retreat couldn't come soon enough.

The departure was at seven in the morning, and the van was scheduled to pick her up at four-thirty. She was already packed and didn't need to get up until three to shower. But thanks to the nightmare, she couldn't get back to sleep. She was ready to go, and at four thirty on the dot, there was a tap on her door. The driver took her suitcase while she locked up.

Time never seemed to matter at LAX. It could have been noon for all the hundreds of people waiting in the security lines. Thank goodness, they all had TSA Pre-check. They had plenty of time before boarding, so they stopped for coffee. Starbucks were everywhere, and this airport was no exception.

While the other women chattered away, Glenda studied her. "Are you okay?" The young woman always knew when something was bothering her, so there was no point in lying.

"I had a hard time sleeping last night, and when I did, I had weird dreams. The last one was a terrible nightmare, and I couldn't get back to sleep."

"What was it about?"

"I don't remember exactly. I just know I was in a hospital and knew I was dying. I think I was in some kind of accident, and I'd been pretty beaten up."

Beaten.

Up.

Shit.

Had the dream been about Dan? He'd been in prison for two years and had another two before he'd get out. No one had told her otherwise, and she hadn't been informed of a parole hearing. The dream couldn't be literal so it must mean something else.

"This will be just what you need, then. It's a very spiritual place. I can't wait to hike into one of the vortex areas."

"Well, I'm looking forward to the massages and meditations." They could keep all that new age, chakra, energy vortex stuff. "I think our hotel rooms all have whirlpool tubs, too. But for what these six days are costing me, I could have had one installed in my bathroom."

"You haven't spent a dime on yourself until now. You deserve this. If you want one of those tubs, you'll find a way to get it, but this is important."

"I haven't spent a dime on myself because I've been paying for school. That scholarship, and my support payments, don't go very far. But you're right. I do deserve this. And after last night's dream, it seems I really need it. I'll find a way to pay the money back to my IRA account."

When they heard the announcement for their flight, they made their way to the gate. Twelve women took over business class. It was extravagant, totally unnecessary, and a great way to start the pampering.

The van ride from Sky Harbor Airport to Sedona was longer than the flight from LAX to Phoenix, but after they left the city behind, the scenery was magnificent. Their hotel was next to the retreat center and reeked of luxury. The views of the flaming red mountains were spectacular, and her mind ran out of superlatives as she took it all in.

After they unpacked, the next order of business was to explore the area. But after wandering around in the blistering desert heat, she went back to her suite to take advantage of the air conditioning and the jetted soaking tub. The picture window in the bathroom looked out at the amazing sandstone formations, and as she soaked away the stress; her underlying fear seemed to drain out into the swirling water.

Yeah, she would be putting one of these in her bathroom someday. Thanks to the relaxing soak, she slept like the dead and woke at dawn to the most gorgeous sunrise she'd ever seen.

"Hey, Elaine! Are you awake?"

She had just finished brushing her hair and glanced at the clock. It was seven-thirty when she opened the door and found Glenda standing there. "Yeah. I was just about to come see if you were."

"You ready for breakfast? It's included, so we might as well."

"Sure. Let me grab my purse."

"You won't be needing it."

Her friend was right. She didn't need her cell phone, either. When they got to the dining room, the other women had just ordered. They talked about the day's events. There was a welcome orientation, a release ceremony and insights — whatever those were — and hydration therapy, which was probably like a massage. It all sounded great, especially the massage.

The orientation turned out to be a tour of the grounds. There were paths to explore, a labyrinth to walk, and benches to just sit on and enjoy the peacefulness of the surroundings.

About a half mile from the center, they came to what the guide referred to as an energy vortex. It was the smaller one. On the last day, they would hike to the big one. They all sat cross-legged on the ground while the guide led them through a meditation to release negative thoughts and anything that blocked the energy flow. It might have been wishful thinking, or more likely her imagination, but she could swear she felt some kind of warm buzzing through her body. But it was probably just the sun on the hot ground.

They walked back to the center and gathered in a large room with vaulted open-beam ceilings, braided rugs with southwestern motifs, and a huge stone fireplace, although there was no need for a fire since it was approaching ninety degrees outside. There were several overstuffed couches arranged in a circle, and everyone made themselves comfortable.

Their guide went into detail about the different methods for self-exploration, such as vision boards, iChing, and Stream of Conscious journaling. Journaling sounded good. The other stuff was too *new-agey* for her.

Next up was the Hydration Treatment & Energy Work. Along with a light massage, there was something called a dry brush technique that was supposed to slough off dead skin and stimulate blood flow. She had plenty of dead skin to slough off. Then she was smothered in essential oils and shea butter. What the heck is a shea? And, because it wasn't hot enough already, the attendant wrapped her in warm towels that were supposed to feel like a "nurturing cocoon to cleanse and renew body and spirit."

The cleansed part was the buckets of sweat. The renewed part came when she escaped the warm towel cocoon and suddenly the ninety-degree heat felt like a cool spring day.

She fell asleep during the guided meditation and the Reiki session which was considered bad form. But that's how relaxed she was. They should have been happy instead of looking at her like she broke some law.

After a long soak in the swirling cool water in her room, her stomach growled for food. The center didn't provide food, and the hotel only served breakfast, so they were on their own, and everyone craved meat. They took the hotel shuttle into town where they found a steakhouse with a southwestern touch.

It was only seven when they got back to the hotel, stuffed, drained, and ready for sleep. She'd never slept longer than eight hours straight before, and it took a while to get moving the next morning. Everyone seemed to be dragging, and they got to the center just in time for the hike to the labyrinth.

After a brief history of labyrinths, they began what was basically a walk through a maze while meditating. She wasn't sure what she was supposed to get out of it, but the walking kept her awake.

Next up was the Emotional Clearing for Wellness session, which was just another guided meditation. She'd just closed her eyes when she felt a touch on her arm. When she opened her eyes, the guide whispered, "You're snoring." At least no one would hit her for that.

The last session of the day was *Horse Medicine, Human Spirit,* and a real horse whisperer helped them interact with the animals. When it was her turn, her horse turned and looked at her as if it could see all her pain and fears. When she rubbed the animal's muzzle, a deep connection seemed to form, so she touched her head to the horse's and felt its lips move on her cheek as if it was kissing her. And when she looked, its nose was wet with her tears. It was a powerful and moving experience which alone was worth the exorbitant price of the retreat. It was something she'd never forget, that's for sure.

That wrapped up the third day, and after cleaning up, they went in search of a Mexican restaurant. Although she'd been born and raised in Southern California and had eaten in some pretty authentic hole in the wall cantinas, the one they found in town made all the others seem like fast-food chains.

She crawled into bed, stuffed and sleepy.

Day four was packed with activities; she was definitely getting her money's worth.

After a fifteen-minute meditation, which she stayed awake through, each of them sat with a life coach. Before her turn came, she was pretty convinced it would be a quick session since she already knew what she wanted to do and how to go about it. When the coach questioned her further, she reconsidered if accounting was what would bring her the most satisfaction. Was it her *calling?* Or was it just a way to make money? And what was a calling, anyway? She didn't have the answers, but she promised to keep an open mind and be alert for other possibilities that might be more fulfilling.

The leader of The Divine Feminine session was a conventional therapist who got her to spill her guts about her ex-husband and the beatings. Through a form of word association, she got past the emotional betrayal that had imprisoned her heart. When it was over, there wasn't a single building she didn't think she couldn't leap over. This, and the horse encounter, had been the most productive and meaningful sessions so far.

Finally, there was the Chakra Health Balancing session. The tuning forks seemed a little silly, but the massage with essential oils made up for it. The guided meditation for clearing her chakras wasn't bad, and it did seem to open up a flow of energy. Or it could have been her imagination, again. Whatever it was, it was soothing.

No one felt like going out so dinner was several pizzas delivered to the large patio. With the outdoor lights turned off, the raucous but soothing clicks of thousands of cicadas filled the air. Without all the light pollution like there was in a big city, she could easily make out the Milky Way and constellations. But between the events of the day, the dry heat, and several slices of pepperoni and jalapeño pizza, she nodded off at the table.

After breakfast they walked to the center and found fanny packs with bottles of water and energy bars. The hike to the vortex was about four miles each way, some of which was a gradual uphill climb. That's what the guides said, anyway. As she struggled to catch her breath, she resolved to make use of the gym at school and get back into shape.

Once they arrived, they sat in lotus position, which after all the practice no longer cut off her circulation, and concentrated on drawing energy up from the ground and through the chakras that had been balanced and cleared the day before. It didn't do much for her, but Glenda looked like she was plugged into a wall outlet. When the heat became too intense, they hiked back to the coolness of the great room.

The next session was a color reading. The guide arranged several cards of different colors before her, and she had to choose which ones appealed to her most. After narrowing all the choices down to blue, the guide gave her a long interpretation and a card that summarized the meaning.

Blue is a masculine color. Dark blue is associated with depth, expertise, and stability; it is a preferred color for corporate America. Dark blue represents knowledge, power, integrity, and seriousness. Avoid using blue when promoting food and cooking because blue suppresses appetite.

Light blue is associated with health, healing, tranquility, understanding, and softness.

So, blue supposedly suppressed appetite? That would come in handy when she was finally ready to lose those last five pounds. She pictured a blue kitchen.

The last session of the retreat was the Mind, Body & Spirit End Integration. They all gathered in the great hall and talked about what their expectations had been when they arrived, and what they'd accomplished. Was it a success? Every woman in her group got something from some or all the sessions, and the verdict was a resounding yes. Would they come back? Again, they all agreed it was a do-over. Shit, she'd come back just for the horse therapy if she could.

Her group wandered back to the hotel and cleaned up for the evening. She chose a blue sundress, and even though it was supposed to cut her appetite, she was hungry enough she could eat a side of beef. This was their last night, and they planned to splurge.

The hotel concierge recommended a French restaurant. The tables were outside next to a rushing creek fed by a natural spring, and the food was definitely French. The menu was *prix fixe,* and they all decided on the four-course option. The server agreed to bring a selection of each entrée so everyone got a taste of everything.

It was the perfect calorie-laden end to a wonderfully restoring getaway. She slept like a log, and then slept through the van ride to the airport, skipped the Starbucks stop, and slept the entire flight. As soon as they landed, she emerged from the plane feeling reborn, renewed, and energized, and she couldn't wait to take on the world. It had been an incredible six days, worth every penny, and now she was home.

The van driver carried her bag to the front door, and she waved to the women she was now so closely bonded with. As she dug her keys out of the bottom of her purse, her mind turned to laundry and grocery shopping. She unlocked the door.

14

―――――――

"Hello, Elaine."

"What are you . . .? How did you . . .? Why are you . . .?"

"What's the matter, darling? Surprised to see me? I told you that day in court I'd make you pay. You should have expected this."

Terror hit her like a freight train. He'd been paroled, and no one warned her. And now he would get his revenge. She was as good as dead. She screamed as she tried to escape, but he grabbed her hair.

"I like your hair long. Makes it easier to grab you when you try to get away."

The first blow hit her cheek. "That's for the first year."

The next blow hit her stomach and knocked the air out of her lungs. As she gasped for breath, he laughed. "That's for the second year."

The third blow hit her jaw and sent her sprawling across the room. But he wasn't done yet. She tried to protect herself by curling into a ball, but he grabbed her arm and yanked so hard the crack was audible. Then the kicking started.

"I told you I'd get you, you cunt. You ruined my life. Thanks to you, my cellmate made me his bitch. Do you have any idea what you put me through? I should rape you the same way they raped me, but I can't stand the sight of you, let alone touch you. You think you hurt now? When I'm done, you'll wish you were dead."

She got off one last good scream before he grabbed her head and slammed it into the wood floor. Then he stepped on her thigh and everything went black.

⅄

"Dr. Green, she's regaining consciousness."

Everything looked milky as the bright lights accosted her eyeballs, and people hovered around her. She heard beeps and felt her chest moving on its own. And what was that thing in her mouth? She gagged.

"Easy there, young lady. Don't try to breathe. Let the machine do it for you."

Machine? What the hell happened? Had she been in an accident? She opened her eyes a little more and saw a portly, gray-haired man with sympathetic eyes looking down at her.

"Hello there, Elaine. I'm Dr. Green. You're at Harbor General. We're getting you ready for surgery, but we need your consent. You have a fractured skull, internal bleeding, a ruptured spleen, several broken bones, and a few fractures. Blink twice if you consent."

She needed surgery? Bandages covered part of her face, and she felt the lump of more bandages on the back of her head. She seemed to be breathing underwater, and every inch of her body burned. If it *was* an accident, she felt sorry for the other guy.

She blinked twice.

"That's good. Now we want to give you something to help you sleep, and then we'll patch you up. The police want to ask you some questions first. Blink twice if that's okay. Otherwise, they'll wait."

Police?

Dan!

Dan had been waiting for her and he'd made good on his threat.

She blinked twice. They had to find him before he found her

again. As battered and broken as she was, next time, he'd kill her. He'd probably meant to do that this time. What had stopped him? Two police officers appeared. The younger one took one look at her and turned away. Boy, it had to be bad if a cop couldn't look at her. The older officer had a notepad and pen and asked if she remembered what happened. All she could do was blink twice.

"I know you can't talk, and we would have waited, but it's Friday, and we want to charge Mr. Jeffers before the weekend. Can you confirm it was your ex-husband who assaulted you?"

She blinked twice.

"Did you know he was there?"

She blinked once.

"Did you provoke him in any way?"

Provoke? What the hell did that mean? And how typical that they thought she'd somehow brought this on herself. Buzzers went off. Beeps sped up. Everything hurt, and she couldn't stop the tears and moans as she squeezed her eyes shut.

"I'm sorry, officer, but that's it. She's in no condition to answer any more of your questions, and I want your badge number. I don't care what else she might have done, she did NOT provoke THIS, and I can't *believe* you would even ask her that! She's in serious condition, and we're taking her to surgery now."

She heard a nurse lay into them as she hustled them out of the emergency room.

"Elaine, do you have an emergency contact in your phone?"

She blinked twice. Her phone had one of those health buttons that contained all her information including blood type and it wasn't password protected. They'd have to figure out how to get to it, though. As they got her ready to move, she heard one of the other nurses talking to someone, someone who was on their way. Then someone injected something into her IV and everything went black.

☒

Machines beeped and someone held her hand. She tried to squeeze it but the pain blazed a path of fire up her arm.

"Elaine? Sweetie? *Oh*, my God! My poor baby girl! Pierre, get the nurse. Our baby's awake! Thank you, Saint Mary!"

There was a buzz of activity, and she gagged as someone dragged what had to be a corncob up her throat. Without the machine breathing for her, she gasped for air and passed out from the pain in her ribs.

The next time she regained consciousness, a pen light blinded her.

"She's conscious and responding. Well, young lady, you gave us a bit of a scare, but you're going to be okay. We'll get you something for your throat, but it's going to be sore for a while so don't try to talk. Just rest. And if the pain gets too bad, press the button on your finger. It'll release a dose of painkiller into your IV. Okay?"

Nodding activated the sledgehammer that pounded away on her skull so she blinked twice, tried out the button, and within seconds the pain eased and the world drifted away.

The next time she opened her eyes, her mother was sitting next to her bed. She was in the ICU and wired for sound if all the machines and beeps were any indication. "Mom?" She tried to whisper, but it sounded more like a frog croaking.

"*Oh*, sweetheart! What do you need? Are you in pain? Of course, you are. Do you need me to get the nurse?"

"What happened?" And why was there coarse grit sandpaper in her throat?

"You should rest. We'll talk about it later when you're better."

Better? The way she felt, *better* was a long way off, and she needed to know.

"Tell me. Did they get him?"

"Dan? They sure as heck did. That monster won't be seeing the light of day for a long time. Your father and I are so sorry we didn't believe you when you told us why you were divorcing him. Sweetheart, we had no idea. What you must have suffered! But you're going to be okay. The doctor said you were very lucky."

"He tried to kill me. Why am I not dead?"

"From what I gather, one of your friends found your small bag of souvenirs in the van, so the driver turned back. You didn't answer the door, and she heard you scream and called 911. Luckily, there was a patrol car right down the street. They broke down the door just as Dan got in one last kick. If you hadn't left that bag in the van . . . Elaine, my precious girl, we came so close to losing you!"

"Mom? Am I really okay? Does everything . . . still work?"

"Let me answer your questions. Do you remember me? I'm Dr. Green. I was there when they brought you in. I just read the surgeon's report, and yes, as best we can tell, everything still works. They had to remove your spleen, but you'll hardly miss it. Your reactions are good, your eyes respond to light, you're coherent, you remembered what happened, and you recognized your mother. As of right now, and unless something new shows up, I think it's safe to say you're going to make a full recovery. But it's going to be awhile before you'll feel up to dancing."

"*Oh*, no! School. My house. My garden. And I don't have insurance! I can't pay for any of this! Shit! What am I going to do?"

Hot lava sizzled in her throat. Buzzers went off, and the beeps sped up.

"Sweetheart, please don't worry about that right now. Your father and I will figure something out. You just concentrate on getting better. That's the most important thing. Now give yourself a hit of pain killer and get some rest."

"Okay, Mom. Mom?"

"Yes, honey?"

"I love you."

"My darling girl. Your father and I love you, too. Everything will be all right. Our Heavenly Father will see to it."

It was a little too late for that.

15

I t was a slow recovery and she couldn't live on her own for the first two months. Her left leg was in a cast from her hip to her ankle, her right arm, which had been fractured in two places, was in a bent cast from her shoulder to her wrist. And several cracked ribs made breathing pure torture.

She was grateful to have her parents there to take care of her. They were patient, and though she lost her temper a lot, she never directed her anger at them. It was laser focused on the man who had done this to her. And she was furious with the justice system that had left her vulnerable.

Her father set up one of the TVs in her old room. Between Judge Judy, NCIS reruns, and reading, she managed to keep from going stir crazy.

With the help of a wheelchair, she attended the trial to the objection of the defense attorney. He said her presence would prejudice the jury to which the district attorney countered with, "She's exhibit A for the prosecution." The judge agreed.

Each day she sat in the courtroom staring at the back of that monster's head wondering if he could feel her hate. Probably not. The few times he'd seen her as the guards led him in or out of the courtroom, he sneered.

The van driver, her friend Glenda, and the first responders all testified, and as the DA had warned her, they presented her as evidence while the ER doctor gave a full report of her injuries and the surgery.

The first tactic the defense came up with was to move for dismissal claiming it was all circumstantial evidence since no one had actually witnessed the alleged beating. The judge denied the request, so the defense tried something so pathetic, she had a hard time hiding her sarcastic laughter, and with cracked ribs, laughing was sheer torture. They called a quack psychologist to the stand. He talked about Dan's childhood and his anger issues which the so-called expert claimed were valid reasons for Dan's behavior.

The judge overruled the prosecution's objection which surprised everyone, but it was soon clear he knew what he was doing. He wanted the jury to consider the so-called expert testimony knowing they'd have none of it. He was right. They deliberated exactly one hour, and she overheard someone say the reason it took *that* long was they were trying to decide where to go for lunch as soon as the judge dismissed them.

Dan received fifteen years in a state penitentiary which would most likely be San Quentin. The soonest he would be eligible for parole would be ten years. The judge ordered him to pay her medical bills. That was great news except he'd moved all his money into an asset protection trust as soon as they'd him released from Corcoran. She'd never heard of that kind of financial trust and accounting had been her major.

Now she owed several hundred thousand dollars in medical bills. There was already a "Go Fund Me" page, but after two months, it had only collected fifty-thousand, which wasn't even a drop in her debt bucket. She would have to sell her little cottage and her car.

So even though he was locked away in prison, he was still beating her.

If only someone had warned her he was getting out. If only she'd known he could legally hide his assets. If only someone had advised her during the first trial.

If only.

In a moment of clarity, she put it all together. As soon as she could walk again, she would go back to school, but not to become a CPA. She would become the thing she'd needed but didn't know was available to her. She would become a Victim's Advocate.

᛭

Two months after she got out of the hospital, the casts came off, and with physical therapy and a lot of determination, she could get around with a cane.

The twenty-thousand from a community victim's fund, plus sixty-thousand from the "Go Fund Me" page still wasn't nearly enough to cover what she owed the hospital. As long as she made regular good faith payments, the hospital wouldn't send her account to a collection agency. But she hated having that debt hanging over her and reluctantly sold her car and her cottage. She had no choice. Between the house, the car, and her IRA, she had enough to pay off the hospital bill with a little left over for an apartment and enough to live on when she went back to school — *if* she was very, very frugal.

She found a place close to UCLA in a not-so-nice neighborhood. The apartment was dingy, and the neighborhood was dangerous at night, but the price was right, and it was near a bus stop. At least her neighbors were friendly. They seemed like a close-knit group and everyone watched out for everyone else, especially after Latesha moved in.

She didn't have a garden anymore, so she filled her tiny apartment with house plants. She'd already sold off most of her valuables; attachments to material things made her vulnerable in that part of town. If she had nothing of value, there was nothing to steal. Her most expensive treasure was an old 19-inch TV so she could watch her beloved NCIS. Her parents gave her a laptop for school, which she hid under her bed whenever she left. She never carried more than twenty dollars so if she got mugged, they wouldn't get much.

This was the reality of her new life much to the consternation of her parents who thought she should have continued to live — safely — with them.

As soon as she was physically able, she signed up for a self-defense class at the local YMCA. Her muscles weren't used to the exercise, and she ached for the first two weeks, but it was a good ache. After every class, she was a little stronger, physically and mentally. She swore she'd never live in fear of another man's fists again. When that class ended, she found a nearby Karate school that accepted monthly payments. Working toward her black belt gave her confidence and great muscle tone. The uniform, called a *gi*, covered her scars nicely.

She applied for, and got, another scholarship. This one was for victims of extreme domestic violence and paid even more than the first scholarship. Then she changed to a double major in psychology and criminal justice. It was a heavy course load, but that was exactly what she needed to keep moving forward. Wallowing in self-pity wasn't how she wanted to spend the rest of her life.

Her neighbors threw barbecue parties by the pool almost every weekend. They invited her, but she was always buried under school books, writing research papers, or studying for exams. Most of the time she was so focused she didn't even hear the knock on her door. But there was another reason. She was just flat out scared of the men. She could defend herself physically, but having to interact with them made her queasy.

☒

It was spring break of the third year after the beating, and most of her support group friends were off on cruises or tours. Getting away sounded great, but she barely had enough money for rent and food, so a day by the pool would have to do. She was a little overdressed in her old lady one-piece bathing suit, but she wasn't ready to deal with the looks and questions. The scars from the sutures where her spleen used to be were still obvious. At least the scar from the hysterectomy wasn't, anymore. There wasn't much she could do about the scars on her legs and arms though.

"Well, Lord ah-mighty! She lives!"

"Hey, Latesha."

"Hey, girl. My, my. For a white girl, you are *painfully* white. Where are my sunglasses?"

"Yeah, I know. I'm probably going to fry which isn't good for my scars."

"Try cocoa butter. Worked on mine."

"You have scars?"

"Yeah, but the cocoa butter helped, and you should have seen *him*. Got him good last time. From what I hear, he still can't talk below a squeak."

"Geez! What did you do?"

"I took self-defense classes after the stitches came out, and when he came at me with a knife last time, I kicked him in the balls and then ran like hell. Asshole tried to press charges claiming *I* attacked *him*, but the cops knew what was goin' on. They'd been to our house enough times. Poor bastard had to stand in the jail cell overnight 'cause he couldn't sit down. Guess he got the hint when he came home to an empty house. Pissed him off, but I had an RO, and he knew better than to try anything. My divorce was final a few months ago. Didn't you hear us partyin'?"

So, *that's* what all that noise had been about. "Yeah, I heard it, but I was studying."

"So, what's with all the school? You planning to be a doctor or a lawyer or somethin'?"

"Victim's Advocate."

"What?"

"Victim's Advocate. Someone who guides a victim of domestic violence through the legal system. Most victims have no idea what resources are available or that they can get restitution for medical expenses for injuries sustained during the attack. In my case, no one told me he could hide his money in a trust so I wouldn't get a dime. Had to sell my house, my car, and everything of value just to pay off the hospital. I'm living off what I had left which isn't much now. I have a scholarship for school, and you've seen my mother bringing care packages of food once a week."

"You know, girl? This is more words than you've said since I moved in. You should talk more often."

"Well, I *have* been super busy. But it's spring break right now. I suppose I could read ahead, maybe start gathering research, but it's such a nice day, I thought I'd get some sun."

"Well, good. Cause like I said, you are pay-*el*. I'm goin' to get a beer. Want one?"

"No thanks. It's a little early for me."

"K. Be right back."

So Latesha was a battered woman who fought back and won. How much courage had that taken? How many times had her husband beaten her before she'd had enough? What kind of scars did she have? A term paper topic formed in her mind.

The beautiful African-American woman plopped back down on the lounge chair. "So, girlfriend, you gotta boyfriend?"

"Nope. Don't have time and don't want one, either."

"They're not all assholes, you know."

"If they were just assholes, I could handle that. Mine wasn't an asshole, he was a monster. Your ex doesn't sound much better."

"Yeah, you got a point. But I think I might have found a keeper this time."

"How can you be sure?"

"Well, I'm not. They change when they know they got you hooked, that's for sure. But usually there are signs; we just choose to overlook them and give them the benefit of the doubt. But after the first time, you tend to be a little more — what's the word? Discriminating? Discerning? Picky?"

"All the above." Would she know it if she saw the warning signs again? Was that a chance she was even willing to take? School wouldn't always be an excuse to avoid relationships. "I don't know. Dan was my first and only. I married him out of high school so I had no one to compare him to. I didn't know what was normal. And I haven't dated anyone since."

"So, like, you haven't had sex with anyone else?"

Embarrassed, she lowered her eyes and shook her head.

"Girl, you need to get you some. Even if you never see the guy again, it's still good for the ego. Nothing like a good orgasm to bring a smile to your face and a sparkle to your eyes. It's good for your complexion, also."

"Orgasm?"

Latesha's eyes bugged out. "*Oh,* my Lord. *Seriously?*"

"What?"

"How old are you?"

"Just turned thirty-nine. Why?"

"And you've never had an orgasm?"

"Is that when he humps for a minute and rolls over and goes to sleep?"

Latesha's mouth dropped open. Apparently, there was more to it than that.

"You Catholic?"

"Not anymore. Why?"

"But you were raised Catholic?"

"*Uh-huh.* But what's that got to do with anything?"

"Did your momma explain what to expect?"

"Not really other than to tell me what my wifely duties were."

"Wifely duties? Lord ah-mighty! You poor thing. I'm gonna loan you some *instructional* videos. Well, they're sorta instructional. I mean, you're gonna learn a lot."

"Really, that's not necessary. I have no intention of ever being with a man again."

"What about a woman?"

"What about it?"

"Maybe you should try being with a woman."

She wasn't *completely* naïve, but the idea of having sex with a woman had never crossed her mind. She wasn't even sure how that worked, and she wasn't curious enough to find out. "I don't think that's my thing. I just have no desire for sex."

"That's 'cause you got no idea what you're missin'. Watch the videos. Then we'll get you a vibrator. If nothing else, you can have sex with yourself. It really is good for you. Ask your doctor."

Ask her doctor about something that intimate? She blushed at the thought.

"See? That's what I'm talking about."

"What?"

"That rosy glow you have now."

"That's not a rosy glow, that's either absolute embarrassment or sunburn."

"Just watch the videos. That's all I'm gonna say."

Thank goodness, because talking about sex was uncomfortable and she needed to change the subject. "So you said your ex used to beat you. Do you mind if I ask you some questions? I need to come up with a topic for my psychology term paper."

"Ask away."

"I'll put together a list and drop it by later."

"Good. Then you can pick up the videos."

Latesha had a one-track mind.

⧗

Oh, my!

After she finished the three *instructional* videos, she was keenly aware of the wetness in her panties and how her breathing had increased. Her thighs involuntarily squeezed together, and her vagina tightened. Was she *turned on?* That had to be it, and it scared the bejeezus out of her. If she let that genie out of the bottle, what then? Ignorance was bliss. If she let herself do what she needed at that moment, would she be setting herself up for a life-time of masturbation? Even though she didn't consider herself Catholic anymore, she would have to overcome a lifetime of indoctrination. But she had to do something or sleep would be impossible.

When she went to bed, she tried a few techniques she'd seen in the videos. It didn't take her long to figure out what she'd been missing.

She slept like a baby.

⏳

She didn't bother asking when she heard the knock on her door. She just opened it and turned back to her postage stamp sized kitchen. "Good morning, Latesha. Want some coffee?"

"Sure."

She poured a cup for each of them.

"Well, did you watch them?"

"What?"

"You know what. Did you watch the *videos*?"

Sigh.

"Yes, I watched them, and yes, they certainly were *instructional*."

"And?"

"And I'm not comfortable talking about something this personal with anyone."

"You did it, didn't you! Couldn't help yourself, could you! I can see it on your face. You get what I'm talking about now?"

Sigh.

"Yes, Latesha. I get it. But I'm not sure what I'm supposed to do with it."

"If a man doesn't make you feel like that, get up and leave. No point wastin' your time. And if you haven't got a man, taking care of yourself keeps you from makin' stupid mistakes — like marryin' a man who doesn't care about your needs."

"I'm never getting married again and I'm never dating. So, thanks to you, now it's just me and my hand, which got kind of tired."

"First off, never say never, and second, that's why you need a vibrator."

"So what, you just walk into Walmart and say, 'Excuse me, where is your vibrator section?'"

"Ha! If only. So there *are* shops that sell them and other toys, but you can get them online if you're too embarrassed."

That was a relief. There was no way she could walk into a store to buy one. Maybe she'd do some research as soon as Latesha left.

"You're gonna look online aren't you?"

Geez, how on earth did she know? "Fine. Yes, I am. Later."

"Good. I recommend the *rabbit*. Hits all the right spots."

Time to move on. "Listen, I don't want to be rude, but I have some reading to do."

"That's a good idea. Erotica is good. Kinda warms you up for the rabbit."

"Seriously. I have *studying* to do!"

"I'll bet."

"LATESHA!"

"Okay, okay, I'm going. Here's that list of questions. I hope you can read my writing. By the way, everyone who didn't go out of town is getting together tonight for a barbecue. If you're not *too busy*, come on out."

"Unless those online shops have same day delivery, I don't think I'll be too busy."

"There you go! Gettin' a sense of humor!"

"Don't you have anything to do besides harass me?"

"Girl, you *need* this kind of harassin'."

When Latesha finally left, she opened her laptop and googled *rabbit vibrator*.

There were over four million search results.

Four million!

Shit.

Even her favorite online bookstore sold them.

There were hundreds of styles, and they weren't cheap. She picked the one with the most five-star reviews and paid extra for next day delivery. She didn't have that kind of money to waste, but hey, she needed to lose a few pounds and eating *was* overrated.

Studying was impossible, so she browsed online for erotica just to see what Latesha was talking about. Within thirty minutes she'd downloaded six free books and spent the day on her couch, reading.

She heard voices coming from the pool area and looked out her window. How was it dusk already? There was a small group of people gathered around the grill. She only had a pack of hot dogs, and she'd spent the last of her money on that vibrator. She considered skipping the barbecue, but then Latesha would notice and pound on her door.

Might as well get it over with and be sociable.

Interacting with men made her nervous, so she changed into some baggy jeans and a sweatshirt, slipped on her beat-up tennies, and ran a brush through her hair. Then she went out to face the crowd, makeup free.

"Well, look who's here! Ya'll know Elaine, right?"

The three men and four women greeted her and asked how she was doing. Did they really want to know? Or were they just being polite? She'd kept mostly to herself after the first time Dan had hit her because of that cobweb. And except for her support group, she didn't have much experience socializing, so she just smiled and answered, "I'm good. How are you?"

She hadn't been able to drink when she'd been on all those pain medications and didn't have money to waste on it now. After she took her first sip from the beer bottle Latesha handed her, she noticed there was a slice of lime in it. "Why is there lime in my beer?"

A deep voice answered her. "It's a cerveza — Mexican style beer. That's how you drink it. Haven't you ever had one?"

He wasn't bad looking, kind of young, with intelligent eyes and olive skin. Probably Hispanic. And he looked at her like she was a one hundred-dollar bill he just found in his pocket.

"I'm not much of a drinker."

"Well, we'll have to do something about that."

"Ease up, Hector. No gettin' her drunk or you'll deal with me."

"Now Latesha, baby, I wasn't goin' to get her drunk — much."

"Yeah, that's what I thought." She pointed two fingers to her eyes and then to him. "I'm watchin' you, boy. I'll mess you up, and you know I can. Leave her alone."

"Fine, whatever." Hector wandered over to a couple of young women who were laughing.

"Don't drink anything unless it comes out of a bottle or a can that you saw being opened. And don't leave your drink unattended."

"Why?"

"Look, these are our neighbors, and for the most part, they're good people. But there's always one, and I think Hector's it."

"I still don't understand."

"*Roofies.*"

"Roofies? What are those?"

"Google it."

She didn't know what roofies were but she would take Latesha's advice. The woman seemed to know everything about how the world outside *her* own self-imposed bubble worked.

"Okay, well, listen, I need to get back to studying. Thanks for the beer."

"Not so fast, girlfriend. Did you buy that item we talked about?"

So much for getting away. "Yes, I did. It should arrive tomorrow."

"Good. Did you get the rabbit?"

"There were four million search hits, so I picked the highest rated one."

"Perfect. And you'll let me know what you think?"

No way.

"Sure."

"What else did you do today?"

"I downloaded some books."

"Oh?"

"Yes, Latesha. I bought some erotic romance novels, or more like short stories. To me, anything less than five hundred pages is a short story."

"And?"

"And nothing. I read some of them. Yes, they were hot. But they're not reality."

"Sometimes we need a break from reality. You're allowed to fantasize, ya know."

"But stories like those set up unreal expectations. Men with washboard abs who are sensitive and affectionate and know how and where to touch but are still responsible and protective? And women who are multi-orgasmic? I mean, last night there was no way I could have done it a second time."

"There *are* men out there like that, but I agree, they're few and far between. That doesn't mean we can't use our imaginations, especially considering you've sworn off men. And you just need practice is all. I can get off four or five times."

Time to go.

"I can't have this conversation right now. I have to go. I'll talk to you tomorrow, or the day after, or maybe next week."

She could still hear the woman laughing as she let herself into her apartment.

Safe!

It was seven when she sat down at her laptop and picked up where she left off. It was midnight when she closed up her computer. By the time she finished all the books, she'd gained a whole new vocabulary and an appreciation for the many ways authors could describe body parts.

16

Despite all the time she spent learning the inner workings of her body, she still aced her exams, and three and a half years after the last beating; she graduated Summa Cum Laude, the highest academic distinction. She cried when she accepted her two degrees while her parents looked and dabbed tissues to their eyes.

She'd survived a violent beating that almost killed her, and she graduated at the top of her class. All she needed was a job now that there would be no more scholarship money.

"Ms. Chambéry?"

"Yes?"

"My name is Paul Drummond. I'm with the District Attorney's office. I was wondering if I might speak to you for a moment?"

He was tall, African-American, slightly balding, with thick *coke-bottle bottom* glasses. "Sure. What can I do for you, Mr. Drummond?"

"It's more like what I can do for you. Dean Matthews said your goal is to become a Victim's Advocate. Is that still the case?"

"Absolutely."

"Good. We have a paid internship position opening next week, and we'd like to interview you for it. It pays thirty-one thousand a year, plus expenses to start, with annual reviews and cost-of-living increases. Would you be interested?"

A paid internship in her chosen field and she didn't even have to send out a single resume. Thirty-one thousand dollars . . . plus expenses . . .

Un-fucking-believable. "You bet! Just tell me where and when."

"How about Monday morning at the Hall of Justice? It's not too far from here. Room 417. Is nine o'clock okay?"

"Yes! Yes, it's very okay. Thank you so much for thinking of me."

"I looked into your background, and based on your coursework and GPA, I know this is a vocation for you. To tell you the truth, this interview is just a formality, but I will still need a resume. Do you have one?"

"Actually, I hadn't gotten that far yet, but I will have one Monday morning."

"Excellent. I look forward to seeing you then. Now I believe your parents are waiting. They are your parents, right? It looks like your mother could use a fresh tissue. Congratulations again on your graduation."

When he was no longer within earshot, she let out a very *un*-adult *whoop*.

"Mom, Dad, you're not going to believe this! I already have a job!"

"Well, your graduation was already cause for a celebration. Now we have another reason. Where would you like to go? It's your choice."

That was easy. The seafood restaurant on the pier near her old house.

Mr. Drummond hadn't given her any job details, but she looked it up on her phone and told them what her new job would be. She giggled so much, she almost couldn't finish her lobster. Almost.

☒

"So? How was graduation?"

"It was okay." She tried to keep a straight face but failed.

"All right, what's up?"

"I have a job interview Monday morning at the DA's office!"

"Well, son of a bitch and shut my mouth! My little girl is all growed up!" Latesha hugged her so tight she could barely breathe, and she really wanted to laugh at the woman's slang.

"This calls for a barbecue!"

And for once, she had to agree.

☒

Her three-month internship had flown by. The work was hard and sometimes heartbreaking, but the rewards were priceless. Now she sat in her supervisor's office.

"I think it's time."

"Time? Time for what?"

"Time for you to take that *intern* label off your business cards. Think you can handle cases on your own?"

That was her goal, her dream, something she'd worked hard for. She tried to contain her enthusiasm but failed. "Mr. Drummond, I am definitely ready! Thank you! Thank you!"

"Don't thank me yet. You won't be working out of this office."

Oh?

"Okay. So, where will I be working?"

"There's an opening in Family Court in South Central. It's a rough neighborhood, but with your black belt confidence, you shouldn't have a problem. The cases will be a real test of your dedication. There are too many women fighting for their homes and their children's welfare. If I had the budget, I could easily staff five more advocates, and they'd still be overloaded. But since I can't hire more, I *can* make the extra work worth it for you, besides the job satisfaction I know you thrive on. How does seventy-thousand a year plus expenses sound?"

Seventy-thousand a year? That was double what she was currently making! Hyperventilation was a distinct possibility. "Are you sure?"

"Am I sure about what?"

"Seventy-thousand? I mean, I'll take it, but isn't that kind of high?"

"Elaine, you are worth every penny. I've never seen anyone so dedicated to helping others navigate their way through the legal system the way you do. You genuinely care about your clients. It's not just a job for you, and you don't know how rare that is. If I could pay you more, I would."

"Mr. Drummond, I'm overwhelmed. I appreciate your confidence in me, and I'll try my best not to let you down."

"I know you'll succeed. If I had any doubts, I wouldn't be offering this to you. But keep in mind, you'll be working with extremely disadvantaged women. Some have already been through the justice and family court system and are still struggling to feed their children while their broken bones and wounds heal. Many have gone back to work because they didn't receive enough to live on and have no other way to feed and clothe their children. Most are living in shelters. Legal Aid is swamped so you'll get referrals to lawyers who take civil court cases, usually on a sliding scale or pro bono basis. I don't know when you'll be assigned those cases. That'll be up to your new supervisor. So, still interested?"

"Does this smile on my face answer your question? When do I start?"

⧖

"Elaine?"

"Yes, sir?"

"Can you come into my office?"

Uh-oh.

"Have a seat."

There'd been rumors of budget cuts, and she almost had enough for a down payment on a little house. It would break her heart if she lost this job.

"First, I want to tell you how impressed I am with how you've handled your cases. You have a genuine empathy for the victims, and they know you know what they're going through. But . . ."

But?

"There's an overwhelming need for advocates with your experience in our South Bay office, and we need to transfer you. Is that going to be an issue?"

South Bay? The courthouse near the beach? Instead of slowing down, her heartbeat raced. "No, sir. That won't be a problem." No problem at all. She wanted to jump up and down and scream but kept her composure. "When do I start?"

"Monday."

Monday?

"*Oh*, and there's a raise that comes with this promotion. You'll be a senior advocate handling the more difficult cases, and your new salary will be eighty-nine thousand plus expenses."

That did it. She burst into tears. The last six years had been a dream come true. The work was hard, sometimes dangerous, sometimes heartbreaking, and not always successful. But it was beyond rewarding. Now she'd be working so close to where she hoped to buy a house, she wouldn't have to get on a freeway ever again. And eighty-nine thousand a year! With the money she'd already saved, she'd qualify for a mortgage!

"Please don't cry. You earned this. Now I want you to take the rest of the day and get your open case files up to date and bring them to me. I'll take care of distributing them. Then I want you to take the rest of the week off — paid, of course — and relax. You haven't taken a day off in years."

"Thank you, sir! Thank you for the opportunity to work with such an amazing group of dedicated professionals. I don't think I would have been so successful without their support."

"Yes, they're a great team, but you did the work. Have the files to me by five, okay? Here's the information on your new position. Good luck, Elaine."

She took the papers and made her way back to her office on wobbly legs.

"Hey, Latesha."

"Hey, girlfriend. What's the matter? You look like you lost your best friend."

"I did."

"You did *what*?"

"Lost my best friend."

"Well, considering that's me, I have to tell ya, I'm not goin' nowhere."

"No, you're not. But I am."

"You am what?"

"I got a new job and bought a house. I'm moving as soon as I get the keys from the realtor."

"Are you shittin' me? I go visit my mama for a few days, and you got a new job? And . . . you're movin'?"

"Yeah. This job pays more than I ever thought I'd make in my life. I went out house hunting the day before yesterday and found a foreclosure on the Strand in Hermosa. The bank approved my application almost immediately. The place needs a lot of work, and it's full of sand fleas, but the price was right, and I'll have plenty left over to fix it up. It all happened so fast, I still can't believe it."

"So, my little girl bought a house and is moving away to the other side of the world. I'm gonna miss you, and Hector's gonna be heartbroken."

Hector never gave up. The more she said no, the more he pursued her. Men like him loved a challenge. She would not miss him at all. "Well, you can come over and hang out at the beach with me as long as you promise not to bring him along."

"Me? Hang out at the beach? *Uh*, in case you haven't noticed, I got enough tan for ten white people. You can come back here for barbecues. Or are you planning to forget your friends?"

This had been her home ever since she could get around without a cane. It was still dingy, but so much had happened while she'd lived there. "No, I'm not going to forget my friends.

And you're more than a friend. How did you put it? I'm your *sistah from anotha mistah*. And my mom thinks of you like another daughter."

"*Oh,* honey child. You've seen me through so many men and so many heartbreaks. How am I gonna deal without you and your mom's cookies?"

They hugged and cried and laughed, and then they cried and laughed and hugged some more. She hadn't expected this to be so tough.

"Look at us, cryin' like one of us is dyin' instead of moving on out of this dump. This is a good thing. Now you'll have no choice but to meet men. They'll be white, but you can't have everything. At least they'll probably have money."

Dan had money, and her life with him had been a nightmare. Money was not high on her list of requirements. "I'm still not looking. I'm very happy with my life the way it is."

"This is probably my fault. I introduced you to the perfect boyfriend. No man's gonna measure up."

The perfect boyfriend — as long as she fed it batteries. Latesha told her a vibrator would keep her from making stupid mistakes, but in fact, she hadn't made *any* mistakes. She worked hard. She came home. Then she worked some more. She watched NCIS. She read steamy romance novels and went to bed with her BOB. And she didn't have to get up and make a sandwich for it after. Nope. No mistakes.

The gang at the apartment building helped her pack and load the rental truck. She wasn't sure how she would get everything into her new house.

⚥

"Thanks, guys! You saved my life. I don't have much cash on me, but you're welcome to it."

Two adorable young surfers with tanned washboard abs had seen her struggling with a heavy box and came to her rescue. They had the truck unloaded so fast, she didn't have to worry about getting a ticket for blocking the alley.

"That's like totally okay, ma'am. Like there was nothing to it. We're totally glad we could help. We're like usually on the beach, so like if you ever need help again, just come get us."

She loved beach people. She could have done without the *ma'am*.

She decorated her new home with a nautical theme; seashells, navy blue and white accents, a pale blue kitchen, and colorful flowers in the window boxes and pots on the patio. She was about to call in the exterminators to take care of the sand flea problem when she pulled up a corner of the carpet and found a hardwood floor. After two months of sanding, staining, and varnishing, it turned out absolutely beautiful, and she beamed with pride and accomplishment.

The small patio in front faced west with a view of white sand as far as the eye could see until it dropped off to the water. After work, she loved to sit on one of her cheap plastic lounge chairs and watch all the adorable young surfers with those tanned washboard abs catch the last waves of the day. On weekends, if she wasn't working, she watched all those adorable tanned bodies play volleyball.

Life really was a beach.

The salt air and barking seals woke her in the morning, and at night, the sound of the crashing waves lulled her to sleep within minutes.

☒

It was Friday evening, six months after she'd moved into her beach cottage, and she looked forward to a relaxing weekend — until a courier arrived with a manila envelope. The return address was Dan's lawyer's.

What now?

She almost dropped the papers when she read the first sentence.

Ms. Chambéry, We are sorry to inform you that Dan Jeffers passed away from cancer on June 27, 2016.

She didn't feel the least bit guilty for not feeling anything except relief. The rest was legalese that could wait until later because along with the letter from his lawyer there was an envelope addressed to her in Dan's handwriting. Her hands shook as she opened it and began to read.

Elaine,

If you're reading this, it's because I'm dead. I found out I had lung cancer a year after I got here. I don't know why I kept you as the beneficiary on my life insurance, but since I found out I'm dying, I've had a lot of time to think. This will never make up for the pain I caused you, and I don't expect it to buy me out of hell, but I hope you'll think a little kinder of me.

Be happy.
Dan

There was a cashier's check attached to the back of the lawyer's letter. The man who had beaten her almost to death had kept her as the beneficiary on his life insurance policy, and she was now five hundred thousand dollars richer. First thing Monday morning, she would deposit most of it in her Roth IRA. The rest she would use to buy a new car. No more bus!

She had no sympathy for Dan and cheerfully hoped he went straight to hell.

Then she remembered she didn't believe in hell and smiled as she imagined worms feasting on his decomposing body.

17

It was pouring down rain, which was unusual for Southern California, so Lisa had to smoke in the garage. She was taking a hell of a chance, but Gerald had just left for the bar, so she figured he'd be gone for at least an hour. She had just lit her second cigarette when the garage door opened.

He didn't say anything, and she was so paralyzed with fear, she still held the cigarette to her lips. She watched him walk to his workbench, grab a can of paint thinner, and before she could move, he hurled it at her. It hit her cheek and splashed her face and neck, which burst into flames from the lit cigarette.

She was on fire!

She slapped at her skin to put out the flames from the chemical and screamed as her skin sizzled. She ran through the still open garage door to their next-door neighbor's house. Joan called 911. She couldn't give the dispatcher any details, only that her neighbor's face was horribly blistered, and she was screaming in pain.

When the paramedics arrived, they called the police who arrested her husband. Then they rushed her to the hospital. The ER doctor got her admitted to the burn unit where they shot her up with painkillers. She could barely talk through her charred lips but managed to give her statement to a detective.

The DA charged Gerald with attempted murder and requested remand. The judge agreed Gerald was a flight risk and bail was denied. Since she suffered third-degree burns, the DA pushed the trial date out three months to give her a chance to heal enough to testify. Gerald spent those three months in Los Angeles County Jail.

The pain was excruciating, and she couldn't function without painkillers. But with the help of a lawyer, she filed for divorce. All she wanted was her medical bills paid and monthly support payments. Unfortunately, with Gerald in jail facing murder charges, the divorce judge denied her settlement request pending the outcome of his trial.

⚥

"The prosecution calls Lisa Weston."

After being sworn in, she focused on the prosecuting attorney's face, but once in a while she glanced at the other people in the courtroom and saw their looks of pity and sympathy. Some wouldn't even look at her. She couldn't blame them.

"Mrs. Weston, please describe the events that took place the day of the alleged assault."

Alleged assault? Describe the events? All they had to do was look at her face. She'd tried so hard to block it all out, and now she had to relive it. The man she'd once loved, who had promised to love, honor and cherish her, hated her so much he tried to kill her by setting her on fire.

The prosecuting attorney had coached her when they prepared for trial. It had been easier to tell her story in the Assistant DA's office, but on the stand, she had a hard time forming complete sentences. Her mind went blank until the prosecutor prompted her and got her talking. Soon, she was able to relate the whole horrible event. Once or twice she brought up the other times he'd been arrested for spousal battery, but the defense attorney objected. The prosecutor argued that her testimony established a pattern of behavior. The judge agreed and overruled.

When the prosecutor had finished questioning her, the defense attorney attacked. "Mrs. Weston, isn't it possible Mr. Weston didn't know you were smoking?"

"Objection, your Honor. The defense is asking Mrs. Weston to speculate."

"Overruled. The witness will answer the question."

"He knew I was smoking. That was what made him angry in the first place."

"Mrs. Weston, isn't it possible he didn't know the cap on the can of paint thinner was loose?"

"Objection, your Honor. Again, the defense is asking Mrs. Weston to speculate."

"Overruled. The witness will answer the question."

"There were many other things on his workbench he could have thrown at me, but he chose the paint thinner. I know the cap wasn't loose when he picked it up because he was always careful about not accidentally starting a fire."

"Mrs. Weston, isn't it possible this was a terrible accident?"

What?

"Objection!"

"Overruled. The witness will answer the question."

"If it was a terrible accident, he would have called 911 himself, but he went in the house as if nothing was wrong while I ran to the neighbor's."

"No more questions, your honor."

"The witness may step down."

"The defense calls Dr. Steinmetz."

After the doctor was sworn in, the defense attorney began. "Dr. Steinmetz, what are you a doctor of?"

"I'm a forensic psychiatrist."

"And how long have you been in practice?"

"Almost twenty years."

"You are considered an expert in your field, is that correct?"

"Yes. I'm often called in to consult on criminal cases."

"Have you met with the defendant?"

"Yes."

"And what is your conclusion?"

"Mr. Weston witnessed his father beat his mother on numerous occasions and developed the belief that violence was necessary to correct perceived wrong behavior."

"So, you're saying the defendant was raised to believe corporal punishment was acceptable?"

"Yes."

"Is this behavior modifiable?"

"In some cases, yes. But it requires extensive therapy."

"Would Mr. Weston benefit from extensive therapy?"

"Objection! Your Honor, defense counsel is asking the witness to speculate without adequately examining the defendant."

"Your honor, Dr. Steinmetz is an expert in his field. He is uniquely qualified to observe and draw conclusions regarding criminal behavior."

"I'll allow it. The witness may answer the question."

"Yes, it is my belief Mr. Weston would benefit from extensive therapy."

"No further questions, your honor."

"Cross-examine, your honor." The prosecutor approached the witness stand. "Dr. Steinmetz, how much time did you spend with the defendant?"

The doctor hesitated.

"The witness will answer the question."

"Thirty minutes."

"And in thirty minutes, you were able to ascertain Mr. Weston was raised to believe beating his wife was acceptable, maybe even encouraged."

"Objection! The prosecution is making a statement."

"Is there a question, Counselor?"

"No, your Honor. I just wanted to make sure I understood. Dr. Steinmetz, is Mr. Weston cognizant of his behavior?"

"I don't understand."

"I'll rephrase. Does Mr. Weston know right from wrong?"

"Objection!"

"Overruled. The witness will answer the question."

"Yes."

"Thank you. No further questions."

With no other options, the defense rested.

The jury deliberated for three hours and found Gerald guilty on all counts.

The judge thanked the jury for their service and imposed the maximum sentence for each count. The assistant district attorney requested Gerald be ordered to pay restitution to cover her initial burn treatments, plus fifty-thousand dollars for any additional treatment she might need. And she would receive twenty-thousand dollars from the *Victims of Domestic Violence Fund.*

"Is that all?"

"Yes, your Honor."

When they originally discussed how much to ask for, the ADA convinced her that if they asked for too much, she could wind up getting nothing. The prosecutor had disagreed, but the ADA filed the motion, anyway.

"Motion granted."

"All rise."

It was over.

⧗

With Gerald safely behind bars, she underwent several reconstruction surgeries. Her injuries were so extensive, she'd never look normal. It didn't help that she couldn't afford the best plastic surgeon. Her medical bills already totaled over two hundred thousand dollars, and she needed more surgeries just to reform her nose. Her lips were so disfigured, it was difficult to talk. A dermatologist tried different methods to smooth out her skin, but the procedures were painful, and the progress was slow.

If the trial judge or the divorce judge had ordered Gerald to sell their house, she could have gone to the best plastic surgeon, and the profit would have easily covered all her bills with a lot left over. As it was, what she would receive wouldn't cover a fraction of what she owed.

Even if she had any skills, she couldn't get a job. All she had was one thousand dollars a month spousal support. Gerald refused to sign a quitclaim, and though that meant she had a roof over her head, she had nothing else and nowhere to turn.

Every day she looked in the mirror and saw a monster.

And every day, wherever she went, she scared little kids.

※

"Well, Lisa. You're healing nicely from the last dermabrasion. The scars are definitely less noticeable."

He was either blind or crazy. She looked in the mirror, and even with thick stage makeup spackled on her skin, she still looked like she'd been trapped in a tornado with a hundred ice picks. Instead of Botox, her lips looked like someone had injected them with cement, and her nose made Michael Jackson's look normal.

The doctor wanted to see her again in three weeks.

The young woman at the appointment desk looked at her sympathetically. "Mrs. Weston, I'm sorry, but your account is over-due, and the charges keep adding up. I'm afraid I can't book your next appointment without at least a partial payment."

"Yes, I know, and I'm sorry. Can we work out some kind of payment plan?"

"I'm afraid that won't be enough. You owe ten thousand dollars already. If you could pay half of that, we could set up a plan for the balance."

Five thousand dollars? And she'd still owe another five thousand? That on top of the two hundred thousand she still owed the hospital?

"But I don't have that much money. I owe the hospital, too. Please? Let me make payments. I'm not a freeloader, and I'm not trying to get out of paying. I can't work until I have a face that won't scare people like I'm some kind of monster. I can't get a job looking like this. Please!"

"I'm sorry. I know you got a raw deal, but there's nothing I can do. But I am curious *why* you got such a bad deal."

"I got the best deal the assistant district attorney said I could get, and he said I was lucky to get that."

"Well, excuse my French, but that's bullshit. Listen, we've seen many other women in similar situations who got all of their medical bills covered and then some. You could have gotten more than enough. Where was your advocate?"

"My what?"

"Your Victim's Advocate. Whoever the DA's office assigned to you should be fired."

"They never assigned anyone, never even told me about it. Would an advocate have helped me?"

"That's what they're for. It might not be too late though. You need to call the DA's office and insist on a referral."

It wouldn't solve her immediate problem, but it gave her a glimmer of hope.

She called as soon as she got home, and after she hung up, she had more than a glimmer. She had an appointment with an advocate the next morning. They were usually swamped, but they had a cancelation while she was on the phone.

Maybe she could sue the ADA for not telling her about her victim's resources.

She tried to ignore the pile of bills that grew as the days passed. It was more than depressing. She avoided looking in the mirror as much as possible. There were days when it all seemed hopeless, and she wondered why she didn't just end it all. Everything was a struggle.

She'd sold her car which, thank God, didn't have Gerald's name on the title. That gave her enough money to keep the lights on for a little while, but it meant taking the bus everywhere. She couldn't stand the looks she got and tried to wear a veil but people looked at her suspiciously thinking she was Muslim.

She'd never paid any attention to how cruel people could be until she was on the receiving end.

Tomorrow she would have an appointment with someone who could help her. With just that bit of hope, she spent the rest of the day organizing and prioritizing her bills in anticipation of the money the Victim's Advocate would help her get. She always believed in the power of positive thinking, and by getting the bills ready to be paid, she was preparing the way for the universe to write checks. That was the theory, anyway.

Before she had a chance to throw out the huge stack of junk mail, she heard a knock. She grabbed the scarf she kept by the entryway mirror, quickly tied it like a hijab, and opened the door to find a very nice-looking man on her porch.

"Can I help you?"

"Lisa Weston?"

"Yes."

"I hope you don't mind. I got your address from Dr. Greenberg's office. My name is Robert Byford, and I'm a plastic surgeon. I'd like to talk to you about your case. May I come in?"

"Can I see some identification?"

"Of course."

He pulled his hospital badge out of his jacket pocket. It looked legitimate, but she asked him to wait on the porch. She closed the door and called the hospital which confirmed he was who he said he was.

"Okay, I'm sorry. Please come in. You have to understand after what I've been through, I can't take any chances."

"I understand."

"Please sit down. Can I get you anything?"

"No thanks. I want to talk to you about an organization I belong to. We're a group of plastic surgeons who donate our time and skills to help women who have been disfigured due to domestic violence. Dr. Greenberg's office called me today and explained your situation. Would you mind removing your scarf?"

Well, he was a surgeon. He probably saw much worse every day.

She steeled herself against the inevitable look of revulsion and pity, but he didn't even flinch.

"Dr. Greenberg's been doing a lot of dermabrasion, I see. That can certainly help, but there's a lot more we can do to smooth out your skin with grafting, and we can reform your nose and lips. We can even transplant some hair from your body and give you back your eyebrows and eyelashes. Yes, I think there's a lot we can do. You won't look like you did before the burn, but we can get close."

"Are you saying you can fix my face for free?"

"Well, in a sense, it won't cost you any money, but we do ask that you pay it forward somehow. Maybe do some volunteer work for a charity."

"*Oh,* my God. Is this for real?"

"Yes, it's for real. Here's my card. Call and make an appointment as soon as possible. I'll let my front office know to expect your call and to fit you in this week. The clinic is open in the evenings and weekends. Now I need to get going."

"Thank you so much. You have no idea how much this means to me."

"*Oh,* I think I do. That's why I do this. I'll see you soon."

After she closed the door, she sat down and cried until someone pounded on the door and scared the bejeezus out of her.

"Lisa! Open up! Are you okay?"

She breathed a sigh of relieve. It was Joan. "Yes, I'm okay," She opened the door.

"What's wrong? I saw a man leaving, and now you're crying. What happened?"

"Nothing happened. He's a plastic surgeon, and he offered to work on my face for free."

"Free? Nothing's free. What's the catch?"

She didn't blame the woman for being suspicious. After all, Joan was the one who heard all the fights, and Joan was the one who called 911 that day her face went up in flames.

"He works with a group of plastic surgeons who volunteer their skills for women like me. I just have to do some charity work after my face heals. But, can you believe it? Just this morning my dermatologist's office said they couldn't treat me unless I pay five thousand on my ten-thousand-dollar-balance. And now, *he* says he can help. It won't look the way it did before, but he thinks he can get close. Maybe someday I'll be able to go out in public without scaring little kids. Maybe someday I'll be able to look in the mirror and not see a monster staring back."

"Lisa, you don't look like a monster. You're beautiful. Under all those scars is a beautiful woman who got a raw deal. Now, it sounds like you have a chance to get your life back."

"*Oh,* and there's more! I found out today I should have had a Victim's Advocate with me the whole time — before and during the trial, even the divorce. I should have gotten a lot more money, and they could have made Gerald sign the house over to me. I'm meeting with someone tomorrow. It's too late for criminal charges; he's already in prison. But they said I can still sue him in civil court."

"That's wonderful! I'm so happy for you. You deserve a break!"

"Well, it's not a done deal yet, but at least it's something. I don't want much, just my medical bills paid and something to live on. If I could just sell this house, that would cover it all — except I'd need to find another place to live. But I'm getting way ahead of myself. The only thing I know for sure is I have to make an appointment to see Dr. Byford as soon as possible, so I need to make a call."

"Okay. Come over for dinner when you're done. I made a pot of chili and some cornbread."

"You've fed me three times this week. I don't want to take advantage of your generosity."

"*Oh,* my dear, Lisa. You're not taking advantage. Let's just call this *me* paying it forward okay? When you have your new life, you can invite me over."

When I have my new life . . .

She'd lived with her scarred face for six months, long enough to forget everything she'd taken for granted before. Her reality was her scars plus Gerald being locked away in San Quentin for nine years with the possibility of parole after five. She had five years to get her life together and disappear where he could never find her. Why hadn't she asked for her maiden name in the divorce? Maybe it wasn't too late.

She called the clinic and made an appointment for the following afternoon. Dr. Byford had told the appointment desk to hold that slot for her.

Tomorrow would be a busy and emotional day.

⏳

Exhaustion seeped through her, but she forced herself to go to Joan's for dinner. If she ever had the money, she would make it up to the woman who saved her life and cared so much.

"I'm so glad you came over. You need to get over this taking advantage baloney."

"I know. But as soon as I can, I'll make it up to you."

"You do what you need to do, but I'd rather you didn't. I'm doing this because it's the right thing to do, not because I expect anything in return."

Tears threatened, but she blinked them back.

"Now, tell me about handsome Doctor . . . what did you say his name was?"

"Robert Byford. I don't know anything about him other than he works at the hospital and has an after-hours clinic with several other plastic surgeons. But he is good-looking, isn't he? But that's something I can only dream about."

"What do you mean?"

"Well, isn't it obvious? Even if he *is* a miracle worker, I'll never look normal, and no man will look at me twice, let alone ask me out. And I'm not sure I'd ever want to get close to another man, even if I could. Gerald didn't show his true colors until we got back from our honeymoon. Although, if I'm being honest with myself, there were signs before the wedding. Little things like criticism hidden behind suggestions. He liked to correct me, but he was usually nice about it.

After the honeymoon, he stopped being so nice. So how do you trust that someone isn't going to turn on you until it's too late?"

"I wish I had the answers, dear. My Allen was perfect in every way. Treated me like a princess. Always made me feel special and loved. Maybe that's why God took him in Iraq — because he was too perfect. That kind of man and that kind of love comes around only once. But I have my memories and his GI benefits."

Joan was quiet, and her eyes glistened. Did she know how lucky she was? "I doubt I'll ever find a man like that. Like I said, who'd want to look at me for the rest of his life?"

Joan sighed. "One more time. Lisa, you are beautiful. Yes, plastic surgery may make you pretty again, but beauty comes from within. No surgery can create that."

She gave up on holding back the tears. "I'm so lonely. As mean and vicious as Gerald was, at least I wasn't alone all the time. I think I miss something I never had."

"What's that?"

"Affection. Someone to hold me, hold my hand, kiss me, and make love to me. Gerald used sex as a punishment. I want to know what it's like to be with a man who genuinely cares about me."

"He's out there, dear. I just know it."

Optimism about paying her bills was one thing. Optimism about finding that kind of man was stupid. "I hope you're right, but I'm not going to hold my breath. Listen, I've had a roller coaster kind of day, and I'm exhausted, so I'm going to go home and try to get some sleep. Tomorrow's going to be even more emotional."

"Okay, dear. Call me or come over as soon as you get home, okay?"

"Of course. If it's bad news, I'll cry on your shoulder. If it's good news, we'll celebrate."

She walked across the grass to her big, gloomy, dungeon.

18

When she'd first called, they said she couldn't do anything more through the criminal justice system, but she probably had a good civil case. Now here she was, about to meet with an advocate.

"Hi, I'm Lisa Weston. I have an appointment with Elaine Cham — Cham — I'm sorry. I forgot how to pronounce her last name."

"SHAMberry. And she's expecting you. Please follow me."

It looked like any other government office. Mostly gray and beige — until she got to Ms. Chambéry's office which was a jungle of green houseplants. They hung in the corners and covered almost every surface. The two walls that didn't have bookcases were covered with framed photographs of the beach and the ocean at sunset. It was a colorful contrast to *government gray*.

Elaine Chambéry was about ten years older and exuded confidence. She was casually dressed, probably to put her homeless clients at ease. Would she understand what her life had been like and how she had to live now?

"Mrs. Weston."

"Lisa, please."

"Lisa, it's nice to meet you. I'm Elaine Chambéry. I'm a Victim's

Advocate. My assistant told me a little about your story, and I think I can help."

"I hope so. I'm desperate." Well, if Ms. Chambéry was repulsed by her face, she was doing a great job hiding it.

"I'd like you to tell me everything, starting at the beginning. And if you don't mind, I'd like to record this so I won't have to slow you down to take notes. Would that be okay?"

"Sure. But how far back do you want me to go?"

"Start when you met your husband."

"That may take a lot longer than this appointment."

"Don't worry about that. Just start at the beginning."

Ninety minutes and a lot of tears later, the confident woman dabbed her eyes. Maybe she *did* understand.

"We have a lot in common. My scars are hidden by my clothes, and he never burned me although I think he would have killed me if he hadn't been interrupted, but I know what it's like to owe several hundred thousand dollars in medical bills. And that was after the divorce settlement. I didn't know I had options then, either."

"How did you deal with it?"

"Well, for a while I made good faith payments to everyone, even if it was only ten dollars at a time."

"I know Gerald has money somewhere, but it's too late to get any of it, and he won't sign the house over to me."

"Well, there are several things we can do, but the best option is to sue him in civil court. I've had very good results with that. I think we can get your medical bills paid. How much is your spousal support?"

"One thousand dollars a month. And that's my only income since I can't work."

"If he's got money somewhere, I'm sure we can petition the court for enough for you to live on until we go to trial."

"How much is this going to cost? I don't have any money. I only eat regularly out of the kindness of my neighbor's heart, and I have to take the bus everywhere since I sold my car to keep the utilities on."

"It's not going to cost you a thing. We work with Legal Aid, and they charge on a sliding scale. It's based on your earned income which you don't have. I'll make some phone calls and prepare the necessary filings. We should be able to meet with a lawyer next week."

"Wow. That's wonderful. Between this and the reconstructive surgery I'm getting for free, my life may just turn around, after all."

"You're getting surgery for free?"

"Yes, there's a group of doctors who volunteer their time after their regular shifts. They provide reconstruction surgery to victims of domestic violence. They use a sliding scale, also. I have an appointment to go over the procedure this afternoon."

"*Hmm.* I wonder if I can refer some of my other cases to them. Let me know when your surgery is scheduled for so I can make sure we meet with a lawyer first."

"Thank you so much. Thank you for taking the time to listen to my sad story."

"Lisa, you have no idea how common your story is. There are a lot of resources that victims like us don't know are available. I certainly didn't, and that's why I do this. Take care, and I'll talk to you soon."

She walked out feeling like things really could get better — until a little girl on the bus pointed to her and said, "Look, Mommy! The mummy!" and giggled. The little girl's mother shushed her and looked at her with pity.

She spent the rest of the ride staring out the window at all the people rushing around living their normal lives. She wanted that so badly she could taste it.

She was early, and Dr. Byford wasn't in yet, so she sat in the waiting room and scanned a magazine. She wasn't alone, and for the first time in a long time, she didn't stick out like a bruised and bloody thumb.

There were five other women with varying degrees of scars. One had a gash that ran from her forehead down her cheek. As deep as it looked now, it must have exposed bone and muscle when it first happened. Other than that nasty gash, the woman was beautiful. But when the woman looked at her, she saw the defeated sadness she knew so well.

No one spoke. No one wanted to talk about what happened to them, nor did they need to.

An hour after she arrived, Dr. Byford walked in, smiled at her, and went through the door to the examining rooms. Soon after, the receptionist called her name.

A long time ago, she'd been friendly and outgoing, but years of Gerald's abuse had made her self-conscious. That, plus knowing what she looked like now, she wanted to shrink into the examining table. Even worse, he was just as drop-dead gorgeous as she remembered.

She showed him a photograph from before the *incident*, and he talked about the extent of her injuries, the scar tissue and thickened skin, her half missing nose, and disfigured lips. He went over the procedure, took photographs, drew on an illustration of a head, and showed her where the incisions would be. He said he would use 6-0 sutures mostly and a skin adhesive on smaller or more visible areas since they would heal with minimal scars. He would implant artificial eyelashes and eyebrows.

There was more, but she'd stopped listening. These details meant nothing to her. She didn't care how he did it. She just wanted it done.

"Do you have any questions?"

"Yes. How long will the stitches be in for?"

"At least two weeks, possibly longer."

"And how long until I look like a person again?"

"You'll look at least eighty percent better as soon as the sutures come out and the incision adhesives take. The swelling and redness may take two months, more or less. You'll want to stay completely out of the sun and use ice packs as much as possible."

"Doctor, be honest with me. Do you really think this will work?"

"Well, I don't want to set your expectations too high, but yes, I think you'll be very happy with the results. So, let's go get you scheduled."

It still seemed like a dream. Suing Gerald for more money. Getting her face — or most of it — back. She tried to contain her excitement, but she couldn't help but smile. Unfortunately, her smile looked pretty grotesque since her lips were so misshapen.

"Mary, we want to get Mrs. Weston in as soon as possible. Schedule at least six hours, and I'm going to want Steve or Bill assisting. Mrs. Weston, I look forward to seeing you again."

"Thank you, Doctor."

He left her to meet with his next appointment.

"Okay, Mrs. Weston, I have next Tuesday open. You'll need to arrive around noon so we can get you prepped."

Tuesday? That would give her a chance to get her house in order, make sure there was some food in the kitchen, and hopefully, meet with Elaine Chambéry and a civil litigation attorney.

As soon as she got home, she called Elaine.

"Lisa, I was just about to call you. Legal Aid is overbooked, but there is a law clinic right around the corner that specializes in cases like yours. I've never worked with them, but I asked around and they have excellent references and a very good record. We can see them tomorrow at ten, and we can walk over there from my office. Can you be here at nine? We can go over some things I've already done before we meet with the attorney."

Tomorrow? She was meeting with a lawyer tomorrow? And she was having surgery next Tuesday? Dizziness hit her, and she had to sit down. Then she remembered she hadn't eaten that day.

"Lisa?"

"Yes, I'm here. This is all happening so fast. I'm having surgery next Tuesday."

"That's wonderful! I'm so happy for you! And tomorrow we'll start the legal process, and soon you'll have your life back. So, nine o'clock in my office?"

"Yes. I'll be there. And I can't thank you enough."

"Well, we don't have that fat check yet, but we'll definitely get you something. I'll see you tomorrow."

As soon as she hung up, she called Joan. "Can I come over?"

"My dear, you don't have to ask. But tell me, is it good news?"

"Better than good. I'll be right there."

Joan had just popped the champagne when she walked through the door. After hearing all about her day, they toasted to her future. Even if she didn't get much, and the surgery didn't completely fix her face, it would still be better than what she had now. And *that* was cause for a celebration.

By the time she got home, she was tipsy and giggling, and she hoped she wouldn't have a hangover in the morning. She had to be at the bus stop by seven-thirty if she was going to make it to the courthouse by nine.

After setting her alarm for six, she fell into bed and a deep sleep. And she dreamed that Prince Charming carried her off on his white stallion. Except Prince Charming wore scrubs.

19

Michael looked at the stack of files in his briefcase. How was he going to fit in another case? The same way he always did — by working too many hours. He *couldn't* turn them down. He *had* to help.

Since that last day of his vision quest he'd been driven, compelled. The only other things he made time for were his AA meetings, his sponsor, NCIS, and his mom, not necessarily in that order. But every once in a while, usually late at night, he remembered what the bear said about the *she* who was working through her own issues and how they'd meet when they were both ready.

He was ready — sort of. But when would he have time for a relationship? He shuddered just thinking about dating. But he'd had this weird feeling lately, like something was right around the corner. Then another day would go by and nothing out of the ordinary happened. He was turning fifty in two days. Kind of old to be starting over, anyway.

He poured a cup of coffee and made himself comfortable on his couch. He looked over the packet of documents from Elaine Chambéry, the Victim's Advocate assigned to this case. He had to put the cup down as he read the transcript of her interview with Lisa Weston, his soon-to-be new client.

Unbelievable. And sickening. His blood pressure rose.

Third-degree burns all over her face. The surgeries, the trial, the ridiculous settlement, the divorce and *its* ridiculous settlement. The woman had been taken advantage of by a system that was supposed to protect her. But the part that really pissed him off was she hadn't been informed of her many options. She'd had no one there to guide her. Based on what the advocate wrote, he knew he could get Mrs. Weston enough to cover everything, plus pain and suffering, as long as that asshole had assets somewhere. He opened his laptop and started his search.

By the time he finished, he had almost everything he needed. He found close to two million dollars spread out over stocks, bonds, properties, and offshore accounts, and that wasn't counting the house he'd refused to sell. It alone had to be worth a half mil.

Despite Gibbs Rule 10 (Never get personally involved.), he lived for cases like this one.

Then he did a little investigating into the woman he'd be working with, Elaine Chambéry, the Victim's Advocate. Her LinkedIn profile page had quite an admirable list of accomplishments and a brief recount of her own sad story.

He studied her photograph for a few minutes. She was beautiful and looked vaguely familiar, but he knew their paths had never crossed. He would have remembered such a beautiful woman. She wasn't much younger than him, and she lived at the beach, probably not far from his house. Maybe he'd seen her in the grocery store? *Ah,* but he would have remembered her, maybe started up a conversation. Maybe even invited her to coffee.

Seriously? He hadn't had a conversation with a woman who wasn't a colleague, client, or family member since Sandy died.

He needed to get some sleep. He had a lot of work to do before he met with Ms. Chambéry and Mrs. Weston at ten, and he was tired.

"*She's* here."

"Didn't I leave you in Oregon a long time ago? And who's here?"

"Yes, and you left without saying goodbye. You hurt our feelings, and I'm not sure those asshole squirrels ever got over it. Anyway, that *she* I was telling you about? Well, you're both finally ready, and we'd almost given up on this ever happening. Don't screw this up."

"Yeah, *uh*, thanks. And drop by again when you can't stay so long."

☒

The bear's laugh woke him. Except it wasn't the bear's laugh, it was his alarm clock. Seven already?

He thought about what the bear said — there it was again — what the bear said. What next? The snake in his bed? A slumber party with the raccoon and the deer? It reminded him of that dark place he'd been in when he went on that vision quest so long ago. That was the catalyst that had brought him to his life's work.

So *she* was here — wherever *here* was. As much as he tried to remind himself that the conversation with the bear wasn't real, he couldn't stifle a rush of adrenaline.

After his shower, he turned on the news and half listened as he drank his coffee and checked his email. Answers to some of his inquiries into Gerald Weston's finances were there, and they confirmed what his searching had already found, but there was much more. The man was worth several million. There were hints of a mob connection, but that would be impossible to prove in civil court. Still, he needed to warn Ms. Chambéry and Mrs. Weston.

If they went after what was her fair share, and if the man was connected to the mob, he might retaliate which would put all their lives in danger. It didn't scare him, but the two women had a right to know the risks.

He dressed in his usual button-down shirt, Wranglers, boots, and a sport coat. Even if the temperature hit ninety outside, he kept his office at seventy-two degrees. He only wore suits when he was trying a case or had a formal meeting with a judge. The other partners were the same way. They all wanted their clients to feel comfortable.

He could afford a new car now, but his BMW Z3 was perfect for zipping around city traffic, and he was meticulous about maintenance. Besides, with the top down, it was a blast to drive the winding roads along the coast, when he had time.

He took back streets from the beach to his office around the corner from the courthouse. Traffic on the main streets was a nightmare of stop and go, and the smell of burning clutches and brakes made his eyes water. It was the one thing about the South Bay area he hated. But in the evenings, when he got home from work, sometimes early enough to watch the sun go down, the traffic and smog were worth it.

He was the first to arrive, so he got the coffee going, made sure there was a bowl of fresh fruit and snacks in the conference room, opened all the drapes, and set up his laptop. A few more answers waited in his inbox, and these were even more ominous. The mob connections were in fact relatives. If he took this case and won, the danger would be real.

If he took this case? Of course, he'd take this case!

He got a cup of coffee and answered his other emails. Then he heard the office door open. It was nine, too early for his client.

"Good morning, Michael." Tina, their receptionist and office mom, called to him from the front area.

He meant to remind her to stop and get some flowers but was pleasantly surprised when he found her arranging a bouquet in a big vase. "Hey, thanks for remembering. I meant to text you before I left this morning. So, I've been digging into my new client's background."

"Lisa Weston?"

"Yes. She's got a hell of a story. Corporal Injury on an Intimate Partner with GBI enhancement."

"Wow. A great bodily injury add-on? We haven't seen one of those in a while."

"Yeah, and this one's going to be worse. She got screwed over badly by the courts. I'm sure I can get her everything she needs. But just so you won't be shocked, I understand she has severe scarring on her face from third-degree burns."

"*Oh*, God! How awful! Here, these are for the conference room. Did you get the coffee started?"

"Yes, *Mom*."

Tina was in her mid-twenties but kept that office running smoothly like his own mother did with her home. He placed the vase on the big table and went back to his email. Maybe he should contact Bruce.

Tina knocked on the door.

"Yes?"

She opened the door a crack. "Ms. Chambéry and Mrs. Weston are here," and in a whisper, she added, "Prepare yourself. It's much worse than you thought."

"Show them in, please."

Terrific.

He could feel his blood pressure rising already.

"Ms. Chambéry, Mrs. Weston, this is Michael Chandler."

Jesus, Mary, and Joseph!

Michael Chandler? *The* Michael Chandler? The man whose wife was murdered while he waited with *her* for the police to come and arrest her husband? *That* Michael Chandler? She caught her mouth before it dropped open.

"Ms. Chambéry?"

She calmed her pounding heart and controlled her breathing then shook his hand and ignored the zing up her arm. She cleared her throat and said, "Please call me Elaine."

"And Mrs. Weston." He shook Lisa's hand.

"Weston is my ex-husband's name. Please call me Lisa. Thank you for agreeing to see us, Mr. Chandler. I'm sure you can tell what kind of case this is."

"Please call me Michael. And yes, Ms. Chambéry, I mean Elaine, sent over your deposition. I read it over last night. Please make yourselves comfortable. Would either of you care for any coffee or tea? Juice?"

He didn't recognize her! Well, it *was* twelve years ago, and she used her maiden name now. But even still, she recognized him immediately. His unusual blue eyes were just as brilliant as she remembered, and he was just as good looking as he'd been back then, maybe even more so with that bit of silver at his temples.

Get it together!

"Mr. Cha — I mean Michael, Lisa is having facial reconstruction surgery next Tuesday and can't go out while she's recuperating. Will you be able to get started quickly?"

"Actually, I've already started. I made some inquiries last night, and this morning I got the answers I suspected I'd get, except for one. It seems Mr. Weston has mob connections."

Lisa gasped. "What exactly does this mean? Have you changed your mind about taking my case?"

"Not at all. We'll just have to be careful, and once court proceedings start, you should plan to keep a very low profile. Maybe even leave town for a while."

"I can't go anywhere for at least a month, preferably two. Do you really think I'm in danger? Will this be putting you and Elaine in danger, too? Because if it will, I don't think I should go through with it."

"I am fully prepared to take that risk. After reading your history, and the judge's sentence, I'm more determined than ever to see that you get just restitution. However, Elaine, you may want to step back from this, maybe turn it over to a superior."

"I *am* the superior, and I don't back down from bullies. This is the worst case of miscarriage of justice I've ever seen — even worse than mine. No, I'm all in. But I'm wondering, if Gerald Weston received nine years in San Quentin, how is he a threat?"

"His mob connections are family on his mother's side."

That could mean a contract which would involve the FBI. Still, if she backed away from this, what did that say about her resolve? This poor woman had no one, not even family. *She* at least had loving parents who took care of her. Lisa had no one. "I don't care. I'm still in."

"Lisa, I want this case. I want to help you. And I know I can win, but the choice is yours. How would you like to proceed?"

"I would feel terrible if anything were to happen to either of you because of me. But it's me he wants dead, and I'm tired of living like this, anyway. Every time I get ridiculed on the bus for wearing a scarf over my face, every time a child points and loudly tells her mommy I look like Frankenstein, every time I look in the mirror, every time I see that stack of bills, every time a doctor's office says they can't help me until I pay down my balance . . . I see his face as he throws the paint thinner at my head. And if he kills me, at least I won't have to live like this anymore. I want to proceed. I've got nothing to lose."

What a brave woman. Brave and desperate. "Okay, what's next?"

"I'll have some documents typed up and couriered to Lisa. She'll need to read them over and sign them. They authorize me to act on her behalf and allow me to proceed with the lawsuit. And I need an itemized list of all your medical and household expenses — basically anything you've spent money on since the incident. There's no way we can get our case in front of a judge before your surgery, and you say you won't be able to go outside for a month, so timing will be tricky. Once I start this, several things need to happen before Mr. Weston can take any action, legal or illegal. And the most important thing is getting his assets identified and frozen, and that will take a court order."

"I'm going to call my doctor today and see about putting off the surgery."

"No, don't do that. We'll figure something out. Maybe there will be a way you can go out — if you're careful."

"I'll call and ask."

"Okay then. I think I have enough to get started. I'll ask the courier to wait until you've signed everything. Don't forget your itemized expenses. I need all of it as soon as possible so I can file motions."

They stood, and Lisa shook his hand, again. "Thank you, Michael, for all your help."

"I haven't done anything yet."

"You've given me hope."

Michael turned to *her* and held out his hand. She didn't believe in that romance novel fantasy shit, but this zing of energy was hard to ignore. From the look on his face, he felt it, too.

"Elaine, would you mind sticking around for a few minutes?"

"I can't. I need to drop Lisa off at the bus stop."

"How about lunch then?"

Lunch? *He* was asking her out to lunch. Her brain froze.

"Elaine?"

"What? *Oh.* Yes. Lunch. *Um,* okay. When and where?"

"Give me your number, and I'll text you. I can pick you up since your office is right around the corner."

Her number? What was her number? And why had her brain turned to mush? She pulled out a business card, wrote her cell phone number on the back, and handed it to him. Then she turned to leave.

"I'll text you around twelve-thirty. That'll give me some time to get Tina started on the forms."

"Okay."

"Okay. I'll see you soon."

"Okay." Was that all she could say? Just *okay?* She needed to get out of there before she turned into a blithering idiot.

20

He dropped into one of the leather chairs What just happened? He'd asked a woman to lunch. A woman who was strikingly beautiful. She was the first woman he'd looked at twice in twelve years. And he didn't know what to do with that.

Should he feel guilty? Was he being unfaithful to Sandy? After a twelve-year sleep, something inside woke up. Was she the *she* the bear told him about?

That they might be destined to meet scared him. As real as those visions had been, the only part of that experience that he completely believed was finding his purpose so he could honor Sandy's memory. Wasn't it the deer that told him to let go of his need to figure everything out? Didn't they tell him to just go with it? And wasn't it just last night the bear said, "She's here?"

His brain gave up. He had no choice but to just *go with it.*

He walked out to Tina's desk. "I need the standard civil lawsuit packet typed up and couriered to Lisa Weston this afternoon. And instruct the driver to wait for her signatures. And I need to prepare a motion to freeze assets. Can you get me an appointment with the clerk?"

"You got it. I'm glad we're taking her case. That poor woman deserves justice."

"If there was any justice in this world, her ex-husband would get the same treatment in prison. But that's up to God to straighten out. We do what we can, and we let God, or whoever is in charge, take care of the rest. Now I'm going to lunch."

"You never go to lunch. What's up?"

He didn't take the bait. She knew what was up. She'd heard what he said to Elaine. "None of your business."

He tried not to smile when Tina smirked. "Don't stay out too late. You have an appointment at two and, hopefully, you'll be able to meet with the court clerk."

His two o'clock was with another battered woman, and as much as he wanted to, his conscience wouldn't let him cancel.

"Yes, *Mom*."

She still couldn't believe it as she and Lisa walked to her car.

"He's a very attractive man, and he sure seems taken by you."

"He knows me. He doesn't remember me, but he knows me."

"How could he not recognize you? Has your appearance changed since the last time you saw him?"

"It was twelve years ago, and I was a little bloody at the time. Remember that story I told you about the beating that sent my ex to prison the first time?"

"Yes."

"He's the man who called the police for me and waited with me until they came."

"Wow!"

"But there's more, and this is going to suck when he *does* remember. While he was waiting with *me*, someone murdered his wife."

"*Oh,* my God! And you're worried he'll hate you when he remembers!"

"Yes. I tried to find him after Dan's trial, and that's when I found the news story about his wife. I know I'm not responsible for what happened, but I still feel guilty. If he hadn't stopped to help me, he would have been home with her."

"You have nothing to feel guilty about. There are two people who are at fault: whoever murdered his wife, and your ex-husband for beating you."

"I bet he blames himself, though. They didn't publish all the details, but the man who killed his wife did it for revenge."

Her phone beeped with a text. "This is him."

There's a deli down the street. How about we pick up some sandwiches and walk over to the park? I'll meet you in front of your building.

Here goes nothing.

Sounds good. Give me about 15 minutes.
Of course.

"Well?"

"I'm meeting him in fifteen minutes in front of my building, and we're walking down to the deli, getting lunch, and going over to the park."

"Are you going to tell him?"

"I don't know. I guess if it comes up, I'll have to. But I'd rather put it off as long as possible."

"You don't strike me as someone who scares easily."

"This is a bit outside the scope of my black belt."

She dropped Lisa off at the bus stop and drove back, pulled into her assigned parking space, touched up her lipstick, and tried to slow her racing heart as she walked to the steps in front of her building.

He was already waiting for her.

♡

A jolt of adrenaline flooded his body when he saw her approach. "Have you been waiting long?"

"No. Just got here. Are you okay to walk?"

"Sure. It's nice to get out of the office, especially when the weather's like this."

"I know what you mean. I shocked Tina when I told her I was going out for lunch. I usually work until she forces me to eat something. And it's always something she brings for me."

"Sort of like your office mom?"

"Exactly."

He set a nice pace, not too fast, but not a stroll, either, and they walked in silence. It should have felt weird, but it didn't. Maybe the bear was right. But he couldn't get past the fact that he knew her from somewhere. He decided to wait until they found a bench at the park before he brought it up.

It was just a coincidence that they both ordered a pastrami on rye and bottled water, right?

Gibbs Rule 39. There are no coincidences.

Damn.

They found a picnic table near the volleyball courts. There was a pickup game going on, probably a bunch of guys who worked together and played regularly. That was something he never had the time for. He used to enjoy playing in tournaments on the beach, but that was with Sandy watching him. "So I have to admit I looked you up on LinkedIn. Do you live at the beach?"

"Yes, Hermosa."

"Really? Where?"

"On the Strand between Tenth and Eleventh."

Now, what were the chances of that?

"I live on the Strand between Eleventh and Twelfth. I knew you looked familiar. I've probably seen you on the beach or at the market."

Sad eyes looked into his as she took a deep breath, then quietly said, "No. That's not where you know me from. I wish it was."

"What do you mean?"

She didn't say anything, just looked at him as if she was trying to tell him something without using words.

It took a few seconds for the knot to form in the pit of his stomach. No, it couldn't be. That woman's name was Elaine, what? Jeffers, Elaine Jeffers. And that was twelve years ago. This had to be some kind of karmic joke, and if he ever got his hands on that bear for not warning him, he'd . . . What? Beat up an imaginary animal?

"I can see by the look on your face, you remember me now." She looked at her watch. "It's okay. I should get back, anyway. Thank you for the pastrami sandwich. I haven't had one in years."

He tried to pull his thoughts together while she wrapped up the rest of her sandwich and grabbed her trash. She was leaving? Why? "Wait. Where are you going?"

"Back to work. I debated whether to tell you, but I wanted to be honest. You deserve to know. You can email me status updates on the case. Thank you for lunch."

She turned and walked toward the litter cans.

"Elaine! Wait!"

She stopped and turned to face him, and when he saw her tears, his brain kicked in. He did a quick review of the facts as he knew them: He helped her when her husband beat her. Her injuries weren't life threatening or disfiguring as far as he could see at the time, and the asshole got a four-year sentence. So who beat her up so badly she spent two months recuperating and accumulated hundreds of thousands of dollars in medical bills?

Christ in heaven.

Her bastard husband had gotten out early, and that's why she became a Victim's Advocate! "Please don't go."

"Michael, you can hardly stand to look at me. It's okay. If I were you, I wouldn't be able to look at me either."

She had it all wrong, and he couldn't let her leave. "Please, wait! I have to talk to you or I'll never get a decent night's sleep again." Because if he fucked this up, seven animals would take turns ripping him a new one every night for the rest of his life.

She stopped walking, hesitated, and then turned around again. "What are you talking about?"

"It's a long story, one you probably wouldn't believe because most of the time I don't believe it either. Please don't go."

With downcast eyes, she walked back to where he stood by the picnic table. "I'm so, so, sorry."

"You've got nothing to be sorry for. In all these years of coming to terms with what happened, it never crossed my mind to blame you for any of it."

"I tried to find you after Dan's trial. I wanted to thank you for helping me that day. I found you on LinkedIn, but you no longer worked at ALL NET, so I googled you. That's when I found the news article about what happened to your wife. I *really* needed to find you and apologize, but you'd disappeared. I never forgot your kindness, and I've thought about you a lot over the years. But this morning, when we got to your office, and I heard your name, I almost turned around and walked out."

"Why?"

"Because I'm the reason you weren't home with your wife that morning. While you were helping me, she was—"

"Elaine! Look at me." When she looked up, a tear ran down her beautiful cheek. "It wasn't because of you. It was because of what I did to that man. I drove myself crazy with *what ifs* for a long time. What if I'd been home? It took a while before I realized I'd probably be dead, too. If I had been there and tried to stop him, he would have shot me instead, or maybe, he'd have shot me and then her. Anyway, it happened because of *me*. Something would have happened no matter what. But it wasn't because of you, and I'm sorry you've felt responsible all this time. It took a long time and a lot of work before I stopped blaming *myself*. And to tell you the truth, if it hadn't happened, I'd still be a cold-hearted, sleazy, trade-mark attorney making obscene amounts of money for ruining other people's lives. Through my pain and guilt, I found myself and a purpose. I put myself through hell in the beginning, and I came out the other side a changed man. I can't make it up to that poor man or any of the others I hurt, and I can't bring Sandy back, but with every person I help, I honor her memory." Geez, now she was sobbing. "Come here."

She walked into his arms, and he held her while she cried. Something inside him shifted. Were the deer and the bear right?

21

Listening to him try to make her feel better broke her heart. What he'd gone through, what she'd lived through, and how they'd survived and channeled everything to make a difference for others . . . it was almost too much to comprehend.

When she got herself under control, she backed out of his arms and instantly missed the comfort and acceptance their shared tragedy brought her.

"Elaine, what happened? He went to prison, but your online profile said you spent two months recovering from a much worse beating. How did he get to you?"

"He got out early, and no one warned me. He was waiting for me when I got home from a week-long retreat. If I hadn't left a bag of souvenirs in the van, and if they hadn't turned around and come back, Dan would have finished the job, and no one would have known. Instead, one of the ladies I went with came to the door with my bag and heard me screaming. She called the police who caught him just as he kicked my ribs in. Until that happened, I was going to school to become a CPA. I was going to open my own office. But lying in bed not being able to move gave me a lot of time to think — and get angry. No one told me he got paroled early. No one warned me. And that's when I decided to become a Victim's Advocate. I needed to help others like me navigate the legal system and understand their options, because no one did that for me."

He reached out and gently wiped the tears from her face. Something between them changed, and she didn't know what to do next, so she stepped back another step.

"I need to get back to the office. I have an appointment in fifteen minutes."

"I do, too. But . . ." He hesitated. "Have dinner with me tonight. Talking to you, sharing this with you, it's, well, it's healing something inside me, and I think for you, as well."

"Okay."

"Okay?"

"Yes, I'll have dinner with you, even though it's against Rule 12. But I have to warn you. I haven't been on a date since, well, ever. In fact, other than my father and doctors, you're the first man to touch me since that day Dan tried to kill me."

"Gibbs? Are you kidding me?"

She smiled at his reaction. "I got hooked while I recuperated from that last beating. I still binge watch rerun marathons, and normally I'd stay home on a Tuesday night, but tonight is a rerun."

"That was the only thing I woke up for. And I reserve Tuesday nights at eight, too. So, Rule 12? *Oh*, yeah. Never date a coworker. Well, we're not exactly coworkers, and I have to warn you, too. I haven't been on a date since college, and you're the first woman I've touched, other than family and clients, since the day Sandy died. What time will you be done today?"

She was the first? In twelve years, he hadn't been with another woman? "My last appointment is at five. I should be done by six, but I'd like to go home and change first."

"Me, too. And since we live so close to each other, I'll just walk over, and we can walk down to Pier Street and grab a bite. How's seven?"

"Perfect. Now I need to get back. My next appointment is probably waiting for me."

When they got to her building, he pulled her into his arms and hugged her. It was one of those hugs that fixed a lot of broken pieces, and she didn't want it to end.

"I'll see you at seven."

"Okay. And thank you for lunch."

"Thank you for sharing with me."

He turned and walked away. And for the first time, she skipped up the steps to her office.

♡

He had a date that night! He'd asked her out, and she said yes. He should have been shaking in his boots, but he smiled and tried not to skip back to his office. As soon as he walked in, Tina was all over him with questions.

"So, how did it go? Are you seeing her again? And look at you! I swear, I don't think I've ever seen you smile like that."

If he had his way, she'd be seeing a lot more of it. "Yes, we're having dinner tonight. Are you happy now? And don't you have work to do?"

He expected the rest of the day to drag on, but his last client's case was almost as bad as Lisa Weston's, and he lost track of time until Tina stuck her head in the door.

"Don't you have a date?"

He checked his watch. Six-fifteen! Shit. He needed to get home, take a shower and try to slow his adrenaline-stoked heartbeat. He grabbed his briefcase, shocked the hell out of Tina with a hug, and ran out the door.

It was five minutes to seven when he walked out onto the Strand. He tried not to jog, but he was just too damned excited. When he got to her house, she was on the patio gazing at the sun as it set.

"You know, there's a green flash just as it dips into the water."

She jumped. "You startled me. Yeah, I've seen it many times."

"Well, you certainly have a good vantage point."

"Don't you have a view?"

"From the front window, but my patio is in back. I get the morning sun, but I'm rarely home to enjoy it." He turned to watch the sun dip, and they both saw the green flash. It was always a challenge since it lasted less than a second. "That was nice. Are you ready to go?"

"Let me get my purse and lock up."

Unlike his house with its entrance in the back, her patio was the front with a gate. It was small but there were flowers everywhere. "I like the flowers. Did you do all that?"

"Yes. I had a beautiful cottage before his last attack but had to sell it to pay off hospital bills. I lived in a dingy second-floor apartment near downtown when I went back to school. No yard. No patio. No flowers. This was a neglected foreclosure, and sand fleas covered my legs when the agent walked me through, but I loved it. I bought it as-is that day for back property taxes and title insurance and spent every minute of my spare time fixing it up. I even refinished the wood floor that was hiding under the really gross, flea infested carpeting. Now it's my haven after dealing with the justice system and battered women all day."

"You did all the work yourself?"

"It wasn't that hard. For a pizza and a six-pack, I got a couple of the neighborhood beach boys to help me carry the carpeting out to the dumpster. But I did the rest. How about you?"

"When I quit my six-figure corporate job, I didn't work for a long time. Sandy's life insurance was enough for me to live on, and when I sold our house, I had enough to buy this one and open my practice. I don't get to spend as much time here as I'd like. Every time we add another partner, we wind up with even more cases. Even with Victim's Advocates like you, it still makes me angry that so many like Lisa Weston slip through the cracks."

"I know. It was the same for me. I had no one to guide me. But my settlement was a lot better than Lisa's, and the court let me sell our house. Hers is locked up. He won't sign it over."

"Well, I think I can get that fixed. If the jury agrees with what I'm going to propose, he'll have no choice. Here we are. Lots of places to pick from. What do you feel like eating?"

"I know this is going to sound weird, but I'd love some fried shrimp and a big lemonade, and maybe we can find a table outside. It's such a beautiful night."

"That doesn't sound weird at all. Let's go to the Shrimp Shack and get two orders to go."

He thought he might be uncomfortable with her, but it was exactly the opposite. That should have scared him, but it didn't. And he decided not to analyze it. He was good with going with it. It was a new experience, and he could hear the animals telling him it was about time. But he had every intention of taking it slow.

♡

He sure was easy to talk to. She expected to feel uneasy since it was her first date, and she'd fretted over what to wear and how to act as she rushed to get ready. But his presence calmed her, and she didn't want to analyze why. She just wanted to go with it. But if anything developed between them, she would insist on taking it slow.

The pier area was crowded with people enjoying the warm summer night. The hot, dry, Santa Ana winds had kicked up, and although the sun had set, it had to be over eighty degrees. They found seats at a table and spread out their food. "You know this heatwave is supposed to last through the weekend. I hope you don't have to work."

"Well, I usually go in, but I think I'll work from home Saturday morning. What do you have planned?"

"I'll be people watching from my patio, and when it gets too hot, I'll make a run for the water."

"*Hmm.* Maybe when I get done, I'll come join you. Or is that being presumptuous of me?"

"Not at all. This is the beach. It's like a great big living room.

That's why I love it here. What kind of beer do you like? I can pick some up."

"Actually, I don't drink. But lemonade or iced tea works. And if that's too much trouble, I'll be good with ice water."

He didn't drink? Most men at least liked a beer or two on a hot day. Would he think she was prying if she asked why?

"You're wondering what's wrong with me because I don't drink. It's not medical. I don't broadcast this, but I don't hide it either. That's one of the benefits of being my own boss. I don't have to worry about being judged. I'm a recovering alcoholic. I just celebrated eleven years without a drink or a drug."

She knew about the twelve-step program. She'd been to Alanon meetings with clients. It was a great way to live one's life. He seemed very comfortable telling her about it which reinforced how relaxed they were together. "That's awesome. I know about the twelve steps. So, you have a sponsor and go to meetings?"

"Yes. Besides work, my family and AA are the only things I make time for except for Tuesdays at eight o'clock. I love what I do, but I have to make time for AA. Without it, I wouldn't have what I have. So, you're okay with me not drinking? I mean if we go out again?"

If they went out again? There was no doubt in her mind they'd go out again. It was impossible to ignore the attraction between them. "I think I had half a beer when I paid the surfer boys for helping me with the carpet. Before that? I can't remember. Maybe a glass of champagne when I graduated college. It just never crosses my mind. Would that be a showstopper if I drank?"

"It would depend on how much and when you drank. It doesn't bother me to be around people who drink. It's my choice, and each day I choose not to. But it would bother me if you were a heavy drinker. You're the first woman I've spent any time with outside of the office or my mom's, and I'm enjoying talking with you. And I'd like to think you'd remember what we talked about the next day. Being with someone who's in a blackout is not my idea of a good time."

"I've never had a blackout. Never had a hangover either."

"What do you think about me going to meetings three or four nights a week?"

How did she answer that without sounding like they were already in a relationship? "What I think shouldn't make any difference. It would be selfish of anyone to interfere. And if any woman you date tries to change that, my advice would be to drop her." Why did the idea of him dating another woman make her uneasy?

"Well, I don't plan to date anyone else, so that won't be an issue."

Unexpected relief washed over her, but when she smiled at him, the look on his face replaced that relief with an overwhelming need to get closer to him.

"Are you going to finish that?"

What?

He pointed to the last shrimp in her basket.

She smirked. *"Uh,* no. You can have it."

When he finished, they gathered up their baskets and cups and dumped it all in a trash bin.

"Feel like taking a walk on the beach?"

Something like butterflies flew around in her stomach. Or was it her dinner?

Is this really happening?

"Sure."

22

D id he just ask a woman to take a walk on the beach in the moonlight? Who was he, and what had he done with the celibate man who swore he'd never get involved with a woman ever again? For a second he thought he could hear all the animals cheering, but it was just the sound of the waves.

They kicked off their shoes and walked down to the water's edge. He would never be able to put it in words because there was no way to describe it. He *had* to touch her. He *had* to take her in his arms and kiss her, but he settled for taking her hand as they skirted the foam that followed the shore waves. It was natural and comfortable.

After they'd walked about a quarter mile, he stopped. He couldn't take it anymore. He turned her to face him. Then he took her face with both hands, leaned down, and when his lips were a hair's width away from hers, he asked, "May I kiss you?"

The corners of her mouth lifted in a subtle, sexy smile which he decided meant *Yes*. So he touched his lips to hers and started slowly. The last time he kissed a woman was so long ago, he'd forgotten how it felt. The kiss was soft and slow but gradually picked up heat when her arms locked around his neck.

Had it been like this with Sandy?

Stay in the now.

All he wanted to think about was how Elaine's lips opened under his, and how their tongues made love to each other. He had to control himself or he'd lay her out on the sand, and that's not what he wanted. When he lifted his head and broke the connection with her mouth, it was like losing a body part.

♡

Stunned. Shocked. Amazed. It all raced through her as his lips parted taking hers with them. It was the most natural thing in the world for her tongue to dance with his. Could he feel her heart pound?

It started out as a slow burn, but the intensity grew until all she wanted was for him to lay her out on the sand. She wanted, no, she *needed* to feel him. She wanted to crawl inside him. It's where she belonged. She had no experience, no frame of reference. This was *nothing* like those books Latesha made her read.

This was the real thing.

He pulled away and left an empty space where his lips had been. She still had her arms around his neck, and he had his around her waist. And when she saw his face in the moonlight, she gave up all thoughts of never getting into a relationship again. She had no choice. He had her heart the same as if he'd reached into her chest and pulled it out with his hands.

"Wow." He tried to catch his breath.

"Yeah, wow. Maybe we should talk about this."

"Nothing to talk about. They told me this would happen. They told me to just go with it. And I thought they were crazy."

"They?"

"It's a long story. I'll tell you about it when it's too late for you to back out."

"Back out?"

"Yeah. When you can't live without me."

"Too late."

♡

He would remember that moment, that profound, life-affirming moment for the rest of his life. Part of him had died with Sandy, and now life flowed through him again, because of this woman. "I need to take this slowly. *We* need to take this slowly. We need to get to know each other. I want to know everything about you."

"I agree. There are things about me you should know."

"Do you sleepwalk?"

The sound of her laugh tickled his heart.

"No, but I might snore, at least Dan said so. Besides him, I haven't shared a room with anyone since high school slumber parties. And I have a black belt in Karate, so you might not want to piss me off."

"A black belt? No kidding?"

"As soon as the casts came off, I started taking self-defense classes at the Y. When I finished those, I continued at a small Karate Studio nearby. It gave me a sense of empowerment and self-confidence that I desperately needed. I still go once a week to stay in shape. And I pity the fool who tries to attack me."

"Wow, I think that's terrific, but I can promise you, the only thing you'll ever feel from my touch is pleasure."

Did I really just say that?

"I mean, I've never laid a hand on a woman in anger, ever."

"I got it, but that brings up a few other things you should know. I have zero experience with men. Dan was my first and last, and let me tell you, there wasn't much in between. Latesha — she was my neighbor where I used to live — she couldn't believe it."

"Believe what?"

"You know, it might be too soon to share this much personal stuff. Let's go back to taking it slow."

"What's the other thing I should know?"

"I'm almost afraid to tell you this."

"No secrets, okay? And I don't want you ever to be afraid to tell me something."

"Okay, here goes. That day you helped me? I didn't know I was pregnant. I miscarried at the police station. By the time I got to the ER, I was hemorrhaging and had to have a hysterectomy. I never told Dan."

Jesus Christ.

He tightened his arms around her.

"It was a long time ago. I just thought you should know, I can't get pregnant."

It took him a second to comprehend what she just said. Was she worried he'd be angry?

"God, Elaine. I'm so sorry that happened to you. You didn't need to tell me, but I'm glad you trust me that much. It doesn't matter to me. I'm just so glad you survived everything."

She shivered. "I guess we should head back. It's starting to cool off."

"Are you cold?" He put his arm around her shoulder as they started back down the beach.

"Not anymore."

She *really* didn't want the night to end, but they'd agreed to take it slow, which was just as well. Other than Latesha's videos and those erotic stories she read, she had no idea what to do or how to act in bed with a real man. She had to be honest with him at some point and putting it off meant not feeling his luscious lips anywhere else. She couldn't imagine what making love with him would be like.

Dan's idea of kissing was to choke her with his tongue. And his technique in bed involved humping as fast as he could, getting off, and rolling over. Then he either fell asleep or made her get up and get him a beer and something to eat. And all that time, she'd thought that was how it was supposed to be.

"Hey."

"What?"

"Why the frown? Are you bored?"

"*Oh*, my, no! I was thinking about how things were with Dan."

"*Oh?*"

"Yeah. I can't believe I thought that's how it was supposed to be."

"How *what* was supposed to be?"

Well, she might as well get it out of the way.

"How about some coffee at my house? I'll explain everything."

He looked at his watch, so she looked at hers. It was nine-thirty. Kind of late for a heart to heart talk about sex.

"Okay. But I can't stay too long. I want to get an early start on Lisa's case, and my first appointment is at nine."

When they got to her house, she let him in and went to the kitchen. He wandered around the living room while she got the coffeemaker going.

"You refinished this floor yourself?"

"Yes."

"Wow, it looks fantastic. I've always wondered why people cover wood floors with carpets. Your house has a cozy, beachy feel. I like it."

Good thing, since she could see him spending a lot of time there. "How do you like your coffee?"

"Hot."

"*Uh*, I meant what do you want in it? I have milk, sugar, artificial sweetener, flavored syrups."

"Maybe a little milk. I like strong coffee like espresso."

"That's good. So do I, and this is strong."

"So, you were going to explain something to me?"

Rats. She'd hoped he'd forget. "Okay, here's the bottom line. I've never had an orgasm with anyone. And until Latesha talked me into watching her porn videos, I'd never had an orgasm at all." The look on his face was priceless. "Bet that's not what you were expecting me to say."

"*Uh*, no. So you were a virgin when you got married?"

"Yes."

"And all you knew was what he taught you."

"He didn't teach me anything. It was always over before I had a chance to think about getting turned on. Look, I only told you this because when you kissed me, something happened. It was something I never felt before. You wanted me to be honest with you, but if this is too much, please say so."

"No, it's not too much. It makes me sad and angry. It was never like that with Sandy. We fell in love in college and learned together how to please each other. Knowing what we had, I can't even begin to imagine what your life was like. Shit, I hope my talking about Sandy isn't upsetting you."

"She was the love of your life, and she's been gone a long time. It doesn't upset me. But I'm sad for you."

"Why?"

"You had it perfect, and because you did a good deed, you lost it all. I can't miss something I've never had."

"I didn't lose it all because I did a *good deed*. I lost it all because of the bastard I was before. So you don't believe in second chances?"

"I don't believe in much of anything."

"What if I told you I've known for a long time we would get together?"

"What? How could you know that?"

"So here's *my* confession. After I sobered up, my sponsor sent me on a vision quest. I was alone in the woods for seven nights. Each night, in my sleep, a different animal came to me, and we talked. Well, they did most of the talking. I was still struggling to make sense out of what happened and trying to find a purpose in all of it. They helped me, and on the last day, I got my answer. That's when I decided to become a civil litigation attorney and help battered women sue for the restitution they were entitled to."

"So where do I fit in?"

"They told me, I think it was the bear, or maybe it was the deer. Anyway, they said I'd find someone when I was ready, that she was going through her own struggles, and when we were both ready, we'd find each other. Last night the bear came to me and said, *She's here.* And this morning you walked into my office."

"But you didn't remember me."

"You looked familiar. I didn't put it together until you told me at the park."

"So you talk to animals, and they talk to you?"

"In my dreams, and they do most of the talking."

"I don't doubt that you think that's what happens, but I'd be more inclined to believe it's your subconscious."

"That's what I thought at first. But they told me things I couldn't possibly have known. And the last day of the vision quest, the wind blew a scrap of newspaper that wrapped around my leg. It was a news article about a woman who'd committed suicide because she couldn't pay her medical bills after her husband threw a pot of boiling water at her face. That's when I knew what I had to do."

It sounded pretty farfetched, but he believed it, so she wasn't about to tell him what she thought. "Well, however you got there, I think what you do is wonderful, and I'm sure your wife would be proud of you."

"You know what?"

"What?"

"I don't want to talk about that anymore. Right now, I need to kiss you."

"*Oh,* okay."

"Okay?"

"Yeah."

He walked over to where she stood, put his arms around her, held her tight, and kissed her until her knees buckled.

"Give me your hand."

He placed her palm over his heart. It pounded like hers. She didn't care what brought them together. She was right where she needed to be.

23

H e tore himself away and, again, it felt like a piece of his body was missing. They had agreed not to rush things, but everything in him begged for her. It was probably good that he had work to do in the morning. "I don't want to, but I have to leave." He could see the conflict in her eyes. She wanted him to stay as much as he wanted to. But they'd just reconnected that morning. As right as he knew it was, he wanted their first time to be slow, and he had to get up early.

"I know. This all happened so fast, but we've got a busy week ahead getting Lisa's case together. How about Saturday? I'll make dinner."

"I should be done around noon. And it's going to be too hot to cook, so we'll go out. Okay?"

Her eyes lit up, and he took that as a yes. *Just go with it.* That's what they'd told him, so that's what he intended to do. He walked to the door, turned, and held his arms open. Without hesitating, she walked into them, and they held each other.

"Good night, Elaine. I'll see you Saturday."

"Good night, Michael. And thank you."

"Why are you thanking me?"

"For dinner and for giving me something I've never had before."

"What's that?"

"Someone to dream about."

"Who's that?" He teased her.

She pulled away and playfully slapped his arm.

"Go. Leave before I change my mind about taking this slow."

Walking out wasn't the hardest thing he'd ever done, but it was definitely in the top five. When he got back to his house, he stopped, looked up at the stars and said, "Thank you." Then he went inside, got ready, and crawled into bed.

They were all there waiting for him. There was even a big banner that read, "Congratulations Michael! You made it," and they wore party hats.

She never remembered her dreams, but this one woke her up laughing. She'd been in a room decorated for a party, and there was a banner that read, "Congratulations Elaine! You made it!" And there were animals wearing party hats. Were these Michael's dream animals?

The week dragged on even though they were both busy with other cases. Finally, Saturday dawned bright and clear. She didn't need to get up that early, but there was no going back to sleep when she thought about seeing him in a few hours. They'd texted throughout the week, mostly with updates on Lisa's case, but there were subtle hints of flirting, and the anticipation of seeing him again distracted her. Several times she thought about walking past his house, but she didn't know which one was his, and if he saw her, he might think she was stalking him.

She put on some cutoffs and a t-shirt, made a cup of coffee, and sat on the patio listening to the waves and nearby barking seals. The beach was still deserted, but in a few hours, it would be packed with people escaping the heat of the city, if only for a few hours. It still thrilled her every time she thought about how she lived where other people came to play.

The sequence of events that had brought her to this point in her life snuck up on her. If Dan hadn't beaten her that morning, she would never have met Michael. If Dan hadn't gotten out of prison early and beaten her within an inch of her life, she would never have become a Victim's Advocate. She would never have found a career that gave her a purpose and fulfillment. She would never have bought this house. She wouldn't have walked into Michael's office with a client last week. And now she was on the brink of another life change.

She owed it all to Dan and the man who had murdered Michael's wife . . . What a mind fuck.

People started showing up. The invasion had begun, and her cute surfer dudes waved as they ran past with their boards. She didn't expect Michael for another five hours, and she needed to find something to do or she'd go crazy with anticipation.

She watered all the plants and straightened up the house. Then she put on her one-piece granny bathing suit that covered a lot of her surgery scars, pulled on that pair of cutoffs and the t-shirt that covered more of the souvenir scars and walked down to the market. As she walked past Michael's block, she wondered what he was doing at that moment.

Something weird was happening inside her. Excitement tickled her heart, adrenaline flowed through her veins, and the butterflies in her stomach danced. That night on the beach had been magical, and she knew it could only get better if she didn't fuck it up. He was honest and sincere, and there were no red flags. She felt safe in his arms, and she couldn't wait to be in them again.

She didn't *need* any groceries, but she bought some snack bars, sodas, eggs, and bacon and walked back. She stumbled when she saw him sitting on the short stucco wall. He was in cutoffs and a t-shirt, and he looked positively delicious.

Please don't let me be drooling.

"Good morning, beautiful."

"Good morning, Michael."

"I was looking out the window when I saw you walk by. How did you sleep?"

"Other than waking up at o'dark thirty, I slept fine. But the other night I had the weirdest dream."

"Here, let me carry the bags. You can tell me about it on the way."

"I thought you had work to do."

"I did. I woke up before dawn and couldn't go back to sleep, so I figured I'd get everything done early. I was hoping to spend the day with you."

"I'd like that."

"So, tell me about the dream."

"This was the other night, the night we had dinner. Your animal friends — I think they were your animal friends — threw me a party. And there was a big banner that said, *Congratulations Elaine! You made it!* My subconscious must have picked up on what you said that night. Anyway, I woke up laughing. I woke up laughing this morning, too, but I don't remember why. I think it had something to do with Rule 39."

Rule 39 was right. It wasn't a coincidence, and it wasn't her subconscious, either, but she would come to that conclusion herself. "So, do you go to church?"

"Not anymore. Why? Do you?"

"Yeah, Saint Mary's."

"You're *Catholic*?"

"Is that a problem?"

"My mother will be thrilled."

"*You're* Catholic? Wow."

"Well, that's how I was raised, but I walked away from all religion the first time Dan beat me and my mother said it was God's will. I guess you could say I'm an atheist, have been since that day. I really don't think about it anymore. Is that going to be a problem?"

Would it? It would definitely make things interesting. He decided to let the evidence speak for itself. Seeing is believing, and all that. "No, it's not a problem other than I go to church on Sundays and holidays."

"I wouldn't mind going with you. And I don't mind going through the motions. Just don't expect me to have faith in God's will and the saints and all that stuff."

Somehow, that would work itself out. He watched her put away the groceries, and when he couldn't stand it anymore, he came up behind her and wrapped his arms around her waist. She leaned back into his body. God, he wanted her. But it was more than lust. Feeling her against him made breathing easier; she was the missing part. Now that she was in place, the machinery of his body functioned again. But it was too tempting. "Elaine, honey, you feel too good, and if I hold you much longer, you're going to feel me. How about we take a walk down to the water? I need to cool off."

He stepped away, and breathing wasn't so easy again.

"Let me grab a couple of beach towels."

They spent the day playing in the warm water and lying on the beach. They made up stories about the people they watched. They talked about NCIS episodes and cast changes. He told her more about his vision quest. She told him about the retreat and living in an apartment in the inner city.

He found ways to touch her. If they were in the water, he held her. If they walked on the beach, he held her hand. If they were sitting on the towels, he had his hand on her knee or around her shoulders. As long as he touched her, he breathed easier.

By three o'clock, they'd had enough sun and surf. "Are you hungry?"

"Yeah."

"Ready to get a bite to eat?"

"Late lunch or early dinner?"

"Does it matter?"

"No, but I could use a shower. I'm kinda grungy."

"Okay. You've got fifteen minutes."

"Why only fifteen minutes?"

"Because I can't stand being away from you." He needed to get a grip, or he would scare her away.

She stood in her doorway, put her hand on his cheek and said, "I feel the same way. And you know what? It doesn't scare me at all."

Had she read his mind? "That's funny because I was just thinking maybe I was coming on too strong. I don't want to scare you away."

"I'm a black belt, remember? I don't scare easy."

He kissed her forehead, and as he turned to leave, he reminded her, "Fifteen minutes."

♡

She should have been terrified, but she wasn't. She was safe with him, though how she knew that, she couldn't begin to guess.

She stripped, frowned at her funky tan lines, and jumped in the shower. No time for anything except a quick shampoo. Her curly hair would have to dry naturally without the benefit of a flatiron. She didn't need much makeup. Just a dab of concealer over the barely noticeable scars on her face and some lip gloss. All that sun gave her a healthy glow. But some of it had to do with a certain sexy lawyer.

She slipped into a sundress, grabbed a light sweater to cover the scars, and had just stepped into her flip-flops when he knocked on the door.

Fifteen minutes exactly.

"Hi."

"Wow."

"Wow?"

"I like that dress. And I like the way you look in it. In fact, I like it so much, I may have a hard time keeping my hands off you."

"Don't try too hard."

She was flirting! It was something completely new to her.

She closed and locked the door, and they strolled down the Strand toward the pier.

"You're not used to a lot of affection and attention, are you?"

"You mean like romantic stuff? In the very beginning, Dan would bring me flowers and hold my hand, but that all ended as soon as we got home from our honeymoon. I like it, but I don't think I'll ever get used to it. But please try." She didn't care if she sounded desperate. She was determined to be honest with him. She never learned how to play the hard-to-get game.

"You deserve to be cared for and loved. We both do. If any two people deserve happiness, it's us."

She couldn't agree more.

"By the way, if you feel like having a glass of wine with dinner, it won't bother me."

"Well, it would bother *me*. Wine makes me sleepy. I told you I'm not a drinker. It has nothing to do with you, I just never think about it."

"Okay. I just want to make sure you know you have the option. Now, what are you hungry for?"

Him. She was hungry for him, and she had no idea where that came from. She'd never felt any physical attraction toward a man before. But this was more than physical. So what did she want to eat? Besides him? "How about a suggestion?"

"Do you like sushi?"

"No. I *love* it."

"There's a place across the highway that's very good. How does that sound?"

She could eat her weight in sushi if she could afford it. "It sounds perfect."

"Then afterward, if we still have room, we can get ice cream and watch the sun go down."

"You're going to spoil me."

"And that's a problem for you? I told you, you deserve it."

"Well, then you deserve to be spoiled, too."

"If you insist. What did you have in mind?"

They were flirting, again. It was new, and it was fun.

Suddenly, he stopped and pulled her close. Then he looked through her eyes and into her soul. "Don't think about it. Just do what you feel. It's okay."

"This is so embarrassing."

"Why?"

"You're the second man I've dated in my entire life, and I don't know what to do or say or how to act."

He stepped back, took her hand, and they continued walking down to the corner. "You're the second woman I've dated since high school. I never learned the games, either, and I'm not about to start now. I know we don't know much about each other, but we have something, and we both know it. There's no point trying to pretend or playing hard-to-get. I want you and I think you want me. And like the snake said — or was it the deer? Anyway, one of them told me to go with it, whatever *it* turned out to be."

"If all that's true, why are *you* holding back?"

He looked surprised. "I don't know. I thought we should take things slow, but now I'm wondering why."

"Life is short. You of all people should know that. If this is meant to be, if we're meant to be, I don't want to wait."

"Let's see how you feel after sushi and ice cream."

She smirked. "Well played, counselor."

24

S he was right. Life was short. He'd waited twelve long years for her even though he hadn't known it at the time. More than anything, he wanted to make love to her, show her how a man is supposed to treat the woman he loves. And he was pretty sure he was heading in that direction — as wild as that sounded.

They fed the morsels of fish and rice to each other by hand since neither was very good with chopsticks, and it quickly became a sensuous game. Licking each other's fingers was so erotic and arousing, all he could think about was how her body would feel under his and how tight his jeans were getting. This meant stopping at the grocery store and buying condoms. He hadn't had to use them since college.

I hope I remember how to put one on.

By the time they left the sushi bar, they were both turned on and trying to hide it. "We need to walk some of this off. You up for a stroll?"

"Yeah, just don't expect me to walk too fast. I can't believe I ate that much. And thank you. You'll have to let me make dinner for you one of these nights."

"That's not necessary, but I wouldn't say no."

"How about tomorrow night?"

"Can't. My mother expects me to come for dinner on Sundays after church. Why don't you come with me?"

"To church? What if I get struck by lightning as soon as I walk in? And isn't it too soon to be taking me home to meet the parents?"

"You won't get struck by lightning. I understand God doesn't do that anymore. Anyway, tomorrow we're celebrating my fiftieth birthday. It'll be just family, and I know my mother would be beside herself with joy. But if you'd rather wait, it's okay."

"When's your birthday?"

"It was Wednesday, but I'll celebrate it tomorrow."

"I won't have a chance to pick up a gift, but I'll go to church and dinner at your mother's with you. But I'm not going to confession or taking communion. Will you be okay with that?"

"Absolutely no gifts allowed, anyway. And, of course, it's okay. I just want you with me. You can meet Father Timothy, the man who saved my life."

"How did he save your life?"

"When Sandy died, I crawled into a bottle, and he got me to see that I needed help. Took me to my first AA meeting where I met the man who became my sponsor. So, got room for ice cream yet?"

"I'm going to gain weight hanging around with you."

"Then we'll just have to find a way to work off those calories."

The look on her face was priceless.

He ducked into the corner market for a few minutes and came out with a small bag. Then they stopped and got ice cream cones, sat on her patio, and watched the sun go down. She only had movies and books to compare it to, but it sure seemed awfully romantic. And that dinner? Feeding each other sushi? Is that what sexual anticipation felt like? It sure was different from watching videos alone.

After they saw the green flash, he stood, took her hand, and led her into her house.

Ah. The moment of truth.

"Elaine, honey, I want you so much I can taste it. But if at any time you want me to stop, just say so. This isn't about me, it's about us, and you have to be a willing participant."

"Michael?"

"Yeah?"

"Kiss me."

"With pleasure."

He did. And by the time he pulled back, they were both panting. Then he picked her up. "Bedroom?"

She pointed down the hall.

He carried her to the bedroom and gently laid her on the bed. Then he looked down at her with what could only be desire. Her panties were wet, something that only happened when she watched those videos and read those books. And now she was living it.

He stretched out next to her, propped up on one elbow, and gazed at her. She held her breath waiting to see what he would do next. She didn't have to wait long.

"Are you scared?"

"No, just a little nervous."

"Why?"

"Because I have no idea what I'm supposed to do, and I'm afraid I'm going to disappoint you."

"Sweet Elaine, you couldn't possibly disappoint me. But you're very tense. I don't even have to touch you to know that. I want you to take off your sweater and roll over."

"What? Why?"

"You'll see. I'm not going to make love to you while you're this tense. I'm going to help you relax. Okay?"

She sat up and removed her sweater. Then she laid down on her stomach and waited.

She heard him in the bathroom rummaging through drawers. Then he grabbed the bag from the grocery store. She heard the click of a cap. Then he was there lowering the straps of her dress and massaging her shoulders.

She'd had a few massages while on the women's retreat, so she could tell he was good at it when her muscles melted under his warm and soothing touch. It was *ah-mazing*.

"Lift up. I want to remove your dress so I can get the rest of your back."

She hesitated.

"What's wrong?"

"I have scars. They're ugly, and I don't want you to be grossed out."

"It won't gross me out, I promise. But I may get a little angry seeing the evidence of what that asshole did. Tell you what, let's turn down the lights, maybe just leave the bathroom light on."

He oozed sensitivity. She could get used to that.

He took care of the lights while she dreaded baring her body. Well, if he rejected her, at least she'd know up front. She sat up and pulled the dress over her head. Then she unhooked her strapless bra and laid back down on her belly.

"You have such soft skin. And a body just made for kissing."

The more he spoke, the wetter her panties got, and the faster her heart beat.

When he finished massaging, the tension was gone, and he leaned over and kissed the small of her back. Then he rolled her over, kissed each nipple, ran his tongue up her chest, past her chin, and lightly rimmed her lips. If he touched her between her legs, she'd surely spontaneously combust. Instead, he kissed her. If she'd been standing, she might have passed out, because that kiss took her breath away.

He sat up, pulled his shirt over his head and laid back down. "Well?"

"*Um*, yeah."

"Are you relaxed?"

"That felt good."

"You've never had a massage before, have you?"

"Twice, but not like that. They were therapeutic, and I always wondered what it would be like with a man. Can I give you a massage?"

"You don't need to. I just wanted you to unwind a little."

"I know I don't need to, but I want to."

He hesitated, then rolled over onto his stomach.

"Would you mind taking your jeans off? If I'm going to straddle your legs, the denim might scratch my skin."

That's my story, and I'm sticking to it.

He chuckled as he stood and stepped out of his jeans. His boxer briefs showed what his trunks had hidden. And he was huge.

The first time Dan thrust into her on their wedding night it felt like his penis was wrapped in barbed wire. The only foreplay had been when he shoved a finger in to break her hymen, and it never got any better. What if it hurt with Michael?

"Hey. What's the matter?"

She sat up. "I'm not scared of making love, it's just been so long, I think my hymen grew back, and I don't want it to hurt."

He crawled up next to her and pulled her into his arms.

"Well, I don't think it can grow back, and it might hurt a little at first. But I promise I'll go slow, and you'll be so turned on you'll hardly notice. I want you to trust me, and if that takes time, I'll gladly wait. Our relationship isn't based solely on physical attraction. I care about you. I care about me, too. And like I said before, we both deserve love and happiness. We've earned it. It's late, so how about we get some sleep? We're going to church in the morning, and this way, I won't have to confess that I had carnal relations outside of wedlock."

"Carnal relations? But you'll have to confess that at some point, won't you? I mean, if we . . ."

"No *ifs*, and I was joking. Knowing Father Timothy, I don't think the penance will be that bad. He'll be happy for me. Now let's get some sleep."

She expected to be too worried to sleep. She wanted him, but his size scared her. And he'd just reminded her she would be going to church and then dinner at his mother's. But at that moment, lying in his arms was so comforting and soothing, she drifted off.

♡

When he first opened his eyes, he didn't know where he was. Then he looked at the woman curled up in his arms. She was beautiful and vulnerable, and he prayed he would do the right thing when the time came. He needed to go home and get ready, but he couldn't bring himself to get out of bed.

She stretched and mumbled, "Good morning."

"Good morning to you, too. You were sleeping so peacefully, I didn't want to wake you."

"I'm usually up before this. Want some coffee?"

"Yes, as long as you don't have to get out of bed to get it." He rolled over, half on top of her, and kissed her as she tried to squirm away.

"Morning breath!"

"Both of us, and I don't care."

Feeling her body under him, her arms wrapped around his neck, his lips locked to hers, as corny as it sounded, he was home again. But when she wrapped her legs around his waist, he had to stop her. "Babe, if you do that, we won't make it to church."

"I know. But I don't want to stop."

"Tonight, when we get home from my mother's. This is going to kill me all day."

"What is?"

"This erection that's going to be difficult to hide."

She smirked. "What time will we be getting back?"

"As early as possible. I've changed my mind. Get me some coffee, wench." As soon as she left the bed, he almost regretted being such a good guy, especially when she covered her body with a robe before she went out to the kitchen. He laid there trying to get his body under control. He needed to go home and take a shower. A cold shower.

He got dressed and found her looking out her picture window, so he wrapped his arms around her from behind. She immediately leaned back into him which didn't help his situation.

"Coffee's ready. I was just about to bring you a cup."

"I'll get it. Then I'll have to go home and shower. Can you be ready to go by eight?"

"Sure. I suppose I should wear a dress?"

"Only if you want to drive me crazy." They sat on her patio drinking coffee, lost in their own thoughts. It wasn't at all uncomfortable. They just didn't need to say anything . . .

"I want to apologize."

What?

"What for?"

"For wimping out on you last night."

He put his cup down, pulled her up from her chair, and lifted her chin so he could look into her eyes. "You didn't wimp out. You have fears, and I understand. You have nothing to apologize for. We'll get there when we're both ready, and when we do, expect to hear angels singing and trumpets blaring."

"Don't you think having an audience would be a little distracting?"

He laughed. "You know what I mean. And I need to get going. I'll be back in about an hour. Kiss me." God, but she had the softest lips. And he desperately needed that shower.

He jogged back to his house, and as soon as he closed the door, he stripped as he ran to the bathroom. He turned on the shower full blast, and when the water was hot enough, he stepped in. He soaped up, wrapped his fist around his cock, and jerked while imagining he was inside her. He hadn't had to do this in years. It only took a few seconds, and he felt a little better. Masturbation was supposed to be a sin, but it eased some of the pressure. Maybe this would keep him from exploding too fast when they finally made love. He had to make it good for her. More than anything, he wanted to give her pleasure and show her what it was supposed to be like.

He had a few minutes before he had to leave, so he called his mother, intending to tease her with hints.

"Michael, is everything okay?"

"Yeah, Mom. Everything is great."

"Then why the call? I'll see you in church in a bit, won't I?"

"I just wanted to give you a heads-up that I won't be alone."

Dead silence.

"Mom?"

"Blessed Saint Mary, you're bringing a woman!"

"Yes, Mom, and you're going to love her."

"Do you?"

"Do I what?"

"Love her."

"We're taking it slow, but I think it'll go that way."

"Is she Catholic?"

"Yes."

"Then I can die a happy woman. She's coming to dinner, yes?"

"That's the plan. Are all my brothers going to be there?"

"Well, no one's said they can't. And I'm sure they'll be thrilled to meet the woman who finally healed your heart."

"I'm not sure I want to inflict this on her so soon."

"They'll be on their best behavior or I'll get my BB gun out. Besides, they're a little too old to be acting up, don't you think?"

If she only knew. "I just don't want to scare her away." He needed to warn her. "Look, I've got to run. I'm picking her up in a few minutes. Save me two seats, okay?"

"Did you go to confession?"

"Wednesday." He needed another week to psych himself up before he confessed what he'd done that morning and what he planned to do that night.

"Okay, honey. See you soon. Love you."

"Love you, too."

Elaine was waiting for him in the alley, and she was beautiful.

"Nice car."

"She's been with me a long time."

"She suits you. So why are we going so early?"

"I want you to meet my mother."

"*Oh,* dear. Did you tell her about me?"

"Not everything. I told her you're Catholic, and she said now she can die happy."

"Well, I told you I don't believe in all that stuff. I hope that's not going to be a problem for her."

"Don't worry about it. But I have to warn you about something."

"*Uh-oh.* What?"

"Three of my brothers and their wives will be there for dinner. John and Jimmy will be alone."

"Five brothers? Well, don't worry about me. I've got a black belt, remember?"

He burst out laughing at the thought of her roundhouse kicking and Karate chopping her way through the Chandler Horde.

"Maybe I should warn them about you."

25

O ut of habit, she dipped a finger in the font and genuflected. It wasn't anything more than an empty gesture. It meant nothing to her.

"I see her."

He led her down the aisle to a pew very close to the front.

"Mom, this is Elaine Chambéry. Elaine, this is my mom, Mary Chandler."

"Nice to meet you, Mrs. Chandler."

"It's wonderful to meet you, Elaine, but please call me Mary. Here, sit next to me. You're coming to dinner, aren't you, dear?"

"Yes, Mom. She is. And I hope you know I meant what I said this morning."

"Actually, John called right after you did. Seems he's been seeing someone and asked if he could bring her to dinner, too."

"Listen, Mom, there's something you should know."

"Not now, dear. Services will be starting soon."

It didn't surprise her when it all came back. She remembered all the prayers and all the responses. After all, she'd had twenty years of indoctrination. But she declined when their pew rose to go take the sacrament. She expected Mary to make a comment, but the woman didn't say a word. She didn't even raise an eyebrow.

When the services were over, they filed out. Michael paused to shake the old priest's hand and introduce her.

"Welcome, Elaine. I look forward to talking with you later."

Later?

"Father Timothy always comes to dinner on Sundays."

"Yeah, and he makes a good referee, too."

"Michael, you're not giving Elaine a very good impression of our family."

"She has a right to know what she might be in for. And by the way, she has a black belt in Karate, so it's your sons you should worry about."

"Michael, you're not giving your mother a very good impression of *me*. I'm sure everything will be fine. We're not talking about teenagers, right?"

"I'll let you be the judge."

Two blocks from the church, he pulled over, got out of the car, and came around to the passenger side. He opened the door, pulled her out, wrapped his arms around her, and kissed her until she couldn't breathe.

"What was that for?"

"I just needed to kiss you. Do you mind?"

"Never. You can kiss me anytime you want."

☒

All five brothers showed up, three with their wives and younger children. John showed up with his new girlfriend. Jimmy, or James as he preferred, was alone. She should have taken notes during the introductions. They all had the same shade of blue eyes, and they were all very attractive. But Michael was just plain hot.

After Father Timothy said grace, and while they passed the food, he asked, "So, Elaine, how did you and Michael meet?"

"Actually, we met twelve years ago when he came to my rescue. We reconnected the other day when I brought a client to meet with him"

The mood around the table changed, but no one said a word until John spoke up. "Wow. Wait to go, Mike. You're dating the woman you were with when you should have been home with your wife. Wonder what Sandy would say about that."

"JOHN GABRIEL CHANDLER! What a horrible thing to say!"

For such a sweet looking-woman, she sure had the *mom* voice down.

"Well, it's true, isn't it?"

John's words stabbed her heart. "Yes, it's true. And we both paid for that day. Michael lost his wife, and when my husband got out of prison early, I almost lost my life. It's taken both of us a long time to come to terms with that. Michael? I'm sorry, but I need to go. Don't get up. I'll call a cab."

"No, you won't! I'll drive you." He threw his napkin down, pushed his chair away from the table, and stood. "Mom, I'm sorry, but it seems John's channeling Dad."

"Michael, Elaine, please don't leave."

"Can't stay Mom."

Just then, John's girlfriend whisper-yelled, "No, no way. If that's how you treat your brother's girlfriend after what she's been through, then I don't want anything to do with you. You're an inconsiderate jerk and I've had it. Don't bother getting up and don't call me. Ever. Again."

Cynthia stood up, grabbed her phone out of her purse, and called what was probably a cab company as she stormed out of the house with John chasing after her.

She shouldn't have said anything, and she wouldn't have if he had only warned her his youngest brother was such an asshole. "Michael, can you please take me home? Mrs. Chandler, Mary, I'm sorry I ruined dinner. I guess I thought everyone would be glad that Michael finally found some happiness after all these years."

Father Timothy touched her shoulder. "Elaine, dear, please don't go. Let's all sit down and finish this lovely meal. Then we can talk."

"Really, Father. It's okay. I should have been more sensitive."

Mark, the oldest said, "No it's not okay. The *runt* was the insensitive one."

Matt, the second oldest, added, "Yeah, the *runt* was way out of line. I know I speak for the rest of us when I say we couldn't be happier that you two got together. Everything happens for a reason, right, Father?"

"That's right. John must have some other issues going on, and he hasn't confided in me, either. Now please, Michael, Elaine, sit down. I know what Michael went through, but I'd like to hear what happened to you."

The last thing she wanted to do was tell everyone at the table how Dan had tried to kill her. But maybe if they knew, they'd understand what a . . . shit. The only word she could think of was *miracle*. Was it a miracle they'd found each other? "Okay. But it's not dinner conversation. Maybe after dessert?"

"Of course, dear. And I'm so sorry about John. I don't know what's gotten into my youngest son, lately. Now please, everyone, eat before it gets cold."

She was a mom, all right. Apologizing for her son's behavior.

The conversation turned to sports and the stock market. After dinner, she and Michael shooed his mother out of the kitchen, took care of the dishes and made coffee.

Michael blew out the big five and zero candles, and everyone ate a slice of ice cream cake which she could barely fit in. There were no gifts to open. He'd told her how years ago he made it clear he didn't want any gifts and would throw them out if anyone ignored his *request*.

While everyone sipped their coffee, she related the whole painful story. When she finished, his brother's wives passed around a tissue box. Even the men seemed to blink back tears. And though he knew what happened, Michael still looked like he wanted to kill someone.

Note to self: never get on Michael's bad side.

Father Timothy was the first to speak. "You're a very brave young woman, Elaine, just like Michael is a very brave young man.

You two have been through your own hell, and now you've come together and found peace, and I, for one, am overjoyed."

Mary wiped her eyes with a tissue. *"Oh,* Elaine, I'm so sorry. What courage it must have taken! And you've accomplished so much, just like Michael. How does that saying go, Father? *From tragedy, the courageous triumph."*

"Yeah, so the next time I see the asshole, I'm going to let him have it."

"Mark Christopher, you will do no such thing!"

"Yeah, I know, Mom. But what he said was cruel and rude. If he knew the whole story . . ."

All the brothers seemed to have the same temper because Luke still seethed. "I don't think it would make any difference. He's too much like Dad." Matt and Luke agreed, and their wives buzzed with righteous indignation.

"I'm sorry I caused problems for your family. It never occurred to me that anyone would blame me for Michael's wife's murder after all these years."

"Elaine, honey, no one blames you. No one ever blamed you. John's just an asshole. Mom, thank you for dinner, but we need to get going."

"Yes, thank you so much for your hospitality and dinner was delicious."

"You're very welcome my dear. Please come back. Michael? You'll bring her back, right?"

"Yes, Mom. But next time, no John."

They were almost out the door when James stopped them and gave Michael a bear hug. Then he turned to her, hugged her, and whispered, "Thank you for making my brother happy again."

"He makes me happy, and I never thought I'd feel this way."

"Come on, Ms. Chambéry. We can still get home in time for the sunset."

"Okay, Mr. Chandler."

They were two blocks away from his mother's house when he

pulled over again, got out, pulled her out, and engulfed her in his arms. "Are we okay?"

"Of course. He just caught me off guard. If I'd known what he was like, I never would have said anything. I would never have ruined your birthday like that."

"Please don't judge my family by that asshole's actions. They're all crazy, and they fight a lot, but the others aren't mean and spiteful like John. I promise, that will never happen again."

"It's okay. Really. Now take me home so we can watch the sunset, and then you can make love to me."

"Your wish is my command."

That asshole hurt her. And if he ever got his hands on his brother, he'd show him how it felt. He needed to make it up to her.

They watched the sunset from the Strand, and then he led her into his house thankful he straightened it up before he'd left that morning. It wasn't anything fancy, but it suited him and the beach. One thing it did have going for it was a big Jacuzzi tub which he hoped to get her into. "Well, what do you think?"

"I like it. It's masculine, but not a man cave."

"Come with me. I want to show you something."

"Your etchings?"

"Funny. No, something better." Her mouth dropped open when she saw the tub. "How about a soak?"

"Naked?"

"Well, yes. Is that a problem? I mean, if I'm going to make love to you, it won't be through your clothes."

"You're right. Sure. Let's soak. But not too long."

"Why?"

"Don't you know what happens to men if they spend too much time in a Jacuzzi?"

"Yes, *I* know, but I'm wondering how *you* know about that."

"Latesha told me."

"What else did Latesha tell you?"

"Lots of things, but I learned most of it from watching her porn collection and reading erotic romance novels."

He needed to put Latesha on his Christmas card list.

He started the water, added some bath oil, and when the tub was full, he turned off the water and started the jets. She kicked off her shoes, and he kissed her as he removed her dress, unhooked her sexy, strapless bra, and pushed her matching panties down. She was bare, something he hadn't gotten to see that morning which was just as well. Instantly erect, he kneeled down and kissed her smooth mound. "I thought you said you haven't been with anyone?"

She gasped at the sensation of his lips on her sensitive skin. "I haven't. Latesha once talked me into getting waxed. I liked it so much, I kept it up. Do you like it?"

God bless Latesha.

He stood up and cleared his throat. "In you go."

She eased her way into the water, and when he was undressed, he climbed in behind her. When she leaned back into his chest, the rightness was overpowering.

"*Ah.* This is wonderful Michael!"

He couldn't speak. He could only close his eyes while gratitude consumed him.

"Hey, are you okay?"

"Yes. Yes, I am. Very okay."

They soaked in silence while the soothing jets of hot water massaged their bodies. After a few minutes, he reached his arms around her and fondled her nipples. The jolt of her body encouraged him to play a little more, and soon she squirmed against his erection.

That had to stop or he'd go off in the bath water.

He eased her forward, stood up, and held his hand out so he could help her up. He wrapped her in a fluffy, white towel and grabbed one for himself. After they were dry, he grabbed a fresh towel to spread on the bed and laid her down on it. Then he laid down next to her.

♡

This is really going to happen!

He kissed her and then slowly, excruciatingly slowly, he worked his way down her body. He stopped to kiss each scar as he went. Then he moved from the foot of the bed and ran his lips up and down each leg, again kissing every scar. He dragged his tongue up her inner thighs, stopping just shy of where she didn't know she needed him.

Frustration and fear combined. Every inch of her skin tingled. Dan never did anything to her down there, and all she knew was what was in those videos and what she'd done to herself and that wasn't even close.

Finally, he spread her legs wide and gave her one long lick, and her back bowed off the bed.

"Okay?"

Her breath caught as she struggled to whisper, "Yeah." She couldn't believe what he could do with his tongue. No matter how many videos she'd watched, no matter how many books she'd read, she could never have imagined how this would feel or how her body would react.

Then he stopped.

NO!

"I want you to orgasm. Okay?"

No problem. Just as long as he went back to what he was doing. It was like nothing she could have imagined. It put the rabbit to shame. And when it was over, her muscles refused to work.

He put on a condom and crawled up her body. When he kissed her, she tasted herself on him. That should have embarrassed her, but he didn't seem to mind. As he continued to kiss her, he positioned himself between her legs and gently edged them apart. "Ease me in, sweetheart."

She reached between them, gently took his rock-hard cock in her hand and aimed it where she needed it to go. Then he slowly pressed. He entered her a little at a time and waited for her to adjust to his size. Between the wetness inside her and the lubricated condom, it was almost painless. When he was all the way in, he propped himself up on his elbows and looked at her.

"You're so beautiful, and you feel so good, I don't know how long I'm going to last. Are you okay?"

"I never imagined it could feel like this. It doesn't hurt at all."

"Do you think you could orgasm again?"

"I don't know. After that one, I don't see how. But you feel so, so, I don't know. But I need you to move or something."

He set a slow pace as he rocked all the way out and all the way in. He kissed her as he moved, and soon that feeling began to build again. She instinctively wrapped her legs around his waist while he kissed her lips, then each of her eyelids, and then back to her mouth. It was intimate and sweet and sensual. And she imagined them enveloped in a cloud of love.

She was close when he said, "Touch yourself, honey. I'm not going to last, and I want you to climax with me."

Touching herself while he was inside her seemed naughty, somehow, but she was too turned on to be embarrassed. She reached between them and stroked herself. He moved a little faster as her breathing became gasps. It wasn't at all like Dan and the way he humped like he was late for a client meeting. This was more like what she'd seen in those videos.

"Baby, I'm going to come."

Something about the way he said it made her insides spasm which lit the fuse.

He pressed in as far as he could and held still while she detonated with him, and they both cried out.

For a split second, guilt flashed through him, but it was gone almost before he realized what it was.

She's not Sandy.

It was different. Not better, not worse, just different, and there was something he never thought he'd ever feel again.

Contentment.

When they each caught their breath, and as soon as he felt himself soften, he reluctantly withdrew. "I'll be right back. Don't move!"

"Yes, sir."

He disposed of the condom and threw some cold water on his face to wake up in case this was a dream. But it wasn't a dream. It was real. He looked up, whispered, "Thank you, God," crossed himself, and went back to the bedroom. She was snuggled under the covers, and he didn't have the heart to wake her up. It was eleven, and they both had to be at work in the morning. Maybe just a short nap.

☧

"MICHAEL! Wake up! Shit! We slept in, and it's late, and I have to get home and get ready to go to work. I have an appointment in fifteen minutes! Wake up!"

She was almost dressed by the time he was alert enough to realize what was going on. "God, Elaine. I'm so sorry. When I came back to bed, you were already sound asleep. I didn't want to wake you. I thought I'd wake up early enough, but . . . Wait! Let me throw some jeans on, and I'll drive you to work."

"No. Thank you, but no. I've got to go — now. Thank you for a wonderful evening. I'll talk to you later."

Before he had a chance to say anything, she was gone.

26

An hour later, he walked into his office to find Tina waiting, tapping her foot impatiently.

"What?"

"You're late. You have to get the rest of Lisa Weston's documents filed this morning. I hope they're done because the process server will be here in ten minutes. And you have an appointment in twenty. And why are you late? You're never late!"

"Calm down. The docs are done."

"Okay. The Lewis file is on your desk, and you're due in court at one for the Richards' case. Since you're late, I'm guessing you had a good weekend?"

"Unbelievable. But I don't have time to tell you about it right now. Besides, it's none of your business. Any chance I can get out of here early today?"

"Your last appointment is at three. And your first appointment tomorrow is at ten although you didn't ask."

"You're right. I didn't. And you're awfully nosy."

"I'm channeling your mother."

"Wonderful. Get me some coffee and some cherry yogurt."

"What's the magic word?"

Sigh.

"Please."

They needed to give her a raise.

He'd filed the complaint and Request to Freeze Assets last week. Once the court order was in place, Lisa Weston would be able to collect the judgment when the judge signed off. He already had the summons with a copy of the recorded complaint prepared. Serving would be tricky since Gerald was in San Quentin.

After he cleared it with prison officials, the process server left. Gerald had thirty days to respond. This would give Lisa time to recuperate from her surgery.

Back at the office, he made a list of supporting evidence for the discoveries which mostly consisted of the police reports, hospital and doctor bills, emergency room personnel depositions, a deposition from her plastic surgeon, photographs of her injuries, and Elaine's testimony.

Since Gerald wasn't going anywhere for the next nine years, he planned to ask for fifty percent of the man's assets. Based on his experience, the man's trial records, the extent of her injuries, and her expense statement, he was confident the jury would find this reasonable.

After his last appointment, he got ready to leave.

"So, where are you going?"

"So, none of your business."

"So, flowers the next day are a good idea."

"So, still none of your business."

"See you in the morning?"

"Don't you have any work to do?" He enjoyed matching wits with Tina. But she had a point.

He stopped at a florist on his way home and picked up a bouquet of colorful daisies in a blue china vase, and since she wasn't home when he got to her house, he placed the vase on her porch.

"*Whoa,* dude! Like who are you and what do you want with Elaine?"

"*Uh,* who are you?"

The taller twenty-something with the sun-bleached hair and

carrying a surfboard answered, "We're her boys. We like help out and totally watch out for her. So like what do you want with her?"

The accusatory tone irritated him, but part of him was glad she had men — well, almost men — watching out for her. It wouldn't be necessary anymore, but that was up to her to tell them.

"I'm not sure that's any of your business, but it's good you're protective. We're dating, and it's serious."

"Like no offense, dude. But how do we know you're not gonna like hurt her like her ex did?"

"She told you about that?"

"Dude. The scars?"

"And like when she first moved in, she was like kinda scared of *us*."

"So, dude, like where do you live?"

"The next block down, on the Strand."

"Cool. Cause like if we find out you hurt her, we'll totally be payin' you a visit."

"I'm not going to hurt her. We have a history that goes back a long time. But thanks for watching out for her."

Surfer number one said, "Later, dude," while surfer number two pointed to his eyes and then pointed at him, the universal warning that they would be *like totally* watching him. He was glad she had them, and he didn't mind that they still kept an eye out for her. But they didn't need to be so diligent, not with him.

It was only four, so he jogged home, changed into jeans and a t-shirt and jogged back. He made himself comfortable on the stucco barrier where he could watch her reaction when she saw the flowers. He hadn't included a card. There were no words to describe how affected he was by everything that had happened since they reconnected.

His stomach fluttered when she turned the corner and let herself into her patio. He waited while she picked up the vase, probably looking for a card. When she didn't find one, she turned around. Maybe she felt him watching her? When she spotted him, her smile beamed directly into his heart.

He walked toward her, but what he really wanted to do was run. When he got to her, he took the vase from her hands, put it down, and kissed her like his life depended on it. Because it did. His new life. The life she breathed into him.

"Wow. Nice greeting. And I love the flowers. Thank you."

"You're welcome."

"What time did you get here?"

"About an hour ago. I got interrogated by your fan club."

"Fan club?"

"Yeah. They watch out for you. Didn't you know that? They wanted to know my intentions. And they threatened me with bodily harm if I hurt you."

"They guessed my story, but we've never talked about it. They're just a couple of sweet kids. I think they think of me as an aunt or something. So why the flowers?"

She opened the door, and he followed her into the front room. "I wanted to. This weekend was beyond words which is why there's no card. Elaine, honey, you deserve the world, and I want to give it to you."

"*Uh,* wow. I don't know what to say. No one except my parents ever wanted to give me anything. Well, Dan liked giving me black eyes and split lips, but I don't think that's what you meant."

No, that's not what he meant, and he had to pretend he hadn't heard her. "Does this attention bother you?"

"No. I just don't know how to react."

"Don't think about it. Just do what you feel."

"Well, I feel like dragging you into the bedroom and showing my appreciation."

"*Hmm.* I guess that would be okay." He tried to act cool, but he couldn't hide his big smile.

She wanted to give him the same pleasure he'd given her, but she didn't know how to get started. All she knew was what she saw in those videos. Dan never demanded that she do anything except lay there, and when he was done, he was *done*. Considering how brutal he could be, that had been a good thing. "I want to do for you what you did for me."

"What's that?"

"This is kind of embarrassing. I've never used words like these before, and I hope I don't sound silly or slutty, but I want to give you a blowjob, except I don't know how."

"You want to? Or you think you should. Because I will never expect you to do anything you don't want to do."

"I want to. I never wanted to with Dan, and he never made me. But I want to please you. Will you show me what to do?"

He looked like he was giving it a lot of thought, and that's not what she wanted. It was time to take things in hand, so to speak. She walked up to him, pressed her body against his, and kissed the closest part of him her lips could reach, which was the hollow of his neck. Then she pulled his shirt out of his jeans and lifted it up to expose his chest with its smattering of silver and abs that would put a man half his age to shame. She heard him sigh as he reached down and pulled the shirt over his head.

Encouraged, she undid his belt and the buttons on his jeans revealing the hard — and getting harder — erection that poked out the top of his briefs. He moved so she could sit on the couch while he stood in front of her. Then he took her cheek in his hand and lifted her chin so he could study her face.

"Are you sure?"

"Yes."

"Just start with what you think I'd like. I'll let you know if you do something wrong. The most important thing to remember is, no teeth."

She pushed his jeans and boxer briefs down to his ankles and came face to face with his cock. His big, beautiful, silky smooth cock. She closed her eyes and thought back to what he'd done to her, so she licked him from the base to the tip like a popsicle. From his gasp, she figured he liked that so she did it again. This time, she swirled her tongue around the engorged head and licked the small drop that formed. It didn't seem to have much of a taste. She wanted to take him in her mouth, but he was so damned big, she wasn't sure she could do it. She tried to disengage her jaw like snakes did and stuffed as much of him in as she could fit without gagging.

"Put your hand around so you can control how deep I can go. I don't want to choke you."

"*Mmm mmm.*"

"Jesus! Don't do that or I'll go off like a rocket."

She maintained suction as she pulled back until she released him. His face was scrunched like he was in pain. "Did I hurt you?"

"No. It feels so good, but it's been a really long time."

She smiled and went back to treating his cock like a cherry popsicle, alternating licking with taking as much as she could in her mouth and sucking. She held him at the base with one hand and gently massaged his balls with the other, all while working him with her mouth. It didn't take long until he began to thrust. She wanted to take more, but that was something she needed to practice. For now, her hand kept him from going too deep.

"Honey, I'm going to come. If you don't want it in your mouth, finish me with your hand." His voice was strained, and he tried to pull away, but she held on while increasing how fast she plunged down and pulled back up. She took a little more each time and listened to his moans. He stopped moving and put his hand on the back of her head, but she kept going.

Jet after jet of warm salty liquid filled her mouth, and she swallowed trying to keep up while he groaned louder. Finally, he held her head still and gradually backed away.

He tripped over his jeans as he made his way to the couch and collapsed next to her while trying to catch his breath.

She wiped her chin and smiled. "Did I do it right?"

Did she do it *right?* The question was so absurd he started laughing, but she seemed to be waiting for him to critique her oral abilities. He needed to get his brain reconnected with his mouth. "Are you sure you've never done that before?"

"I watched Latesha's videos and thought about what you did to me. Was it okay?"

"*Uh,* well, *okay* isn't how I'd describe it. Give me a minute." He never expected her to do that, and he needed to send flowers and candy to Latesha. Elaine was unbelievable. Innocent and experienced at the same time. They were perfectly matched, just like the animals had said.

When he could move without trembling, he stood, pulled his jeans up, and took her hand.

"Where are we going?"

"Your bedroom. Your turn."

"I didn't do that because I expected to take turns."

"I know. But right now, I need to taste you."

Her eyes widened. Then without saying another word, she followed him. When they got to the bedroom, she reached to unbutton her jeans, but he stopped her.

"Let me."

She nodded her head, and he went to work removing her clothes like he was unwrapping a present. Then he laid her on the bed so her legs draped off the side. He spread her open with his hands and took a taste.

Honey and heaven. The other night had not been his imagination.

He caressed her with his tongue until she panted and squirmed, then he put one finger in and found her G-spot. She cried out, so he increased the pressure of his tongue and finger. She cried, "*Oh,* fuck, I'm going to pee!" She squirmed to get away from him, but he held her in place with his other arm. She groaned until her body stiffened. Her juices, her female ejaculate, spilled out of her, and she screamed.

When she quieted, he removed his finger and gently kissed her smooth skin.

"Fuck."

"Was that okay?" he teased.

"I have no words."

"Then I'll take that as a yes." Kneeling at the foot of the bed he helped her sit up. Everything under her was wet. "I think we made a mess of your bedspread."

"It'll dry. But if you're going to do that to me again, I'll keep towels in here."

"So what should we do, now?"

She playfully punched him in the arm and tried to stand up, but her legs wobbled.

"Whoa! I think my bones melted."

They heard growling which seemed to come from her stomach. "Hungry much?"

"Starved. Just give me a minute to get my brain cells back."

"Now you know how I felt." He gathered their clothes and helped her dress. While she pulled herself together, he got a towel and tried to blot up the evidence. "Do you want to go out somewhere or call for a pizza?"

"Pizza sounds good. I'm not sure I can handle dealing with the outside world right now."

"Sausage, mushrooms, olives, and . . .?"

"Make them black olives, and that's perfect. I have sodas in the fridge."

He called in the order.

"Good timing. The driver was about to make the last deliveries for the night. It'll be here in thirty minutes. After we eat, and you can think again, we need to talk about Lisa's case." He walked out to give her some privacy.

When she came into the living room, he forgot what they needed to talk about. Her hair was bed-messy, and she had that unmistakable glow of a woman who was completely and thoroughly satisfied. He wanted to keep that look on her face for many years to come — one day at a time.

"So what's the next step? You filed the complaint, and he's been served, and now we have to wait for the response. What can we do in the meantime?"

His brain synapses started firing again. "I need to collect the rest of the depositions. I'll need one from her neighbor, the ER doctor, and her plastic surgeon. And you, too. And I want to talk to the original prosecutor. Something's been bothering me about the way they handled her case."

"Like what?"

"Like the DA's office is usually more vigilant about the victim's rights and securing more than adequate restitution. She didn't get anything close to what she needed or deserved, and she knew nothing about her options. She didn't know about your department, and that's just not typical. My sponsor, Bruce, is kind of a private investigator. I think I'm going to have him do some digging."

"You think there was collusion?"

"I don't know, but my gut says something's not right, and I always listen to my gut."

"Is that a Gibbs thing?"

"No. It's a Chandler thing. So as long as we're waiting for the pizza, I might as well call Bruce now."

"So late?"

"It's not that late, and he won't mind."

As soon as he got off the phone with Bruce, the pizza arrived. He told her about the conversation as they sat on the floor with the box on the coffee table. "Well, it seems there are others who are looking at this assistant DA. This isn't the first time he's screwed over a domestic battery victim. Bruce is going to meet with his team tomorrow and start digging."

"Wow. Well, that would explain a few things. I hope he finds concrete proof. Meanwhile, she's going in for surgery tomorrow. I offered to take her, but her neighbor will be with her. This is an outpatient procedure, so she'll be home tomorrow night."

"How long is the recuperation?"

"At least two weeks for the stitches and probably months before all the swelling goes down. She's one brave woman. Every time I look at her or think about what she's gone through, I realize how lucky I was that my injuries were below my neck and easy to hide. Someday I'll look into doing something about these ugly scars."

"Yes, she's brave, but so are you. You took a tragedy and turned it into a triumph. And your scars are *not* ugly. They're a reminder that you survived. You have no idea how beautiful you are, do you?" She blushed and looked down at her lap. "Come here."

She got up, came around to the other side of the coffee table, and sat on the floor next to him. He put one arm around her, took her chin in his other hand, and lifted her face so he could see into her eyes. "You're incredible. You're brave and beautiful and smart. And you seem to like me." He kissed her lightly.

"No, I don't like you."

What?

"I love you. I'm not going to question it. It just feels right, like I've always loved you. I know you're still in love with your wife. I understand. But that doesn't change how I feel, and I want to be honest with you."

He knew she loved him. She'd said it before. He loved her, too. But he needed to reconcile that with how he'd loved Sandy. Was it possible to love two women that much? Was it cheating? Was he somehow betraying Sandy by admitting his love for Elaine? He needed to talk to someone. "Elaine, I . . ." He didn't have the words to tell her how he felt.

"It's okay. You don't have to say anything. You show me with your actions. I know you have things to work out. Like I said, it doesn't change anything. Are you finished with the pizza?"

No, it didn't change anything, but it bothered her that he couldn't express how he felt. His wife had been one lucky woman. Maybe someday he'd feel the same way about her. It didn't matter though. There was nothing she could do about it, and she wouldn't pressure him.

They cleaned up the living room and stored the rest of the pizza in the fridge. "Let's sit out on the patio. It's warm, and the stars are out."

He took her hand. "Elaine, honey, I want you to understand."

"You don't have to explain anything. Nothing you say or don't say will change how I feel. It doesn't matter, so please, don't worry about it."

"I care about you. I care about you so much. And it probably is love. I just never thought I'd meet someone, and I'm struggling with this feeling, like I'm being unfaithful — which is stupid since she's been gone for twelve years."

"Look, the last thing I want is for you to feel bad about how you feel about me. Let's just let it go. You'll work it out when you're ready."

"I don't want to hurt you."

"You can't."

They watched the stars in silence for the next hour.

"I need to get home. I have a discovery to write and motions to prepare."

"Okay."

"I'll call you tomorrow."

"Okay."

He stood, pulled her out of her chair, and kissed her for a long time. "I don't want to leave you."

"But you have to."

"Yeah." He hugged her, let go, and let himself out onto the Strand.

"Thank you."

"For?"

"The orgasm and pizza."

He laughed. "Anytime."

She hoped he meant that.

She went inside and got ready for bed. Then she stripped the sheets and comforter and started a load of laundry that would finish in the morning. She didn't want to wash away the signs and smells of what he'd done to her, but there would be other times. She just had to be patient.

After she remade the bed, she laid down and closed her eyes.

"He really loves you, you know."

"Who are you?" She didn't need to ask. It could only be one person.

"It's okay. I couldn't have picked a better woman for him. Just be patient."

She woke with a start. She still didn't believe in that mumbo jumbo stuff, but that had to be his dead wife. What should have freaked her out comforted her. She just needed to be patient.

27

He was having one of those dreams again. He should have expected it.

"You love her."

"Yes, I do, but I love you, too."

"I know you do, but it's way past time for you to move on. She's perfect for you, and there are terrible things coming, and the two of you will need each other."

"What do you mean, terrible things?"

"Danger."

"What kind of danger?"

"You need her, and she needs you. Don't lose her."

"What kind of danger?"

"She loves you. Don't let her go."

"Wait! Sandy!"

He woke in a sweat. Danger? Was Elaine in danger? Did it have to do with Lisa's case?

It was two in the morning.

Shit.

There was no way he could go back to sleep after that dream so he got up, made a pot of coffee, and sat down to check his email.

Bruce had been busy, and it was worse than he thought. He

didn't want to know how many laws his sponsor had broken in the process, but he'd found a connection between Gerald Weston and the assistant DA to the tune of a hundred thousand dollars. This was the ADA who hadn't asked for nearly as much restitution as he could have. In a nutshell, the man had taken a bribe. Bruce found proof of the transactions and dug deeper. It was likely this wasn't the first time this ADA had colluded with a defendant.

His priority had to be getting justice for Lisa Weston. As a civil litigation attorney, he couldn't go after the ADA himself, but he had friends in the DA's office who would do their own research and find corroborating evidence. What Bruce found, and the way he found it, would not be admissible as evidence and it would be best if no one knew about his methods.

By the time he finished all the documents for Lisa's case, it was seven. He got ready to drive to the office and sent Elaine a text telling her he had news and asked if she would have lunch with him. Five minutes later, she answered with a smiley face, so he sent "12:30?" and got back another smiley face.

It was a busy morning. He had briefs to prepare for five other cases besides Lisa's. When he finished and was about to answer emails, Tina stuck her head in the door.

"Elaine's here."

How was it twelve-thirty already? "Send her in, please. And hold my calls. And could you get us some food? Maybe Chinese?"

"She's in the conference room, and food won't be necessary."

When he walked in, Elaine was spreading a checkered tablecloth over the big table. "What's all this?"

"I thought I'd bring lunch to you. There's a place a couple blocks away that makes up these baskets. There's chicken salad, tuna salad, different breads, an assortment of condiments, and ambrosia for dessert. I added bottled water. They even include plates, napkins, forks, and knives. I hope this is okay."

"Okay? This is great! And a good idea since I have a lot to tell you. There's a new development, something I would never have thought possible." He told her about Bruce's findings while they made their sandwiches.

"Wow. I sure didn't see that coming. But it answers a lot of questions. What are we going to do?"

We?

"*We* aren't going to do anything about that. I just sent the information to some people I know in the fraud division at the DA's office. They'll know how to proceed. But yeah, this sure answers a lot of questions. And it means I have to push for an early trial."

"Why?"

"Because their investigation could hold up our case while they put their case together, and that could take months. If my trial date is set, they'll wait before they subpoena any of my files."

"So where do we stand?"

Tina stuck her head in the door. "Sorry to interrupt, but this just arrived. It has Lisa Weston's case number on it."

"Thanks." He opened the envelope, and his jaw dropped.

"What is it?"

"It's Gerald Weston's answer to the complaint. No contest."

"No contest?"

"Yeah. I asked for two million which he's agreed to."

"That doesn't sound like a man who is doing nine years in San Quentin. Something's not right."

"I know. But I've got to get this recorded before we dig too deeply. Excuse me a minute while I give Tina the information for the forms."

He stepped out and gave the envelope back to Tina. "I need a Request for Summary Judgment prepared. And see if you can get me an appointment with the clerk today. I want to get this recorded as soon as possible."

"Will do. *Oh,* and your appointment this afternoon just canceled."

Perfect. Now he had more time to spend with Elaine. He walked back to the conference room and sat down. "My next appointment canceled, and Tina's preparing the Request for Summary Judgment docs and getting me an appointment with the court clerk. All I have to do is file the request."

"That's great, but I have an uneasy feeling about this. It was too easy."

"I know. A man as vicious as Gerald Weston doesn't just agree to pay his ex-wife two million dollars unless . . ."

"Unless he's got a way of getting it back."

"I think I'll ask Bruce to dig a little deeper into Mr. Weston's finances."

After he sent the text, she said, "So? What's next?"

"What does your afternoon look like?"

She checked the calendar on her phone. "It appears I'm open. I have some paperwork to finish, but that can wait. What did you have in mind?"

"How about after I make that stop at the courthouse, we go for a ride up the coast?"

"Sounds like fun."

"I'll pick you up as soon as I'm done."

The clerk of the court could fit him in at two o'clock and agreed to expedite the process. With any luck, Lisa would have her money by the time the bandages came off.

It was a warm day, but with the schools in session, the roads weren't clogged with teenagers cruising the beaches. He held her hand as he drove and they sang along with the radio.

Next stop: Santa Barbara for dinner at Castagnola's on the pier.

Lisa was somewhat aware of her surroundings, but when she tried to talk, it came out muffled like she was underwater. The anesthesia was wearing off.

Dr. Byford was by her side. "Hey, Lisa. Welcome back! The surgery was a complete success. I'm going to call your neighbor and let her know she can come pick you up. By the time she gets here, you'll be able to walk. Don't try to talk, now. The bandages around your mouth need to stay in place. I'm sending you home with pain medicine that will help you sleep. That's the best thing you can do right now."

Too many words.

What he said about the surgery filtered through the fog. A complete success? She wanted to ask about it, but the anesthesia fog kept her brain from functioning, and the bandages kept her lips from moving.

She wanted to thank him, but all she could do was moan. Maybe tomorrow.

Joan was there. Now she could go home and sleep it off.

"She's going to be very swollen for a while, and starting tomorrow, she needs to keep ice packs on both cheeks, her lips, and her eyes. There might be a little oozing, but that's normal. If she starts to bleed a lot, call me. And if the pain is too much, rather than take too many painkillers, I'll prescribe something stronger."

"Thank you, Doctor. Come on, Lisa. Easy does it."

Dr. Byford and Joan got her up and into Joan's car. She slept on the way home, and as soon as Joan got her into her guest bed, she went right back to sleep — until sometime in the middle of the night. At least she thought it was the middle of the night since she could only open her eyes a crack.

Every inch of her, from her neck up, throbbed and burned. She didn't want to wake Joan, but she couldn't stop moaning. It hurt almost as bad as the burns from the fire had.

"Hey, Sweetie. Are you okay? Need some painkiller?"

All she could do was groan.

"Okay. Here you go. Open up." Joan pushed a tablet on her tongue where it would dissolve. "The doctor said if one dose isn't enough, he'll write a prescription for something stronger. I guess too many of these might hurt your stomach. Now try to get some sleep, and if it hurts too much, groan. I'll hear you."

She tried to stick it out, but after a half hour the pain was still unbearable, so she groaned.

"Not working? Okay. I'm going to call the doctor."

She didn't want Joan to wake the man up, but she didn't have a choice. She heard the woman on the phone talking to him, but the pain was so bad she couldn't focus on the words. She drifted in and out of consciousness.

"Lisa? Wake up, dear. Dr. Byford is here."

"Hey there. Joan tells me you're in a lot of pain and the painkiller isn't working. Using your hands, tell me what the intensity is, zero being no pain and ten being unbearable."

She opened and closed both hand three times.

"How long ago did you give her the last dose?"

"About an hour."

"Okay. Lisa, I brought you something stronger. Joan, watch me."

He used a plastic syringe, the kind mothers used to give cough syrup to babies. "Fill it to here and then place the tip next to her tongue and press the plunger. Got it?"

"Yes, Doctor. Thank you for coming. I know Lisa didn't want me to call you since it's the middle of the night, but she's in too much pain."

"You did the right thing. She needs to sleep. I want to wait a few minutes and see if the morphine helps, and I might as well change her bandages while I'm here."

He was a dreamlike shadowy figure. Whatever he gave her was working nicely.

"Lisa? How's the pain now?"

She raised four fingers just before she fell asleep.

When she woke up, she could open her eyes a crack without passing out. Her head throbbed, but it was a seven and bearable.

"Joan?" She could move her lips a little but they were numb, and her voice was barely more than a whisper.

"Good morning, sweetie. No talking yet, okay? How's the pain?"

She raised seven fingers.

"Dr. Byford said if it's anything more than a six, I should give you another dose of morphine."

She whispered, "Not needed."

"He told me you'd try to downplay it, and if you said seven, it was probably more like eight. He sure is a nice man, and very easy on the eyes, don't you think?"

If she could have, she would have laughed. It seemed absurd to think about him like that while she probably looked and sounded like Boris Karloff in the original "The Mummy." When the morphine kicked in, and she could think about something besides the pain, she wondered how the civil suit was going.

Mr. Chandler asked for two million hoping to settle for one million. He was so confident about winning, she let herself imagine what she'd do with the money — what would be left after she paid off her medical bills, anyway. She definitely wanted to donate some to Dr. Byford's clinic.

If Gerald hadn't ruined her, she might have considered getting to know Robert Byford better, but thanks to her disfigurement, she had a hard time looking any man in the eye. Besides, wasn't it considered unethical for a doctor to take up with a patient? Of course, she wouldn't be his patient forever — not if the surgery was successful. He was so good looking and so nice, he was probably married, or maybe gay. Next time she saw him she needed to check his ring finger.

That painkiller was good for some awesome fantasies.

She slept the better part of the week, waking for baby food, water from a sippy cup, and to go to the bathroom. The pain had eased considerably, and she didn't need the morphine anymore, just some ibuprofen. She could talk but her lips were still numb.

"Lisa, dear, there's a Michael Chandler and Elaine Cham — Cham —"

"SHAMberry."

"Anyway, they're here, and he said he has something important to tell you. Can I show them in?"

Why not? The bandages had to look better than her face had. "Okay."

Joan led them in and propped her up on pillows.

"How are you feeling?"

She tried not to slur. "I'm okay. My lips don't seem to work yet, but Dr. Byford said the surgery was a success. It was very painful though. Thank God for morphine."

"This should make you feel better. Gerald isn't contesting. He's agreed to our settlement figure. I've filed his response and submitted the request for summary judgment. As soon as the judge approves it, we can arrange for payment. Lisa, he agreed to the full amount! Two million dollars!"

What?

"Joan? Did you sneak morphine into my juice? Mr. Chandler, there's no way he would give me the bird, let alone two million dollars. There's a catch. There has to be."

"No catch. And no counteroffer."

"Then he hid his assets well, and you'll never find the money."

"Actually, he didn't hide it well at all, and his net worth is considerably more than two million."

"Then why did the assistant DA tell me not to ask for more during the trial?"

"Well, that's a good question, and I have people looking into that. It appears there may have been collusion. But that's not something we're going to get involved with, and I don't want you to worry about it. I've already turned over my source's information to my contacts in the DA's office. The court clerk is expediting our settlement request so the judge should have it in front of him to sign today or tomorrow. Then we'll serve Gerald's bank with the court order, and if that goes smoothly, you should have two million dollars in a week or two."

"There's no way. I know him, and there's no way he'll agree to that."

"He already has."

"And I'm telling you, he's up to something. The man tried to burn me alive, and now he's going to give me two million dollars?"

Elaine spoke up. "Lisa, do you have life insurance?"

"I don't think so. Wait. Now that I think about it, he made me sign something. And an envelope addressed to me came in the mail last week. I forgot all about it. I thought maybe it was junk mail from one of those insurance companies. I didn't get a chance to throw the junk mail out."

"So you still have it?"

"Yes, but it's at my house, and I'm not supposed to do any walking except to the bathroom."

"Could Joan let us in? Does she have a key?"

"Yes, of course. Joan? Could you let Mr. Chandler and Elaine into my house? And show them where I keep the mail."

"Sure, Sweetie."

"I'll make a deal with you," he smiled. "If you'll call me Michael, I'll call you Lisa. Okay?"

Why couldn't she remember that? "Okay."

28

"She keeps her unopened mail on the desk in the den."

"Michael, here's a pile of junk mail, and I think this is what we're looking for. It's from Consolidated Life Insurance, and it looks like a policy envelope, not advertising. Should I open it?"

"Who's the envelope addressed to?"

"Lisa."

"Joan? Would you do the honors?" Since Joan was Lisa's caregiver, they avoided any questions regarding federal mail tampering laws.

Joan handed the form to Elaine who looked it over. "What does it say?"

"It's a confirmation of a policy Lisa took out naming Gerald as the beneficiary. It doesn't look like her signature's forged. But get this. The policy is dated one week before he attacked her."

"Let me see." He scanned the attached form and found the amount. One million dollars with an accidental death rider for another half a million. How could Gerald pull that off while he was in prison? Insurance companies were usually very thorough when investigating large payouts and possible foul play.

"Well, I don't know how he thinks he's going to pull it off, but it

MARY A. NASON

would seem Mr. Gerald Weston is planning to have his ex-wife killed for a million and a half dollars."

"How can he do that if he's in prison?"

"I don't know, but we need to get her some protection, like right now!"

"Wait. Mr. Chandler? There are two other envelopes from other insurance companies."

"Bring those, too."

They ran back over to Joan's house where Lisa was resting comfortably. He called Bruce, explained the situation, and got the phone number of a security company Bruce had worked with in the past, just in case.

The other two envelopes contained confirmations for two other life insurance policies, each for one million plus riders for an additional half a million. All were addressed to Lisa and had her signature. All named Gerald Weston as the owner and sole beneficiary.

"I'm going to keep these in my safe at the office. Lisa, do you remember signing three forms?"

"It was only one. I thought it was medical insurance, but Gerald had said one got lost in the mail and the other was a duplicate I had to endorse for his doctor."

"Did Gerald tell you why you needed the insurance?"

"No. But he said he had a life insurance policy on himself, so if anything happened to him, I'd be provided for. Kind of ironic, isn't it?"

"Do you remember seeing an envelope addressed to him?"

"No. Mr. Chan — I mean Michael? Am I in danger?"

"I'm not going to lie, Lisa. You have insurance policies totaling four and a half million dollars, and he's the owner and beneficiary on all three. I'm going to read them over and see what they say about accidental death and if they're payable in case of foul play. In the meantime, I can have a security company watch your home, and there will be someone with you at all times."

"See? Now you know why he agreed to the two million so fast. With me out of the way, he wouldn't have to pay any of it. I told you he was up to something. And I don't want to do anything that would put Joan in danger."

"He needs to get you out of the way before the summary judgment gets recorded or the two million will go into escrow, and he won't be able to stop the transfer. Listen, I know you're recovering, but we really need to get you moved to somewhere he can't find you."

"I still don't understand how he can do anything from prison."

"He's probably hired someone. I'll have my friend look into this, too. There's usually an upfront payment, like a deposit, and if there's a money trail, he'll find it. I need to meet with your doctor about getting you moved."

☒

"Hey, Bruce. What did you find?"

"Yeah, so this Weston guy is a real piece of work. No money's changed hands yet, but with the mob ties on his mother's side, my bet is he's going to have *Uncle Vito* take care of the details. Of course, they're smart enough to hire someone outside the family so none of it can be traced back to Weston. But lucky for you, I have my sources."

"Don't tell me. I'm sure your methods are completely legal. So keep digging. There's four and a half million and a life at stake. In the meantime, I've got to move Mrs. Weston someplace safe, and she just had facial reconstruction surgery."

"So other than that, how's life? We haven't met for a while, but I'm hoping you'd call if there were problems."

"Life is wonderful. Even the nocturnal animal visits are good. They all seem to think I've found *the one* they told me about during the vision quest."

"So you finally believe they're real?"

"If it was anyone but you, I'd say, of course not. But since it *is* you, and you can't have me committed, well, I have to admit, I do think they are. There *is* such a thing as sponsor-sponsee confidentiality, right?"

"There would have to be, or no one would do a complete fifth step. So, when do I get to meet the lady?"

"Maybe a Sunday dinner at Mom's as soon as I get Mrs. Weston safely hidden — or you find enough evidence to stop whatever her ex is up to. Okay?"

"Sounds good. Well, let me get back to it. Take it easy, Michael. I'll be in touch."

"Thanks for your help, man."

He disconnected and turned back to Lisa. "I need to talk to your doctor right now."

Even with the bandages and swelling he could see the fear in her eyes as Joan said, "I'll call him."

Elaine looked at him with one raised eyebrow. "Can I talk to you in the other room?" He followed her into the kitchen where Lisa wouldn't hear. "What did your friend say? I can tell by the look on your face it's not good."

"It's not. Bruce is still digging, and so far, there's no trace of money changing hands, but he agrees. With Gerald's family's mob ties, it's a safe bet that he's planning to have Lisa killed. I need to move her."

"*We* need to move her. She's my client, too."

"Elaine, sweetheart, this could get dangerous. I don't think I'd survive if something happened to you. I don't want you involved."

"Gibbs Rule 15. Always work as a team. I'm already involved. Besides, I have a black belt, remember?"

"Gibbs Rule 38. My case. My lead."

"Gibbs Rule 51. Sometimes you're wrong."

"Gibbs Rule 5. You don't waste good."

"You win." He pulled her into his arms and kissed her. He was in love with her and told her so with his lips and tongue. And she answered.

"Excuse me. Dr. Byford is on his way over."

"Good. Can you pack up some of Lisa's clothes?"

"Yes, and I can go next door and get more. How many days do you think?"

"I don't know. It could be a week, maybe two. I think Weston will move fast since once they record the judgment, the court will try to collect the money on her behalf. I'll call the clerk's office and see where we're at in the process."

Wasn't it bad enough Gerald had tried to kill her before? Now she had to worry about hitmen and life insurance policies. She just wanted her medical bills paid and enough to make house payments with since he wouldn't let her sell. Was that too much to ask? And now she had to hide while putting other people in danger — all because of Gerald's greed. In the ten years they'd been married, had the man ever loved her?

"Lisa, Dr. Byford's here."

"Hey, how are you feeling?"

"A lot better, and the pain isn't nearly as bad."

"Good. Let me check your bandages." He removed the old ones and checked the sutures before applying new bandages. "Looks very good. You're healing well. Now I understand we need to move you. Do you have a place to stay?"

"No. The few relatives I have live in New York, and I can't travel that far like this."

"No, you can't, but I may have a solution. Let me talk it over with Mr. Chandler."

Anything was better than sitting around waiting for whatever Gerald was planning.

Michael and Elaine walked into the guest room. "You have an idea?" Michael looked hopeful.

"I have a cabin up by Big Bear Lake. It's only accessible by four-wheel drive. Lisa can stay there."

"But I'd be alone!"

"No, you wouldn't. I can take time off from the clinic. That way I can keep an eye on your face as it heals."

"I couldn't ask you to do that. I already feel bad about all the hassle everyone has to go through just because of my ex."

Dr. Byford lowered his voice. "It's not a hassle. I want to take care of you."

What?

♡

She'd been a beauty, and he'd felt compelled to give that back to her. But it wasn't just about her physical beauty hidden under those burn scars. Was it her vulnerability? Her loving heart? Her refusal to hate or seek revenge? In her civil suit, she asked for what he considered reasonable compensation for the horrible damage her husband did to her face, and consequently, her life. And she never spoke about him other than her concern that he agreed to the two million without a fight and her fear for her friends.

The oozing had stopped, so he didn't need to replace several of the bandages which gave her a little more freedom of movement. She thought she was hideous, which couldn't have been further from the truth. If she was in danger, he had to protect her.

He had two weeks off from the hospital and the clinic, and then Michael and Elaine would arrive to take his place while he went back to his practice for a few days. He picked up enough groceries to last three weeks and several sippy cups. Then he picked her up from Joan's.

Once at the cabin, he helped her unpack and got her settled on the couch in the great room. She stared at the view of the lake through the floor to ceiling windows, so he built a roaring fire in the giant stone hearth to keep her warm.

"Thank you, Dr. Byford."

"I think we're beyond formal titles, don't you? Please, call me Robert, or Rob. And you shouldn't be trying to talk."

"You're still my surgeon, and I'm afraid you're putting yourself in danger."

"How about you let me worry about that? Yes, I'm your surgeon, but I'm also your friend. Let me take care of you. This way, I can make sure your face is healing. And speaking of, I'm going to get some ice packs. We want to keep that swelling down as much as possible."

When he got to the kitchen, he stopped. What was he getting himself into? He was more than just her surgeon, more than her friend, and more than her protector. But now was not a good time to speculate on what it all meant. Instead, he unlocked the gun cabinet and loaded one of his hunting rifles — just in case.

He brought the ice packs from the freezer and gently placed them on her face.

"How about a protein shake?"

"How am I going to drink it?"

"I picked up some sippy cups."

"I wish you wouldn't do this."

"Do what?"

"Take care of me like this. I'm not used to it."

"Lisa, if you don't stop talking I'll bandage your face again so you can't open your mouth."

"Is it a diet shake? I've been cutting back on sugar since I seem to be a few pounds overweight."

"Who told you that?"

"My ex. He told me I was fat. It was one reason I took up smoking. I'm even heavier now because of the stress."

"Okay. In my professional opinion, you are not overweight. Now as a man, I can unequivocally state, you're perfect. And no, it's not a diet shake."

"Okay."

29

He was just trying to be nice and cheer her up. The man was hot, and she figured his beautiful girlfriend wouldn't be threatened by him taking care of a burn victim. She fought the sadness that always crept up on her when she thought about couples in loving relationships. Couples like handsome Michael and beautiful Elaine, and Robert and his probably stunning girlfriend. That was never her experience and never would be.

She closed her eyes and fell asleep.

"Lisa. Lisa, honey. Wake up. I want you to drink another shake."

His gorgeous brown eyes looked intently into hers. It reminded her that no man would look at her like that — willingly. He was just concerned because he was her doctor.

"Hey. What's wrong? Are you in pain?"

Yes. But not the physical kind.

"No, I'm fine. Just groggy from all the sleep."

"Okay. If you're sure. I have some pain medication in case you need it. Don't be a martyr."

"Yes, *Doctor.*"

"Here, let me help you."

This beautiful man helped her sit up so she could drink the

protein shake, and the sippy cup was a thoughtful idea. The more she thought about it, the more she envied his girlfriend.

"It's supposed to snow tonight."

"Really? I've never seen snow fall."

"Seriously?"

"I was born and raised in Los Angeles and never made it up to the mountains. I bet it's beautiful." He had that look again. The part of her face that wasn't covered in bandages was covered in sutures, and yet . . . "Robert, is this," she gestured at the space between them, "going to cause problems with your girlfriend?"

"My *what?*"

"Your girlfriend."

"What makes you think I have a girlfriend?"

"Well, you're very handsome. You're very nice. And you're a doctor."

"And all the women I've dated since I opened my practice seemed to zero in on the doctor part. None of them ever wanted to get to know *me*. So to answer your question, there is no girlfriend. If there was, I wouldn't be here with you. I'm not the kind of man who would treat a woman he cares about like that."

No girlfriend? She had to put that thought out of her mind before she humiliated herself. She got up intending to wash her empty cup, but he steered her back to the couch in the great room and added a log to the fire.

"You rest. I'll clean up."

"I feel guilty with you waiting on me like this."

Uh-oh.

"One more time. I want to take care of you because I care about you. You have nothing to feel guilty about. I'm not doing this out of pity or because I'm your surgeon. Okay, maybe being your surgeon is part of it. But I genuinely care about you. Now please, just rest, okay? We'll have a longer discussion about this someday when I'm not your surgeon anymore."

Well, okay, then.

She dozed off and dreamed of her knight in shining scrubs who carried her away to a beautiful castle overlooking the ocean. She woke up the next morning alone in a big bed, all cozy and warm.

What the —?

She was wearing a large t-shirt, but she hadn't brought one. It was one of his! He'd seen her naked! Well, of course, he had. She'd been naked on the operating table, too. And yet he told her she was perfect. Maybe she should be concerned that her plastic surgeon needed glasses.

She threw on her robe and wandered into the kitchen. "Good morning."

"Good morning, sleepyhead."

"I know. Sorry for conking out on you last night."

"Don't be sorry. You obviously need more sleep, and it's good for you. Want some lukewarm coffee? I can put it in the sippy cup, and when you're done with that, I'll whip up a shake."

She wanted to tell him to stop spoiling her, but that would probably get her an argument. "Yes, please."

"Sit. Cream and sugar?"

"Yes, but do you have no calorie sweetener?"

"Nope. A little sugar won't kill you." He handed her the cup of tepid but very aromatic coffee. "It snowed last night. Looks like it might snow again today."

"Really? I need to see."

"Go ahead and take your cup with you."

Just as she walked into the great room, it began to snow again. It was magical. She felt him behind her and stopped herself from leaning back into his body. It would have been humiliating when he pushed her away in disgust.

"It's really something, isn't it?"

"I could sit and watch this all day."

"Well, there's no reason why we can't."

"Don't you have important things to do?"

"Important things? Right now, there's nothing and no one as important as you."

What?

"As a matter of fact, after your breakfast shake, I'm going to take a look at your stitches. I think some of them can come out, maybe not today, but tomorrow. The scabs from the deep dermabrasion are almost done peeling. Now, drink up."

She needed a shower, and her hair was greasy. But she couldn't do it alone. "I have a small problem."

"What's that, honey?"

Honey?

"Joan has been helping me shower and wash my hair. I can manage the shower, but I'm afraid to wash my hair. I don't want to get my face wet."

"So, what's the problem?"

"My hair is greasy."

"If it bothers you that much, I can help you wash it."

Well, after all, he is a doctor.

"Are you worried I'll take advantage of you?"

Yes. No. Did she want him to?

"From your silence, I'm guessing you are."

He lifted her chin and looked into her eyes. There was that look again. What did it mean?

"I promise I will not act inappropriately while you're my patient."

She fought back the disappointment. Wait. Why was she disappointed?

"Okay."

He removed all the bandages and helped her into the shower. After she soaped up and rinsed, she opened the curtain so he could lean in and wash her hair. It was awkward physically and emotionally, but she slowly relaxed, especially when he massaged her scalp.

Once she was dressed, he dried her hair and pulled it into a ponytail to keep it off her face. "Thank you."

"You're welcome."

"Can you put some mouthwash in a sippy cup? I think I have dragon breath. I guess it's going to be awhile before I can brush my teeth."

When she was done, he asked, "So, what would you like to do? We could watch movies, or play Scrabble. I have a deck of cards around here, somewhere. What'll it be?"

"Well, all of that sounds fun, and maybe later, but right now, I just want to sit by the fire and watch it snow."

"Okay, honey. You go sit and get comfortable."

"What about the bandages?"

"I think we can leave them off. I can't believe how fast your skin is healing. Take a look."

She couldn't bring herself to. Even when she rinsed her mouth out, she made it a point not to look. She was afraid of what she'd see.

"I want to wait until all the stitches are out first."

⅀

For the next thirteen days, they watched a lot of movies, played a lot of Scrabble, and talked. When he was sure the incisions around her mouth were healed enough, he made oatmeal and scrambled eggs for her. And when she promised to be careful, he let her brush her teeth.

He stood her in front of the bathroom mirror while she kept her eyes closed. She felt the pulling as he removed the last of the stitches.

"Open your eyes, honey."

"I can't."

"Sure you can."

"Am I still hideous?"

"You were never hideous."

"You're sweet to say that, but I know what I looked like. I saw how little kids reacted to me."

"Lisa! Open. Your. Eyes."

In a million years she could never have been prepared for what she saw. Except for some redness around her eyes and where the last of the stitches had been, and some swelling around her nose, she looked like herself — before the incident. She sank to the floor and cried.

"Lisa, honey, why are you crying?"

"I never . . . I never . . . I never thought I'd see *my* face again! You said you could do it, and I hoped there'd be some improvement. But, I never expected this. *Oh,* my God! I don't know how to thank you!"

♡

He kneeled on the floor in front of her.

This poor beautiful woman!

And he'd done this.

Some people thought plastic surgery was for the vain, and surgeons were only in it for the money. This was the real reason. This right here.

"Sweetheart, don't cry. It's bad for your eyelashes. And the look on your face just now, that's all the thanks I need."

If he hadn't made that promise about not acting inappropriately as long as he was her surgeon, he would have kissed her. But *she* needed to feel safe with him, even though *he* knew she was.

His priority had been her surgery and healing. Now the most important thing was keeping her safe. There would be time for them to explore their feelings. Based on her body language when he got close, she felt the same way.

He helped her up. "Come on. Let's go take a hike in the snow so you can experience it. Let me put some sunblock on your face and find you a hat. You know, Michael and Elaine will be here this afternoon."

"That's right. And you have to go home."

"Only for a few days, then I'll be back."

"This whole thing seems silly. There's been no sign of any trouble. You should call Michael and tell him you're bringing me home. There's no sense in staying here."

"When they get here, if Michael feels it's safe, we'll all drive down. So, how about that hike? Just a short one to get some fresh air. Sound good?" She smiled. It was the first smile he'd seen on her face, and it was breathtaking.

She hadn't brought anything heavy, so he bundled her up in one of his jackets. It was too big, of course, but she looked adorable in it. With hats and gloves on, they headed out for a slow, easy hike.

♡

"*Oh,* Michael. It's so beautiful up here. And look at all the snow!"

"Yeah. It's a good thing the road's plowed, or my little sports car wouldn't make it. I think we still have to hike to get to the cabin."

"Can't wait."

Yes, it sure was gorgeous. Maybe he should look into buying or building a cabin, but it needed to be more remote. There was too much resort traffic on the four-lane highway.

It was too bad they were on their way to deliver bad news. The judge assigned to Lisa's case had died a week ago under what the police were calling suspicious circumstances, and the new judge was backlogged with hundreds of cases to review. There was no doubt the final judgment would be signed and recorded. It was just going to take a while longer.

"There's a lot more traffic than I expected. I guess this is a popular ski area." He glanced at his rearview mirror in time to see a big, black SUV race up on his tail, then veer left to pass him. As it came up alongside, the SUV swerved to cut them off. No, not cut them off. Run them off the road! And there was nowhere to go but down.

Just as the SUV sideswiped his little car, Elaine screamed, "MICHAEL!"

He prayed to God, Jesus, and Saint Mary as they rolled down the embankment. When his car came to a stop right side up, he sent a silent thank you to Sandy for making him get the optional roll bar.

"Elaine? Baby?"

No answer.

He smelled gasoline.

He unlatched his seatbelt, leaned over and unlatched hers, and still, there was silence.

He refused to consider any other possibility except maybe she'd been knocked unconscious. The frame was mangled, and he had to force his door open. He ran to her side, but no matter how hard he pulled, he couldn't get the door open. Now he could hear the gasoline as it hissed and poured from the ruptured tank he'd just topped off. He had to get her out and away before it blew up.

He needed a knife. There was one on his keyring! He grabbed his keys from the ignition and ran back to her door. His hands shook as he sliced the heavy canvas top enough to let him lean in and lift her. With lousy leverage but superhuman strength driven by terror, he pulled her out and carried her as fast and as far as he could before what was left of his car blew up and knocked them to the ground.

Seconds and inches.

The woman in his arms groaned. "Elaine, sweetheart, talk to me!" Her eyes fluttered open, and he cried with relief.

"What happened," she whispered.

"Thank God! We got run off the road, but we're alive!"

Her eyes widened with shock. "*Oh*, no! Your car!"

"Fuck the car. We're alive!"

She groaned again.

"*Oh*, shit! Are you hurt?"

He scanned her body looking for any obvious injuries but didn't see anything.

"I ache all over, and I think I hit my head."

"Hang on. I hear sirens." Just as he finished saying a silent prayer of thanks, he heard voices yelling.

"Hello down there! Was anyone still in the car?"

"No, but we need medical assistance!"

He didn't want her to move until they checked her over. It was a miracle they survived considering the mountain rescue team had to rappel down to lift them out. The paramedics examined Elaine. No broken bones but she had a mild concussion.

"Okay, sir. Your turn."

"There's nothing wrong with me."

"Well, sir, you've got a good laceration above your eye which probably needs a stitch or two."

It wasn't until that moment that he noticed all the blood on his shirt. It wasn't Elaine's, so it must be his. "Can't you just clean it and slap a butterfly on it? We need to warn our friends."

"*Oh,* Michael! What if those were the men who are after Lisa?"

Those men had a good head start already, and he didn't want to think about what they'd find at the cabin. But what he knew with absolute certainty was that life really was too short. He loved her, and he wanted to spend the rest of his life with her.

After taking their statements, the deputy sheriff called for backup and gave them a ride in his Jeep to Dr. Byford's cabin.

30

"I hear sirens, but they're not very close. I hope it's nothing serious. If it was summer, I'd say maybe it's a forest fire, but that's not likely with all this snow."

"Doesn't that look like smoke over there?"

"*Hmm,* yeah." It was just a thin wisp of smoke. Probably someone burning trash or leaves. He checked his watch. They'd walked for almost an hour. It was time to turn back. She stumbled, and he grabbed her hand to steady her. He held it like it was the most natural thing in the world to be holding her hand, and they walked in a comfortable silence

They were almost to the front door, but he held her back. Something seemed off. There were no visual signs, but the hairs on the back of his neck stood up. He whispered, "Let me go inside first."

"Why? Is something wrong?"

"I don't know. It's just a feeling. Probably nothing. Stay here." He went around to the service porch entrance and grabbed his rifle. Then he walked through to the kitchen. So far, so good.

When he rounded the corner into the great room, he heard a gunshot and felt the burn as a bullet grazed the side of his left arm. He kept hold of the rifle as he glared at the man in the ski mask who pointed a handgun at him.

"Don't even think about it. We just want the woman."

"Sorry. I can't do that." Then he yelled, "RUN, LISA!"

"She can't." Another thug, also in a ski mask, held her wrists behind her back and pushed her into the room.

Thug One pointed his handgun at her. "Drop the rifle, or I'll shoot her."

"Shoot him, Robert! He's going to kill me, anyway!"

He put the rifle down as the siren got louder. Then car doors slammed, and Michael yelled through the front door, "Dr. Byford? Robert? Lisa? Are you in there?"

Thug Two yelled, "Yeah, they're in here, and we'll shoot 'em if you open the door."

"What do you want?"

"We're coming out. Then we're leaving. And if any of you move, we'll kill both of them." Thug One grabbed him while Thug Two continued to hold her with her arms behind her back.

They were human shields! They must have had a car nearby. How had he missed it? He'd heard three car doors slam. Someone else was there. He had to stall. "Why are you doing this? What do you want?"

"We don't want anything except our cut. It's not personal. We don't even want you. You just happen to be in the way. And lady, I gotta say, your husband is an idiot. Why he'd want a bitch who looks like you dead . . . Well, none of my business. Let's go."

"How much is he paying you?"

"A mil. Seems he's set himself up for some insurance payout if you die, and he has some powerful family."

"Joey! Shut the fuck up!"

"What? No one heard me, at least no one who's gonna live, anyway. Now, quit stalling."

"I'll go with you. You don't need him."

"Lisa, no!"

"*Aw,* ain't that sweet. True love. No deal. Move."

Thug Two kept Lisa in front of him as he opened the door and walked out behind her. Thug One pulled him in front, and they followed.

A County Sheriff's SUV blocked the snow-covered dirt road. "Hold it right there. Drop your weapons."

"Come any closer, and we'll kill them."

"They're going to kill us, anyway. Shoot them!"

"Lisa, honey, they can't kill us. We're what's keeping *them* from being shot."

"Go ahead, Sheriff. There's one of you and two of us. Now, just let us go, and the man might live. Can't say the same for Mrs. Weston here. Too bad. Such a pretty face."

"NOW!"

Two shots rang out, and the thugs dropped. Then deputies swarmed the front door.

They were safe, and he desperately needed to hold her and kiss her.

♡

It happened so fast, her brain couldn't register it, but her body did. When he pulled away, she struggled to catch her breath. "Does this mean you're not my surgeon anymore?"

"It sounded like a good idea at the time. But seeing that goon with his gun aimed at you? I realized how much I care for you. Damn it. I didn't mean for this to happen." He let her go and backed away.

"I don't understand."

"Lisa, honey, you have your life back. You're free. You need time to go out in the world and experience life. And I don't want to hold you back or get in the way."

"I still don't understand."

"Excuse me, Mrs. Weston? I have a few questions."

"Yes, of course, Sheriff. But Robert? We'll talk later?"

"Sure."

Why did that sound like a brush off?

When she finished answering questions, she tried to find him. Maybe he was outside. But when she went out there, Elaine was waiting for her.

"Where's Robert?"

"He said he had to leave. He didn't say why, but he sure seemed upset. Did you two argue?"

"No. We didn't get a chance to. He kissed me, and then he told me I had to be free to get my life back, and he didn't want to hold me back and get in the way. I don't . . . I don't understand. When we first got here, I thought he only cared about me as a patient and I was too ugly. And then, thanks to him, I'm not ugly anymore, and he kissed me, and he said he cared for me. And now he's gone. Why did he leave?"

"I don't know, Sweetie. Men do strange things sometimes."

"I should pack and get out of here. Wait! I've been so caught up in my little drama, I just now noticed your bandages. What happened to you?"

Elaine's jaw dropped. "You call this a little drama? Your ex-husband hired two hitmen who held you at gunpoint and were about to kill you for insurance money. Nothing *little* about that!"

"But what about you two? How did you get hurt?"

"They ran us off the road, but we're okay now."

"And Michael's car?"

Elaine looked at the floor and shook her head as a tear rolled down her cheek. Michael appeared at her side and put his arm around her. "It's insured. It was time to update my transportation, anyway."

"*Oh*, no! I'm so sorry you two got dragged into this! When I get the settlement, I'll reimburse you."

"Well, actually, there's something we have to tell you."

After he explained what happened with the judge and the delay it was causing, he excused himself. "I need to talk to the Sheriff," and hurried off to find him.

"By the way, you look stunning! Is this how you looked before?"

"More or less. I really hoped . . ."

"Lisa, are you in love with Dr. Byford?"

"Am I? I don't know. We got very close these past few weeks. He took care of me, and he promised he wouldn't do anything inappropriate, like take advantage of me, while he was still my surgeon. But after he kissed me, I thought that changed. At least, he said it had. How are we going to get home if Michael's car was destroyed?"

"His insurance company is sending a car. It should be here soon."

Anger replaced her pain. "Good. The sooner I'm out of here, the sooner Robert can come back. If he wants to avoid me, that's fine with me."

"Lisa, men do this sometimes. They think they know what's best for us, and they make decisions for us, except they don't bother asking us what *we* want. He probably thinks he's doing the right thing by taking himself out of the picture. I saw that kiss, and I'd bet money that man really cares for you, probably even loves you. Give him time."

"Give him time? Sure. Thanks to him, I've got all the time in the world now."

♡

Lisa was asleep in the back seat as Michael maneuvered the rented Escalade through the winding roads and freeways. Neither of them knew what to say to the brokenhearted woman, anyway.

She reached for her purse then remembered it had blown up with his car. Her mind raced through all the details she would have to deal with when they got home. She needed a new phone. New ID. And please let the hidden key still be in the potted cactus, and boy was she grateful she hadn't brought her laptop with her. "Do you have your phone?"

He found it in his jacket pocket, undamaged, and as soon as they had a signal, she called her parents. The last thing she wanted was for them to hear about what happened on the six o'clock news.

"Mom?"

"Sweet Jesus! Are you okay? Where are you?"

Shit. The story must have made it onto the five o'clock news.

"Michael and I are on our way home. We're okay."

"Michael?"

"Yes. It's a long story, and I owe you a visit. I want you to meet him."

"Oh? Is it serious?"

"Yes."

"Is he Catholic?"

"Geez, Mom. What if he wasn't?"

"He is! *Oh,* the saints be praised! This is wonderful!"

"Slow down. We're not to that point yet. But I do want you to meet him."

"How about dinner tonight?"

"Not tonight. We're both pretty banged up. Maybe next week? I'll call you when I know what our schedules look like."

"Okay. But, honey?"

"Yeah, Mom?"

"We're happy for you, but you know your father will probably interrogate him."

"I know. And I'll warn him. I'll talk to you soon. Love you, Mom."

"Love you, too, darling."

She disconnected and handed the phone back to him.

"So you want me to meet your parents?"

"Yes. That is if you want to."

"I want to."

"Well, Mom said to warn you. My father will put you through the wringer with the third-degree and all."

"Why? You're old enough to make your own decisions."

"Yes, but they didn't believe Dan could be that cruel until I almost died, and they got a wake-up call. My father needs to make sure you're not like him. Is that okay?"

"Sweetheart, I'm glad they're concerned, and I'll happily subject myself to his questioning. How are you feeling? Do you want to go to Urgent Care?"

"No, I'm fine. The ibuprofen worked, and if it wears off, I'll just take more. What about you? That cut needs stitches or you could wind up with a scar."

"It'll just add to my rugged good looks."

She burst out laughing. "If you get any more good looking, I may have to chain you to my bed."

"Promise?"

Hmm. They hadn't talked about it in a while, but they didn't need to define their relationship. They both knew how they felt, and as far as she was concerned, it was love. She didn't need anything else.

"Want to help me buy a new car?"

"Don't you want to research first? Make sure you're getting what you want? You don't strike me as an impulse buyer."

"Well, my impulses haven't done too badly. Which reminds me, there's something I want to talk to you about later."

"Oh? Give me a hint."

"Not right now. Right now, I want to remove your clothing, slowly, one piece at a time, kiss every inch of you, bury myself in you, and show you how much I love you. *After* we take Lisa home."

Well, alrighty, then.

"Are we there yet?"

They dropped a groggy Lisa off at Joan's and told her what happened. Then he broke a few speed limits on the way home.

The hidden key was right where she'd left it, so he dragged her inside, picked her up, and carried her to the bedroom. Then he gently laid her on the bed and crawled up next to her. "God, Elaine. I was never so scared in all my life as I was when I had to cut the top and pull you out of the car. If I hadn't had a knife . . ."

She felt him shudder and tried to lighten the mood. "Rule 9. Always carry a knife." She was safe. He was safe. And all was well in their world.

"*Hmm.* I never thought of that. Anyway, you were unconscious, and all I could think about was how I couldn't lose another woman I loved. And I was never so happy and relieved as when you groaned and I knew you were alive. It made me realize just how precious you are to me and how much I love you."

"I feel the same way. I love you. I really, truly, do. What happened today was another reminder of how short life can be and how everything can change in an instant. I don't want to lose you, ever. Make love to me, please."

31

He did exactly what he said he would. He removed one piece of her clothing at a time and kissed every inch of her skin as he uncovered it. When he got to her toes, he sat back and gazed at her. No hesitation, no residual guilt. This was right. And he could almost hear Sandy agree.

He took off his clothes, grabbed a condom, and lay back down beside her. She was bruised and hurting, and the last thing he wanted to do was put his weight on her, but he had to have her. He had to have that confirmation that they were alive.

He gently rolled her so they were face to face then draped her leg over his hip, and as they stared into each other's eyes, he entered her. It was slow and emotional. And when he couldn't hold back anymore, he reached between them and stroked her. It wasn't more than a minute before she came apart in his arms, and he joined her.

When their breathing slowed, she whispered, "Wow. It just keeps getting better. When I remember what it was like, I mean, it's unbelievable. And it blows me away when I think if he hadn't beaten me almost to death, I wouldn't have walked into your office that day, and I wouldn't be in your arms now. I don't know if I'll ever get over that. And today, we almost lost it all."

♡

She couldn't hold back the tears. It was all so overwhelming — how the chain of events had to unfold the way they did to bring her to this point with him.

"I know, baby. If it wasn't for Father Timothy dragging me to my first AA meeting where I met Bruce who sent me on a crazy vision quest, I probably would have drunk myself to death. Instead, I turned my tragedy into a purpose, and then you walked into my office with the same purpose. Like you said, life is short. I know we haven't been together long, but I don't want to waste anymore time. I want to marry you."

What?

"Wait. I wasn't fishing for a proposal. I mean, I love you more than I ever thought possible, but I don't know about marriage."

"Why? What are you afraid of?"

How could she explain it? "I don't want you to be mad or misunderstand."

"Misunderstand? Only if you don't explain it to me. And I could never be mad at you. I want you to always be honest with me, and God knows, I never want you to be afraid to talk to me."

Their bodies were still joined as she took a deep breath. "Okay. I know you're not him, but Dan wasn't always cruel. He hid it until we were married. And like I said, I know you're not him, but I'm scared you'll change on me. It isn't you, personally. I'd be scared with any man. This is screwed up, I know. And I'm sorry, but the man I once loved, the man who vowed he'd love, honor, and keep me, tried to kill me."

He pulled out of her body but kept her in his arms. "Baby, I understand your fear. I suppose if I were you, and had survived what you did, I'd be afraid, too. Tell me, what will it take for you to trust me? What can I do?"

"I don't know. Maybe I just need time."

"I'll wait, even if it takes a lifetime, as long as I can spend it with you."

The other thing that held her back was religion. He was devoutly Catholic, and she was devoutly not. Other religions were somewhat tolerant of non-believers, but Catholicism was not one of those. If they married, he'd want it in the church. She could pretend, go through the motions, say the words, but only the vows would mean anything. How would he feel about that? It was a conversation they needed to have — but maybe not in the afterglow of an unbelievable orgasm.

"What else is bothering you?"

"How do you do that?"

"What?"

"Tune into me like that."

"It's easy. Your face is very expressive. So, what is it?"

"I don't think we should discuss this in bed after having sex."

He got up to dispose of the condom. "Talk to me. Tell me what else is bothering you." It was probably the Catholic thing. She considered herself an atheist. She was probably worried he'd insist on a church wedding. That would be his preference, of course, but there were ways to compromise.

"Where would we get married?"

He was right. It was the Catholic thing. He crawled back into bed. "Well, my first choice would be the church, but if that's a show-stopper for you, there are other options. Living without you isn't one of them. It matters, but you matter more. How about we worry about that after you say yes?"

So what would he do if she said no? Nothing. They'd just continue with the way things were. The alternative would be to break up, and he refused to consider that. He needed some advice, and tonight would be a good time for the animals to get talkative.

"Okay. But you need to give me some time. We need to get to know each other better."

"And to do that, we have to spend more time together. So whose house should we live in?"

"What?"

"We should live together."

"But . . . what would your mother think? What would Father Timothy say?"

"I know my mother would prefer that we get married first, but I think she would understand. Besides, I'm a little too old to worry about my mother grounding me or cutting my allowance. Father Timothy wouldn't like it either, but again, I'm a big boy."

"Please let me think about it."

"I told you, I'll wait forever if I have to. Listen, we've had a long, emotionally and physically draining day. I'm going to make us something to eat and then we're going to get some sleep. I need to be here with you tonight."

"I love you."

"I love you, too. You'll never know how much."

They watched some late-night talk shows and ate peanut butter and jelly sandwiches in bed. Then he held her until they dozed off.

He wasn't worried when they showed up. Maybe he should be worried that he wasn't worried anymore.

"She'll come around."

"Yeah. She didn't survive everything just to run scared for the rest of her life."

"She'll see."

That was reassuring. "How do I get her to trust me?"

"You just keep being you. She'll get it on her own, and it won't take long. Don't worry about that. But you should think about the ceremony. The chances of her accepting Catholicism again are probably nil. It bothers her, so how far are you willing to go?"

"I don't know. I know I don't want to live without her. I guess I should talk to Father Timothy."

"That's probably a good idea. And sooner rather than later."

"What's that supposed to mean?"

"Nothing."

"Wait, a minute! Don't drop that on me. Tell me! Is he going somewhere?"

"Eventually."

What did they know that he didn't? Was the old priest ill? Was he moving to Florida? What?

"Really, Elaine. After everything you two went through, after all the tragedy and pain, do you really think he could turn violent?"

"No."

"Then what's the problem?"

"I don't know. Nothing, I guess."

"Then tell him *yes* for cryin' out loud!"

"You know, for a cute, furry raccoon, you're terribly rude."

"You know, for a beautiful, intelligent, compassionate woman, you're terribly dense."

"Hey, Rocky. Ease up a bit, will you? Look, Elaine. The man went through hell, and not once did he ever take it out on another person. He turned it in on himself, instead. I know for a fact he'd cut off a nut before he'd hurt you or anyone else. We told him about you years ago, about how you two would meet when both of you were ready for each other. And now you're making us look like rookies with bad timing."

"How can a bear and a raccoon look like rookies?"

"Hey, don't forget us!" That's when the snake, deer, beaver, skunk, and two huge birds circled around her.

They were Michael's vision quest animals, and she'd hurt their feelings. "I'm sorry. You're right. He's been nothing but loving and understanding with me, and he's been nothing but compassionate with Lisa. And he risked his life to pull me out of a car that was

about to explode. He says he loves me, and he shows it in everything he does."

"So what are you scared of?"

"I guess, nothing. There's just that other little problem, though."

"You're an atheist. Or so you say. But if that's true, then there's
no such thing as spirit animals."

"That's right."

"So who are you talking to?"

The bear had a point.

And that, that right there was the crux of the matter. Bears
weren't supposed to have points.

Fate. Destiny. Good or bad luck. Making a wish and blowing out
birthday candles. All of that had to do with something beyond her
five senses, so was there something else going on here? Something
she didn't understand? And just because she didn't understand, did
that mean it didn't exist?

Did other people have philosophical discussions with spirit
animals in their dreams? "Okay, maybe I'm not an atheist. Maybe
I'm an agnostic."

"Or maybe you can just be spiritual and not put a label on it.
Stay open-minded. Go to church. See beyond the dogma and glitter
and absorb the positive energy. Say their words if it'll make him
happy. Words aren't what's important. It's the intention behind the
words that counts."

"Wow. So now I understand what Michael was trying to explain
about that vision quest. You guys *are* good."

"*Shh!* Don't tell anyone! We're already booked until next fall."

Ⴟ

She woke up laughing.

He pulled her to his side and wrapped his arm around her.
"Funny dream?"

"Your menagerie is quite entertaining."

"What did they say?"

"That I'm beautiful, intelligent, compassionate, and dense, and they're booked until next fall."

"So?"

"So the answer is yes, I'll marry you. I'll even marry you in the church if that's what you want."

"You would do that?"

"It's just a room, and according to the bear, the words aren't important. It doesn't matter where or how. What's important is we love each other, and we want to commit to a life together. If you want to get married in the church, I'm okay with that."

"Remind me to give them a good review on Yelp."

"I'm sure they'll appreciate it."

"I asked Tina to cancel my appointments for today. After what we went through yesterday, I think we're entitled to a day off."

"I don't have any appointments, either, and I agree."

"Would you mind going with me to talk to Father Timothy?"

"You want to talk to him about marrying an atheist?"

"That was my original intention. I was going to ask him about a compromise, but that doesn't seem to be necessary now. I just want to stop by and visit. It was something the bear said."

"Oh?"

"He said not to wait too long, but he wouldn't tell me why."

"Okay. Let me grab a quick shower."

"I didn't say right now."

They spent the next hour celebrating their engagement.

Now it was time for a shower. He turned the hot water on. "We need to go shopping."

"I just stocked my kitchen the other day. What do you need?"

They soaped each other up. "Not for food. For an engagement ring."

She rinsed the shampoo out of her hair and applied conditioner. "I don't need a ring."

"No one *needs* a ring, but I want you to have one, and I want you to pick it out. You're going to wear it for a long time, so it needs to be something you like."

She rinsed the conditioner out, and he turned off the water. They dried off, and then he took her in his arms. "I love you. You have no idea how happy I am that you said yes."

"*Oh,* I think I do."

"We both deserve to be happy, and being with you, knowing you love me and will be my wife, I can't tell you how that makes me feel."

"You don't have to. I feel the same way."

"*Hmm.* Let me check."

32

"Hello? No, dear. Did you try her cell phone? Well, Dr. Byford. I don't know what to tell you. Maybe she's out living her life like you wanted her to."

Bless Joan. The woman hadn't agreed with her, but she'd honored her request, anyway. The man had broken her heart, and she didn't want to talk to him. He probably just wanted to explain and that would be too humiliating.

It had been almost a month since that horrible day in his cabin. Her scars were hardly noticeable, now. It just took a little concealer to cover them. She still hadn't received any settlement money, but now there was an investigation into the attack at the cabin. The FBI couldn't tie it directly to Gerald, but his family was implicated. Meanwhile, the judge was still behind in reviewing cases, and according to Michael, it might be another week or two.

Michael also told her the original Assistant District Attorney was under investigation for collusion and dereliction of duty which meant Gerald's chances of early parole were now dead.

She'd hoped to buy a car with the settlement, but at least now she didn't mind taking the bus. Elaine told her about scholarships for domestic abuse victims, and she had an appointment that afternoon with the finance officer at the local community college. She'd

MARY A. NASON

always wanted to be a nurse, and they had an excellent program. If she got the scholarship, it would cover her first semester. The rest would depend on her grades.

Joan hung up the phone.

"Well, what did he want?"

"The same as before. I think you should talk to him."

"Why?"

"Because he's hurting. He knows he made a mistake, and he wants to talk to you about it, maybe beg your forgiveness."

"He's hurting?" She couldn't help but laugh, but it was bitter. "He made a mistake? Gee, that's too bad. I know the feeling."

"Lisa, dear. Men do this. They're fixers. They think they know best how to fix something, and they have to be proven wrong before they'll admit they made a mistake. He knows he was wrong. He did what he did because he honestly thought it was best for you. Won't you at least talk to him?"

"I don't know what I'd say."

"Wait until you hear what he has to say before you worry about that."

"I'll think about it. Right now, I have to go home and get ready for my appointment at the college, and then I have to get to the bus. Thank you for the coffee."

"Let me know how everything goes."

"Don't get your hopes up."

She walked across the lawn to her house, and when she got inside, she saw her cell phone laying on the desk with ten missed calls and five messages. That wasn't new. He'd left messages for two weeks, and she'd deleted them without listening.

Fine. I'll listen. Then I'll have a good laugh and an even better cry.

Just as she was about to press the voicemail icon, the doorbell rang. She wasn't the least bit surprised when she looked through the peephole and saw him. If she ignored him, he'd just keep trying.

Might as well get it over with now.

"What do you want?"

"May I come in?"

"I don't think that's a good idea, nor is it necessary. My face is just fine. It's healed nicely. The scars are hardly noticeable, and I don't scare little kids at the grocery store anymore. Thanks for checking up on me though."

She tried to close the door, but he stuck his hand out, pushed it open and barged in. He grabbed her around her waist and kicked the door closed.

"I need you to listen to me."

"I did. I listened to you. And what you said was you wanted nothing to do with me. I got it, Robert. I understand."

"No, you don't, and that's not what I said."

"You said you want me to go out and be someone I never was and have no desire to be. Date all the men who never were interested in me before and still aren't. You want me to have a social life that I don't need or want. You decided what was best for me, and you took away the one thing I really wanted — the first man who proved I could trust him — until I couldn't. But that's okay. I'm fine. In fact, I'm fabulous. So you can go now. I have to get ready."

"Ready?"

"I have an appointment at the college. I'm going back to school. Seems I've got tons of free time trying to juggle my non-existent social calendar." She opened the door for him to leave, but he didn't move.

"What time is your appointment?"

"Three, but I need to be at the bus stop by two."

"I'll drive you."

"No, you won't."

"Please. You have to let me explain."

"You already did."

"But you don't understand."

"Sure I do. And I told you. I'm good."

"But I'm not! I made a terrible mistake, and I miss you, and I didn't realize until it was too late."

"Didn't realize what?"

"I didn't realize I'd fallen in love with you."

What?

"*Oh,* don't be silly. We spent three weeks together, and for the first week, my face was hidden behind bandages. You know, I never would have said or done anything about it if you hadn't made the first move. I never felt worthy. But you made it so I could look in the mirror and not gag, and I thought maybe now that I wasn't hideous anymore . . . and at first I thought you wanted me, but you left without saying a word. It is what it is, Robert. Now, if you'll excuse me, I need to get ready."

He dropped his head, and his shoulders sagged, but he still didn't move to the door. And when he looked up, her heart cracked. Beautiful, brave, gifted, Dr. Robert Byford had tears in his eyes.

Shit

"Robert . . . I . . . I . . ."

"It's okay. You have every right to be angry. I did what I thought was best for you, and you'll never know how sorry I am that I assumed you'd want time to be on your own. Maybe someday you'll forgive me."

He walked to the door and paused as if he wanted to say something else. Then he walked out.

Oh, my God. What have I done?

♡

"I want Latesha to be my maid of honor. Is that okay?"

"Of course, it is. And I owe her."

"What?"

"I owe her for teaching you about sex."

"Oh. Well, she'll be thrilled that her lessons paid off. What about your best man?"

"It has to be Bruce."

"Not one of your brothers?"

"No. First, they can be assholes, though nothing like John. Second, how would I pick one? And third, I owe my life to Bruce — and Father Timothy. This is nice."

"What is?"

"Lying in bed all morning making wedding plans. Neither of us has anyplace we have to be." Just as he rolled over to pull her to him, his cell phone rang. It wasn't his mother's ringtone, so he thought about not answering, but considering everything that had happened, he probably should.

"You should answer that. It might be Lisa."

"It's not her number, but you're right. Hello?"

"Michael Chandler?"

"Yes, this is he."

"This is Rose Mayweather, Judge Connolly's assistant."

He sat up, alert. "Yes, Ms. Mayweather. What can I do for you?"

"It's what I can do for *you*. Mr. Chandler, the judge just signed your petition for summary judgment in the Lisa Weston case. Congratulations! I wanted to let you know now because your case files are about to be subpoenaed."

"So the DA is going ahead with the bribery case?"

"Yes. But I don't believe it will involve you, just your files."

"That's wonderful news. Thanks for calling."

"My pleasure. Have a nice day."

"You, too."

"Who was that?"

"That was the judge's assistant. Lisa's judgment is official. Now she can get the money."

"That's wonderful! Let's call her with the good news."

"Okay, but there's something I need to take care of, first."

"*Oh?* What's that?"

"This." He pulled his future wife to him and kissed every inch of her skin until she panted and cried out for more. And by giving her what she wanted, he got what he needed — peace and joy.

The doorbell rang, and her stomach flipped.

Please let it be Robert!

She looked through the peephole and disappointment punched her in the gut when she saw the courier. She opened the door. "Yes? May I help you?"

"Lisa Weston?"

"Yes."

"I have an envelope for you. Please sign here."

She signed for the manila envelope, thanked the courier, and closed the door. It was from the clerk of the court. What could be so important it had to be delivered on a Saturday?

Joan came out of the kitchen. "What is it, dear?"

"It's from the court. I'm afraid to open it. Would you do it for me?"

She handed the envelope to Joan who opened it, scanned the cover page, and began to cry.

"It's over, dear. You won. First thing Monday you need to contact the clerk with your bank information so they can transfer the money to your account."

♡

"Hello, you've reached the lovely Latesha. She's a little tied up right now, so please leave a message, and she'll call you back as soon as she gets the knots undone."

"Hey, girlfriend. Call me as soon as you can. I have news and a big favor to ask —"

"Hello? Elaine, honey, is that you?"

"You got those knots undone pretty fast."

Latesha giggled. "Yeah, he was just leaving. So, what's up?"

"I'm getting married."

"Lordy, girl! When did this happen? Who is he?"

"It's a long story. Can we come over?"

"You want to bring your squeeze to the old hood? What color is he?"

"White."

"That's a shame. I always thought a brother would be perfect for you. *Oh,* well. Sure, you can bring him over. That way I can decide if he's good enough for my little girl. When?"

"How about right now? It'll take us about a half hour to get there."

"Okay. Bring your suits. We'll have a pool party."

"We'll see."

"Hector will be brokenhearted, you know."

"He'll get over it. I think you're going to like Michael. He says he owes you his undying gratitude."

"*Oh?* OH! You found someone who appreciates a good blow job!"

"Well, I wouldn't put it exactly that way, but he's definitely grateful for the things I learned thanks to you."

"This is so excitin'! So yeah, get your skinny white butts over here!"

"See you in a few." She disconnected and turned to her fiancé. Her fiancé. She loved the sound of that. "She wants us to bring our suits, and she wants to throw a pool party and barbecue."

"Sounds fun."

"I have to warn you. This isn't the greatest neighborhood. In fact, it can be a little rough."

"Honey, I'm not some sheltered preppy. Don't worry about me. Besides, my fiancé has a black belt."

"And Latesha wants to check you out and make sure you're worthy of me."

"I'll charm her just like I charmed you."

"Well, don't go that far, please. I don't want to have to hurt her."

He laughed as he grabbed his keys. "Let's go."

When they arrived, she made him take the faceplate off the stereo. His beautiful new Range Rover was insured, but she still didn't want anything to happen to it. They planned to do a lot of traveling.

Latesha and the gang were already gathered around the pool, and when they saw each other, they squealed and ran into each other's arms. "Lordy, girl! Look at you! You're positively glowing.

And no wonder you weren't interested in any of the brothers. Look at those blue eyes. This man is downright delish!"

"Yes, he sure is. Latesha, this is Michael Chandler, my fiancé. Michael, this is Latesha Chester, my *sistah from another mistah.*"

He took her hand, shook it, and then pulled her into a hug. "Thank you. Thank you from the bottom of my heart."

"*Oh,* my. But what are you thanking me for?"

"Well, first, for being such a good friend to Elaine, and second, for helping her learn things her ex should have taught her."

"Well, bless your heart! Aren't you sweet. And from the looks on both your faces, I can see she learned well. Hey, everyone! Come here and meet Elaine's fee-awn-SAY!"

Hector approached her, pulled her into a hug, and whispered, "I'm happy for you, Babe. We coulda had some fun, but I'm glad you found what you wanted."

"Thanks. Someday a woman's going to come along and snag you."

"Not if I can help it."

He watched the interplay between Elaine and the good looking Hispanic man.

"Don't you worry about him. He tried. They all did, but she wasn't interested. Seems she was holdin' out for you. She just didn't know it yet. So, tell me, why should I give you my blessing?"

He gave her a very abbreviated recap of his life and what had brought them back together. When he finished, Latesha dabbed her eyes. "*Oh,* my Lord. I'm speechless, and that *never* happens. Yeah, you passed my inspection. So, when's the big day?"

"We haven't set a date yet."

Elaine touched his shoulder. "Hey. Can I talk to my *sistah* for a minute?"

"Sure. I'll go make sure all those men drooling over you know you're mine."

"Trust me, they know. Girlfriend? Can we talk in your apartment for a few minutes?"

"Of course, *girlfriend*. You need some advice or somethin'?"

"No. I just want to tell you what happened."

♡

As soon as Latesha closed the door, she told her everything that had happened since the day she moved away.

"Good God, Girlie! You two . . . you deserve each other. If ever there were two people who paid their dues, it's you two. What a story!" She grabbed another tissue to wipe her eyes.

"Yeah. What a ride. So, I've been thinking, and Michael agrees, there's no one I'd rather have as my maid of honor than you. What do you say?"

"Child, I'd be honored. I feel like we've come full circle."

"As soon as we set a date, I'll call you, and we'll get together."

"I can't believe my little girl is gettin' married, and to the perfect man."

"He's not perfect, but he's perfect for me."

♡

"Lisa, you need to call him."

"I can't. The last time I saw him, he left in tears!"

"Call him! He made a mistake. You made a mistake. Don't spend the rest of your life regretting and wondering. Call him!"

"What would I say? I need an excuse."

"No, you don't but you got the settlement money. Didn't you say you wanted to donate to his clinic to pay him back?"

"Yes, I did. I guess I could drop in at the clinic and give him a check. But what if he won't talk to me?"

"Then at least you'll know you tried."

"You're right. Okay. I'll do it."

"Good. Now go home and make yourself even more beautiful than you already are. And wear something sexy."

"I am not going to get all sexed up to go to a plastic surgery clinic for battered women!"

An hour later she stood at the reception window wearing a conservatively tailored skirt and jacket and low-heeled pumps. It would be a long time before she felt comfortable wearing anything that drew attention to herself.

"Is Dr. Byford in?"

"He's with a patient right now. Can I give him a message?"

Disappointed, she answered, "No. Just give him this."

She held out the envelope with a check for two hundred thousand dollars but stopped when the door to the waiting room opened, and a woman with a large bandage over her nose and two black eyes walked out.

Her hand shook while adrenaline raced through her, and her mouth was as dry as desert sand.

He looked shocked when he saw her. "Lisa! Carol, hold my calls. I'll be in my office. Lisa, please come with me."

She followed him into his office where he closed and locked the door. Then he just stood there looking at her, waiting for her to say something.

"Thank you for seeing me. I wanted to give this to you."

He took the envelope, opened it, and read the check. "You didn't have to do this."

"Yes, I did. And I also have to apologize for the things I said."

"I'm the one who should be apologizing. You were right. I made a lot of assumptions, but I cared about you more than I thought possible."

"Cared? Past tense?"

"I still care. I'm sorry, but I do."

"I care about you, too, more than I realized. I was hurt and angry, and I said things I shouldn't have, and I've regretted it every day since. Can you forgive me?"

"Can you forgive me for pushing you away?"

She looked at him through her tears and whispered, "Yes. I understand why you did it, but I've missed you. I don't know how it happened. We were only together a few weeks. Did I ruin it?"

He closed the distance between them and reached to wipe her tears with his thumb. "No. I don't know how it happened either, and I never thought I'd see you again. But now that you're here, I don't want to let you go. I love you, Lisa."

"I love you, too!"

"May I kiss you?"

Before she could say yes, she was in his arms with his lips fused to hers. It was heaven.

There was a knock on the door. "Dr. Byford? Is everything okay?"

He broke the kiss and sighed. "Yes, Carol. Is my next appointment here?"

"No, Doctor. She canceled. You don't have any more appointments today. Shall I lock up?"

"Yes, thank you. I'll see you Monday."

"Goodnight, Doctor."

"Good night, Carol." He turned back to her. "Now, where was I?"

He kissed her again, probing with his tongue until her lips parted. It was wild and wonderful, until he broke the kiss, again, breathing hard. "Not here. The first time I make love to you won't be on my desk."

"Make love?"

"*Oh*, hell. Did I assume too much?"

"No. I want to. I want you. I've just never had these feelings, and I don't know what to do with them."

"Let's go home, and I'll show you."

She followed him to his house where he showed her exactly what to do with those feelings.

33

H e held her as they caught their breath. From the moment he saw her at the clinic, he knew this would happen. It was magnificent. *She* was magnificent, and he was just about to tell her how much he loved her when her cell phone rang.

She glanced at the display. "I need to take this. I'm sorry." She picked up her phone and pressed the *Accept* button. "Hello?"

He couldn't hear what the other party said, but he saw her face go white and her mouth drop open.

"Thank you, Warden. Yes, please send the paperwork to my attorney, Michael Chandler. Yes, you have the address. Yes, and thank you for calling."

She dropped the phone and looked at him with wide-open eyes.

"What is it, honey?"

"He's dead."

"Who?"

"Gerald. An inmate killed him in the shower this morning. My ex-husband is dead." The corners of her mouth tipped up. "Gerald's dead!" She jumped out of bed and began to dance around the room, naked. "It's over! It's all over. *Oh,* my God, Robert! I'm free! The nightmare is over! He can never hurt me again!"

He lay propped up on one elbow and watched her dance and

laugh. It hadn't occurred to him until that moment just how awful her life had been with that monster. And now she was free. Free to love him without reservation. "Come here, honey." She stood by the side of the bed grinning until he reached for her hand and pulled her down next to him. "Yes, baby, it's all over, and I'm so happy for you."

"But?"

"No buts. It just hit me how badly the attack affected you. Now, you never have to worry about him again. We should celebrate."

"What did you have in mind?"

"Well, I'd say we should make love again, but I only had that one condom in my wallet, and it was probably expired. Don't worry. I don't think it leaked."

"It's okay. I can't have children. I never used birth control with Gerald although that was a pretty stupid chance to take. My periods have never been regular, and I never got pregnant, and he's the only man I've been with since we got married ten years ago."

"I've never not used one. Too many gold-diggers looking to trap a rich doctor into marriage."

"Well, I'm not looking to trap you, and I have my own money, so I don't need yours."

"Then bareback it is."

There was nothing like it, and he vowed never to use a condom with her again.

"I'm hungry, so you must be starving."

She rolled into his arms. "Not starving, but I could eat. I guess we skipped dinner."

"Let's shower, and I'll take you out for breakfast."

"*Oh*, but I need to go home first. I can't wear the same clothes I wore yesterday."

"Okay. Shower first, then I'll follow you home, and *then* I'll take you out for breakfast. How's that?"

He had a big, beautiful shower that could fit four people, and they used every inch of it.

An hour later, she mused, "I love your bathroom. Maybe now that Gerald is dead, I'll finally sell that monstrosity and buy something more modern. It's so dark, like a dungeon. Or maybe that's because that's how it always seemed. A dungeon I could never keep clean enough for him."

"Why don't you hold off on any major decisions for a while. If things go the way I hope, you won't need a house."

"Why, Robert! Are you asking me to move in?"

"It's a little soon for that, but that's how I see things. What do you think?"

"I think you're probably right."

"By the way, did you buy that little car?"

"I'm renting it short term. I don't know enough about cars to buy the right one. Maybe you could help me?"

"Sure! It'll be fun car shopping with you."

No doubt there'd be lots more fun in the future.

The future.

With her knight in shining scrubs.

♡

"Mom?"

"In the kitchen, dear."

She led him into the kitchen. "Where's dad?"

"Where else? Manning the grill. I hope your friend likes chicken."

"Mom. This is Michael Chandler, my *fiancé*. Michael, this is my mother, Grace Chambéry."

"Pleased to meet you, Mrs. Chambéry."

"Call me Grace, dear. Wait, a minute! Your *what*?"

"My fiancé. Michael asked me to marry him, and I said yes. Look!"

She held out her hand to show her mother the two-carat ring.

"*Oh*, Blessed Jesus! PIERRE! Come here!"

"Calm down, Mom."

Her father ran into the kitchen. "What is it? Are you okay? Elaine! When did you get here?"

He kissed her on the cheek as her mother cried out, "She's engaged! Look!"

"Dad, this is Michael Chandler, my fiancé. Michael, this is my father, Pierre. Michael and I are getting married."

"This calls for champagne!"

"Mom, Michael doesn't drink."

Silence.

"Grace, Pierre, it's okay. *I* don't drink, but you certainly can."

"Wait, I think we have some sparkling cider somewhere." She dug through the refrigerator. "*Ah*, here it is. Pierre, get the glasses."

"Mom, this can wait until we eat. Dad, you better get back out there before the chicken goes up in flames."

"Good idea. Michael, why don't you join me?"

"Dad, be nice. He's one of the good guys. Don't scare him away."

"It'll be okay. Your father just wants to get to know me."

I hope you know your blood type.

After they left the kitchen, her mother turned to her. "Okay. Tell me everything. How did you meet? How long have you known him? Are you getting married in the church?"

"One question at a time. It's a long story."

It wasn't quite as bad as a police interrogation. After he finished telling his story and answering questions, her father gave him a bear hug. But he felt as grilled as the chicken.

"Welcome to the family, Michael. I'll be proud to call you my son-in-law."

"Thank you, sir. That means a lot to Elaine. She's an incredible woman, and I'm in awe of her strength."

"Yes, her mother and I weren't there for her when that animal put her in the hospital the first time. We almost lost her the last time, but with the help of St. Joseph, we've been very close ever since. We better get this into the kitchen. The womenfolk are probably worried about you."

♡

"So have you two given any thought to the wedding? Like a date? Or a location?"

"Not yet. I would like our parish priest to conduct the ceremony, but we haven't discussed where or when, yet."

"Where do you go to church?"

"Saint Mary's in Redondo Beach. My family has always gone there, and Father Timothy has been there as long as I can remember."

"What about your family? Do they know yet?"

"Well, it's just my mom and my brothers, and I plan to tell them tomorrow at dinner."

"He has five brothers, Dad."

"Six boys? Your poor father!"

"I'm sure he saw it that way. He passed away several years ago."

"Will one of your brothers be your best man?"

"No. It would be hard to choose, and I'm closer to my AA sponsor, so I'm going to ask him."

"AA? My brother, Phillipe has been sober for what? Twenty? Twenty-five years? From what I know about it, and what it did for him, it had to be divinely inspired."

"There are a lot of people who would agree."

"Well, Michael, I need to call your mother and start planning an engagement party."

"Mom, please don't go to all that trouble. This isn't a first marriage for either of us, and you already gave me a big wedding with all the trimmings."

"Nonsense. You have a second chance at a *happily ever after* so you should have it all. And this time, I know you'll be much happier. I assume Latesha will be your maid of honor?"

"Of course."

"Good. She's been a good friend to you. She's such a character, I'm surprised she doesn't have a man."

"I'm not surprised at all. Every man she dates tries to tame her, and she's too much of a free spirit."

When it was time to leave, Michael shook hands with her father and kissed her mother on the cheek. "Mrs. Chambéry, Grace, please don't call my mother until Monday. I want a chance to tell her, first."

"Of course, dear."

♡

"Well, what did you think?"

"I like them. They obviously love you very much."

"I hope my father didn't give you too bad of a time."

"Not at all. He asked a lot of questions, and I told him my story, and I'm pretty sure he got choked up. At least he kept clearing his throat. So, we should talk about where and when. Want to stop and see Father Timothy and see when he can do this?"

"Sure. And maybe I'll go to confession."

"Seriously?"

"Seriously. It was something the bear said the other night. I'm willing to keep an open mind."

"I love you."

"I know." She winked.

Father Timothy wasn't hearing confessions that day, but the new priest was. Father Stephen had been there for several years already, but everyone still referred to him as the new priest.

In the three months they'd been together, his confessions hadn't varied much. And his penance was always the same. He had no idea what she would confess. It probably had something to do with pre-marital sex, although hopefully, she wouldn't be too graphic. It didn't matter. There was no way either of them would be contrite about that.

When they finished with their identical penances, they found Father Timothy in his office. "Father, are you busy?"

"Never too busy for you, Michael. And Elaine! So good to see you! So, what can I do for you two?"

"We want you to marry us."

"Right now?"

"No, although that would sure simplify things. No, you know my mother would be heartbroken."

"Mine, too."

"Do you want to get married here?"

"Well, we haven't gotten that far in the planning. But just in case, is it possible to have the ceremony somewhere else?"

"Well, you know there's a lot that goes into the rites of matrimony. I'm afraid it wouldn't be a Catholic wedding if it were someplace other than a church. Is that a problem?"

"No. We just wanted to know what our options were."

"Elaine, does your family have a church they attend?"

"Yes, but I know it would mean a lot to Michael if you performed the ceremony. My parents won't mind. They're just thrilled Michael is Catholic."

"Okay. What kind of time frame are you looking at?"

He remembered what the raccoon said. It needed to be sooner rather than later, and he didn't want to dwell on what that meant. "Next June? What do you think, honey?"

"Since it's a second wedding for both of us, it should be something simple, although my mother will disagree. So yeah, with our work schedules, we should be able to pull something together by then."

"Excellent. How about June 10?"

"That's right after my AA birthday. That would be perfect. Is that okay with you, honey?"

34

They grabbed some Chinese food to-go and ate it on her patio. Her mind raced. A June wedding! Well, at least they had the date nailed down, she had her maid of honor lined up, and Michael had his best man. There was the guest list, invitations, dresses, the reception, so many details and decisions. She couldn't remember doing all of that the first time which gave her a new appreciation for her mother's organizational skills. "What about a honeymoon?"

"Baby, every day with you is a honeymoon. And where would we go? Hawaii? Mexico? We already live at the beach. I say we just disconnect from the internet and turn our phones off for a week. We can take a drive out to the desert or someplace else. Whatever you want."

A whole week, just the two of them — and thousands of people frolicking in their front yard. Heaven.

"Speaking of cell phones, I think I hear yours."

She raced into the house and dug her new phone out of her purse. She hadn't had a chance to restore her contact list, but it looked like Lisa's number. "Hello?"

"Elaine? This is Lisa Weston. How are you?"

"Lisa! I'm great. We're great. But, how are *you*?"

"Couldn't be better. I just wanted to let you know that Gerald was killed in prison, and because his assets were frozen thanks to Michael, he never could change his beneficiary. I'm now a multi-millionaire!"

"*Oh*, wow! How wonderful!"

"And that's not all. Robert and I are together."

She let out a squeal loud enough to bring Michael running. "Michael! You're not going to believe this!" She gave him a quick summary. "Hey, can you two come over next Saturday?"

"I'll have to check with Robert, but I'm sure that would be okay. Saturday night?"

"Why don't you come for the day, too? We can hang out on the beach and then barbecue."

♡

So someone shanked Gerald Weston in the shower. Bruce had spent time in San Q. Shit. Did he really want to know? Would it change anything? He called his sponsor, anyway.

"Hey, Bruce."

"Michael! What's new?"

"Well, besides you being my best man, did you hear about Gerald Weston?"

Silence. Well, that answered *that* question. "Bruce? Did you have anything to do with it?"

"No, of course not! I might have mentioned the case to one of my partners. What he did with that, I couldn't tell you. So, you're getting married! Congratulations! And yes, I'd be honored to be your best man, but won't your brothers be pissed?"

He decided to take Bruce at his word. Maybe it was just that simple. "Probably, but too bad. They're drinkers, and I'm going to need someone sober. Listen, I have to go, but I'll call you next week sometime. Meanwhile, pencil in June 10, the Sunday after my sobriety birthday."

"Will do. And Michael? I'm really happy for you."

He turned back to Elaine who was eyeing him suspiciously.

"What was that about?"

"Gibbs Rule 39."

"There are no coincidences. *Oh,* shit! Do you think —?"

"He said no, but he might have mentioned Lisa's situation to someone who might have told someone. You know he did time in San Q. I think he still has friends there. But he claims he had nothing to do with it, and I'm going to let it go. So, how about we fool around in the shower?"

♡

When Lisa and Robert showed up at ten, the temperature was already in the eighties. The surf was up and Robert had brought his board. She and Lisa sat on beach chairs watching their men put the kids to shame before the waves died.

When her surfer boys ran by, the cute blondie yelled, "Yo, Elaine! Your dude is totally awesome! And his friend like kicked ass out there! We approve!"

They were still laughing when Michael and Robert stalked up carrying their boards raining salt water all over everything.

"What's so funny?"

"My boys just gave both of you their approval."

Robert collapsed next to Lisa. "This was fantastic. I haven't surfed in years. Babe, we should buy a beach house."

"*Uh,* is there something you two haven't told us?"

Lisa laughed. "No. We've just been kicking around some ideas. Now that Gerald is dead, I can dump that medieval monstrosity. I wouldn't mind living near the beach, just maybe not right on the sand. It's kind of noisy and crowded, don't you think?"

"It is. But I love watching the people, and it's not noisy at night unless it's a holiday. What about a place up on the bluffs?"

Robert liked that idea. "Yeah, I could see that. Close enough but not too close."

"Well, let's see how much I can get for the dungeon."

"Listen, it's a little after noon. We should think about getting the barbecue going. I have a feeling these two are going to need naps soon."

"Yes, a nap sounds good — right after I dunk you."

Michael picked her up, ran into the water, and dropped her. She sputtered as she came to the surface, and the water fight was on.

☒

Between her mother, his mother, and Latesha, everything for the wedding came together perfectly. Grace and Mary were pretty much inseparable ever since they'd bonded over martinis. The families even spent Christmas together. Christmas Eve was a difficult time for Michael and his mother since it was the anniversary of Sandy's and his father's deaths, but Mary insisted on making the holiday joyous.

In March her parents threw them an engagement party at a country club that one of Michael's partners was a member of. That night the animals threw parties for both of them — separately, of course, and they laughed about it the next morning.

The reception would be a beach party catered by one of the local authentic barbecue restaurants, complete with hushpuppies and sweet potato pies. And there would be tubs of ice-cold sodas and sparkling apple cider. Neither of them wanted the trouble alcohol and the hot sun could cause. If people wanted to bring their own booze, that was fine, just as long as they confined the consequences to the sand. Guests would be encouraged to bring beach clothes and change at the church.

She refused to have a bridal shower or a bachelorette party and opted for a girls' day of beauty at a local spa, instead. She invited all the ladies she went on that retreat with plus several others from the office, and Lisa, and, of course, her mother and soon-to-be mother-in-law. It was supposed to be relaxing which was damn near impossible since Latesha kept everyone laughing.

Michael's brothers, several of his male friends from AA, and the law firm partners spent the day before the wedding at a baseball game. Someone knew someone who had a private box right above home plate at Angel Stadium. As usual, his brothers got drunk. They were still a little perturbed he hadn't asked one of them to be his best man.

A week before the wedding they met with a young woman and her son. The woman's story was gut wrenching and reaffirmed why they'd chosen the paths that had brought them together. Jennifer was in danger and Michael had been working on her legal case. If he could get them some support he planned to rent his house to her. He didn't want to sell it. He'd paid peanuts for it and it was worth a fortune now. Renting it out would be the perfect solution.

They turned their cases over to coworkers and prepared for a solid week of nothing but peace and quiet on the beach, along with thousands of their closest friends. No phones, no laptops, and no TV except for Tuesday night at eight.

The night before the wedding, she stayed at her parents' house while he stayed with his mother. It was a silly tradition, but both mothers insisted. They texted for hours until neither could stay awake.

$\heartsuit$

"Well, bro. I hope you know what you're doing. I still have a hard time believing you're marrying the woman who basically killed Sandy."

"Get him out of here."

"What? I'm just saying what everyone else is thinking."

That's when the *old man* stepped in. "Speak for yourself, *runt*. And if you don't shut up, Matt and I are going to *escort* you out on your ass."

"Why don't you escort him out now? I don't want to hear his shit. I only invited him because Elaine wanted me to. You know what, jerk? That attitude is why you can't find a woman who will stick around longer than two dates."

"Their loss."

"No, they dodged a cannonball. Now, everyone, *out*. I need some quiet time."

"Hopefully, you're having second thoughts."

"OUT!"

When he was finally alone, he dropped to his knees on the prie-dieu in the groom's room and prayed.

Heavenly father, I don't have the words to express my gratitude that you saw fit to lift me out of my despair and bless me with Elaine. Help me to be a good husband and never take this blessing for granted.

In the name of the Father, the Son, and the Holy Spirit, amen.

"Hey, Michael? You in there? It's time."

Bruce didn't have to worry about him getting to the altar. He couldn't wait.

♡

"Let me check you, girlie. Hair's good. Dress isn't tucked into your panties. Makeup isn't smeared. Yeah, you're good to go."

"Thanks. Remind me to give you a good review."

"Appreciated."

"Well, I guess I better go take my seat. Robert is probably wondering where I am."

"Okay. And Lisa, in case I don't see you before we get to the beach, you make sure you're there to catch the bouquet! That goes for you too, Miss Latesha."

Lisa laughed as she closed the door behind her. Seconds later they heard a muffled scream. When they yanked the door open, a man had his hand over Lisa's mouth and was trying to drag her outside.

"I don't fucking think so, asshole!" She stepped on the man's foot and when he let go of Lisa, she roundhouse kicked him in the groin burying her stiletto heel right where it counted. When he bent over, she dropped him with a knifehand strike in the neck. He fell to the floor in agony.

"Who the fuck are you?"

"*Oh,* my God, it's Gerald's brother!"

"Latesha, go tell my father to call the police. And let Michael know I'll be a few minutes late and not to start without me."

"You got it, *sistah!* That was some nice moves!"

The man was still curled up on the floor, crying when the police arrived.

After a short delay so she could touch up her makeup, the ceremony went off without another hitch, and afterward, people buzzed about how the bride had saved her friend from certain death.

"Come here, wife."

"Yes, husband?"

He led her into their bedroom and closed the door.

"Michael, we can't stay in here too long. Someone might come looking for us or need to change."

"They can wait. We haven't had a minute alone since yesterday morning, and I haven't had a chance to tell you how proud and scared I was when I found out what happened. But I wish I could have seen that guy's face when you kicked him with that shoe."

"Well, there was no way I was going to wait for the police. He probably would have killed Lisa in the parking lot long before they showed up. Told you I had a black belt."

He kissed the smile off her face. When he broke the kiss, she collapsed in his arms, and he had to hold her up. When she caught her breath, she whispered, "Hold that thought. I'll meet you back here in a few hours."

"I don't know if I can wait that long."

"So why didn't we change clothes at the church? That could have been the perfect excuse for some privacy."

"Next time."

"Sorry, husband. 'Till death do us part.' No *do-overs* allowed."

They walked hand in hand outside where the reception had spilled out of the patio and onto the sand. Everyone seemed to be having a great time, and the food was a hit. As he held his wife and watched friends and family enjoying themselves, peace and happiness filled him to the point of bursting.

"Mr. Chandler? Elaine?"

"Jennifer?"

"Sorry to crash your party. Congratulations, by the way. Remember, you told me about your house for rent? Well, I just checked it out, and I'd like very much to rent it."

"That's great. We'll call you next week and work out the details."

"I really need it sooner, like tomorrow. Eddie is getting out of jail soon and we can't stay at that shelter."

"It's okay, honey. Jennifer, we'll call you in the morning. We can get you moved in probably in the next day or two. Right, honey?"

"Right. And I'll make sure there's a restraining order in place before he gets out."

"Thank you. Now, I'll let you get back to your party."

Seconds later John the asshole walked up to them. Instead of the snide remarks they expected, he watched the woman walk away.

"Who is she?"

"Don't even think about it. She's got enough going on. She doesn't need you causing her any more pain."

But he saw the look on the *runt*'s face. He knew that look. Maybe she was just what John needed to find something worth redeeming in himself. He didn't know whether to warn her or let it play out. But at the first sign of trouble, he had no problem incapacitating his brother.

"Lisa, honey. Let's take a walk."

He led her down to the water where they skirted the waves. He hoped his shaking hands weren't too obvious, and he shoved one in the pocket of his shorts to assure himself the ring was there. He'd bought it the other day intending to ask her to marry him when the time was right. It was bad form to propose at someone else's wedding, but after almost losing her at the church, he couldn't wait.

When they reached a less crowded stretch of beach, he led her to dry sand, turned her to face him, and dropped to one knee. "Lisa, my love, I realized today how precious every minute of my life with you is. I almost lost you again, and the thought of living without you terrified me. I'd planned to wait until we got home, but I just can't. Lisa, my heart, my life, my love, will you marry me?" He held the ring out to her.

She was quiet, and her silence scared him. Just as he was about to stand up, she kneeled in front of him. "Today reminded me of how it used to be. You've shown me what love is supposed to be, and I love you more than I ever thought possible. So, yes. Yes, Robert. I'll marry you."

His relief nearly knocked the air from his lungs. With shaking hands, he slid the ring on her finger. Then he stood and helped her up. He took her in his arms and kissed her as if his life depended on it because he'd learned that day that it did. When he broke the kiss, she asked,

"Should we go tell Michael and Elaine?"

"I guess. But I don't know if we should steal their spotlight."

"I don't think they'll mind. They've been hoping for this since the ordeal at your cabin."

"Then let's go tell them. I'll race you!"

"Are you gonna throw that bouquet or what?"

"I was hoping Lisa and Robert would get back from their walk — *Oh*, there they are. Okay, so go gather up all the single women, yourself included."

"*Uh-uh.* I like being single. So many *bruthas*, so little time."

"You mean there are some left whose hearts you haven't broken yet?"

"*Hmm.* You have a point."

When all the single women had gathered, she turned around and tossed the bouquet into the air. Then she heard a man laugh.

"Good timing!"

She turned around to see a beaming Lisa holding the flowers while Robert had his arm around her. Then she saw the sparkle on the woman's left hand.

"HOLY COW! You're engaged!"

EPILOGUE

"**B**reakfast in bed for my fiancé."
Lisa took one look at the eggs and one sniff of the bacon, ran for the bathroom, slammed the door and barely made it to the toilet in time.

"Honey? What's wrong?"

Between retches, he heard her yell, "I'm okay! I think I —" She vomited again just as he opened the door.

"No! Don't come in!"

He ignored her and held her hair back. When the heaving stopped long enough, she mumbled, "I think it's the flu."

"Are you achy? You don't feel like you have a fever. Do you have a headache?"

"No," was all she could get out before the dry heaves hit, again. When they finally stopped, she sat back exhausted while he got a wet washcloth and gently wiped her beautiful face.

"Honey, I don't think it's the flu."

"How do you know?"

"I'm a doctor, remember? Do you think you might be pregnant? When was your last period?"

"I don't know. I told you I'm not regular. Pregnant? No way. I can't have kids."

"I think you should take a test."

"*Oh,* Robert. What if I am?"

He saw the fear on her face, and it saddened him. "Then we'll look for a bigger house with a big backyard in a good school district."

"You wouldn't be angry?"

"God, no! I'd be overjoyed. But let's see if that's what it is, first. Let me get you back to bed with some tea and crackers, and then I'll run to the drugstore."

They sat on the patio and watched the sun go down. It was his favorite time of the day, except for waking up with her snuggled into his side every morning.

"Are you happy, baby?"

"I never knew life could be so wonderful until you came along."

He was just about to echo her words when his cell phone rang. It was his mother's obnoxious ringtone.

"That's my mom. I told her we were unplugging from the world for a while."

"Then it must be important. You better answer."

He had a feeling he knew why she was calling, and he dreaded hearing the confirmation. "Hi, Mom. What's up?"

"Michael, honey. Father Timothy passed away last night."

Damn. The animals had warned him so he shouldn't have been surprised. Still, a rock formed in the pit of his stomach.

"Michael? Are you there?"

"Yeah, Mom. I'm sorry. What do you need me to do?" He hoped her answer was *nothing.* The priest had saved his life. Maintaining around her would be damn near impossible.

"Would you and Elaine take me to the funeral?"

"Of course, Mom. Let me know the details when you have them. And Mom?"

"Yes?"

"He lived a good life and now he's in heaven."

"I know, sweetheart. But it's a reminder I don't have much longer, either."

"I'm hanging up now. I don't ever want to hear you say things like that. Call me later if you need anything and let me know when the services are."

"I will. I love you, son."

"Love you, too, Mom."

♡

She could tell what it was about from his side of the conversation and the look on his face. The priest had seemed tired but still healthy when he officiated at their wedding last week. What could have happened?

"Did she say what happened?"

"He died in his sleep. He was close to ninety, so I guess God said it was time for him to come home."

As hard as she tried, she still couldn't bring herself to believe in all that heaven and hell stuff, but she nodded, anyway. She promised the bear she'd keep an open mind and would support her husband no matter what he needed.

When her cell phone rang, she saw Lisa's number on the display. "Hey, Lisa. Everything okay?"

"Well, sort of. I'm pregnant."

And the cycle of life continued.

♡

John walked past his older brother's house hoping to catch a glimpse of the new tenant, the beautiful woman with the sad but beautiful green eyes. He'd never been so affected by a woman, and it wasn't lust, either. Yeah, he was attracted to her, but it was much more than that. There was something about her that brought out something in him he didn't even know was there. He was the youngest of the Horde, the spoiled screw-up, the proud king of snide and hurtful remarks. Yet, when he thought about her . . .

Jennifer peeked through the blinds. The man with the unusual blue eyes and muscles stood on the Strand staring up at her big picture window as if trying to see inside. She pulled the heavy drapes closed and checked that the door was dead-bolted.

John and Jennifer's story continues in SAFE WITH ME, available at www.books2read.com/safewithme

If you enjoyed this book, please consider leaving a review. Then read on for more books by Mary A. Nason.

ALSO BY MARY A. NASON

BELIEVE

She's still waiting for her happily ever after.
All he wants is someone to love again.

If it's real, it's worth fighting for. After all, it only took fifty years for destiny to come full circle.

After three divorces, Annie Rogers never thought she'd spend her *golden years* alone. Now she's settled into her dream home in the Pacific Northwest, but every day is *Groundhog Day* predictable. Every day she cares for her dog, laments about her lack of a social life, and checks her empty mailbox. Every night she sleeps with her *magic wand*. Use it or lose it, right?

Sam Baker had it all. A beautiful wife and two beautiful but spoiled daughters. Now he's a widower, and the girls are grown and on their own. He's active and hopefully still virile, and it sure would be nice to have someone to make love to again.

Together they find the freedom to explore every aspect of a loving, trusting, relationship, a freedom neither had ever had before. This is it. They've found their happily ever after. But ageism, con artists, and illness conspire to drive them apart.

Can they find their way back to each other? Will destiny win? And just how long is happily ever after?

BELIEVE is the standalone first book in the Second Chances series. It's a love story for and about the Silver Generation.

Buy Now: www.Books2Read.com/believe

REMEMBER

She's a reformed bitch and busybody. Understandable since her ex made her that way.

He's a happy-go-lucky guy, except when it comes to commitment. Understandable since his ex made him that way.

After a stressful week playing *bridezilla* whisperer, Becky Montgomery unwinds with her sidekick, freelance photographer Justin Williams, over too many tequila shooters. Was it the alcohol that lowered the defenses around her heart and allow her to spill her guts? And did she really tell him he's hot?

Justin had never shared with anyone what it had been like living with a narcissist. But Becky had such a sympathetic ear, it just spilled out. But he didn't hear anything after she said he was hot. He'd loved her ever since he first laid eyes on her, but he'd hidden it for years. Was this his chance? Maybe taking her along on a photo shoot will give them both a new beginning, and he can convince her he'd never do anything to hurt her.

Instead, the wilderness holds a nightmare from his own past: a crazy ex who'll use every dirty trick in the narcissist's handbook to get him back. Only this time she's adding a new dangerous chapter — erasing Justin from Becky's heart and memory and if that doesn't work erasing Becky from Justin's life. Permanently.

He could make her forget her past . . . If his past wasn't stalking their future

REMEMBER is the second book in the Second Chances series. To avoid spoilers read this after BELIEVE.

Buy Now: www.Books2Read.com/remember

SMILE

She lives vicariously through the characters she writes in her romance novels. She can only imagine the endings. Those happily ever after stories don't come true for women like her.

He's retired now but ever since he was a boy he's dreamed about a woman. A woman he needs to help. Is that why he became a cop? And where is she?

Abby Randall needs to make this getaway ski trip. But why now? Is it fate that makes her stop at her usual gas station? In the restroom she helps an adorable little girl. Of *course,* she's adorable. Her waiting grandfather is drop-dead gorgeous. Yeah who is she kidding? Happy endings only happen in her books not to women like her. Yet this man sparks an attraction she hasn't felt in years and it scares her to death. So she runs just like she always does.

Retired detective Ted Taylor may have just blown it. The pretty lady with turquoise eyes has slipped away before he can even ask her name. She'll think he's crazy but her face haunts his dreams. If he can find her in Lake Tahoe his lonely days and nights might be over.

When Mr. Tall Hot and Silver sits down next to her in the casino Abby isn't sure what to think. Ted is just like the heroes in her books. Maybe . . . with him . . . she can pretend the past that broke her never happened. Just for a few days.

Ted knows this woman has secrets that are painful and deep. If he lets slip that he's loved her all his life she'll run — and he won't be able to protect her from her worst nightmare. A nightmare no one deserves to live through alone.

Can he slay her dragons?

Can she triumph over her hideous past?

He could be her silver lining — unless her nightmares swallow her whole.

SMILE is the standalone third book in the Second Chances series.

Buy Now: www.Books2read.com/smile

THE GOOD DEED

Have you ever heard the saying *No good deed goes unpunished?*

Michael had it all, a successful career and a loving wife. Then a brief stop and a simple good deed took it all away.

Elaine was a housewife with broken bones and a fractured spirit. A stranger's good deed helped send her husband to prison, and she moved on with her life — for a little while, anyway.

His good deed saved her but at a terrible cost. Can they overcome their guilt and find the happily ever after they've earned?

Not so fast. . .

THE GOOD DEED is a spicy later-in-life romance and the first book in the Chandler Horde series.

Buy Now: www.Books2Read.com/thegooddeed

SAFE WITH ME

She's running from her ex.

He's running from his reputation.

John is the youngest of the Chandler Horde, the spoiled brat. He gave his heart twice, got it back in pieces both times, and swore off women forever.

Jennifer is the youngest of the Finley sisters, the quiet bookworm. She gave her heart once, got broken bones in return, and swore off men forever.

Now she and her son are in hiding, on the run from her ex and his family. Can she trust the man with the reputation and unforgettable blue eyes to keep them safe?

John has finally found his purpose: protect the green-eyed beauty and her son with his life. But can he convince her they're safe with him?

SAFE WITH ME is a spicy later-in-life romantic suspense and the second book in the Chandler Horde series. To avoid spoilers, read THE GOOD DEED first.

Buy Now: www.Books2Read.com/safewithme

ALL I WANT

He has everything a man could want but does he have what he needs?

Andrew Chandler goes undercover to expose corruption in a shelter. Posing as a homeless veteran, he experiences firsthand how quickly reality can change. If he doesn't finish this assignment soon, he'll lose his sanity. Just when he is about to give in to the madness, a beautiful angel appears.

Marie-Thérèse Chambéry has everything

she needs. A home. A satisfying career. Friends and family. But something's missing. She's drawn to the homeless man in the park and feels compelled to help him. Just when she thinks he's going to open up to her, he vanishes.

Their paths cross again unexpectedly. He's overjoyed. She's humiliated. With a little help, they just might get it all.

ALL I WANT is a spicy later-in-life romance and the third story in the Chandler Horde series. To avoid spoilers, read this after SAFE WITH ME.

Buy Now: www.Books2Read.com/ChandlerHorde2-5

NO PARKING

All's fair in love and parking places.

She doesn't own the whole street. And if that brat touches his truck one more time she won't be able to sit down for a week.

Why does that jerk have to park his ugly, diesel fume belching truck in front of her house? And why does he have to be so gorgeous?

What's a little sabotage between enemies? The more she fights him, the more he pushes her. Pissing off the green-eyed beauty is just too much fun — until the day it blows up in his face.

Relationships can be full of potholes, and this is more than just a battle of the sexes. It's a battle between dominants and both are determined to come out on top.

One of them will lose the battle. Can both of them win the war?

NO PARKING is a spicy romantic comedy and the fourth story in the Chandler Horde series. To avoid spoilers, read this after ALL I WANT.

Buy Now: www.Books2Read.com/no-parking

ABOUT THE AUTHOR

Mary A. Nason is a feisty member of the Silver Generation and retired geekette. She writes spicy romance for seasoned ladies. Originally from Los Angeles and then Silicon Valley, California, she now lives in a small town in Central Oregon.

When Mary's not writing, she loves playing with her dog and traveling. She has a vivid imagination and finds story ideas and character inspirations through her friends — who are nice to her so she won't write them in and then kill them off.

There's a little bit of Mary in all her heroines, but alas, so far, the heroes have been pure fantasy. She is currently single and enjoying it. Besides, writing is a jealous lover.

For information about Mary's upcoming books be sure to sign up for her mailing list at www.maryanason.com. You can also write to her at info@maryanason.com.

Be sure to follow her on:

Facebook www.facebook.com/MaryANason/

Mary's Spicy Ladies (and gentlemen) group at www.facebook.com/groups/291053078037228/

Goodreads www.goodreads.com/maryanason

Bookbub www.bookbub.com/profile/mary-a-nason

LINKS AND RESOURCES

- Gibbs Rules
- Color meanings: http://www.color-wheel-pro.com/color-meaning.html
- Alcoholics Anonymous. (2001). *Alcoholics Anonymous, 4th Edition.* New York: A.A. World Services, http://www.aa.org
- Al-anon: https://al-anon.org
- Adams, Douglas. 1980. *The Hitchhiker's Guide to the Galaxy.* New York: Harmony Books.
- "Great bodily injury" (sometimes referred to as "GBI" or "great bodily harm") is a legal term that means significant or substantial injuries. http://www.shouselaw.com/gbi.html
- http://family.findlaw.com/domestic-violence.domestic-violence-victim-resources.html

THE TWELVE STEPS OF ALCOHOLICS ANONYMOUS

1. We admitted we were powerless over alcohol — that our lives had become unmanageable.
2. Came to believe that a power greater than ourselves could restore us to sanity.
3. Made a decision to turn our will and our lives over to the care of God as we understood Him.
4. Made a searching and fearless moral inventory of ourselves.
5. Admitted to God, to ourselves, and to another human being the exact nature of our wrongs.
6. Were entirely ready to have God remove all these defects of character.
7. Humbly asked him to remove our shortcomings.

8. Made a list of all people we had harmed and became willing to make amends to them all.

9. Made direct amends to such people wherever possible, except when to do so would injure them or others.

10. Continued to take personal inventory and when we were wrong promptly admitted it.

11. Sought through prayer and meditation to improve our conscious contact with God as we understood Him, praying only for knowledge of his will for us and the power to carry that out.

12. Having had a spiritual awakening as the result of these steps, we tried to carry this message to alcoholics and to practice these principles in all our affairs.

Made in the USA
Middletown, DE
07 May 2021